ALSO BY SARAH FINE

Of Metal and Wishes
Of Shadows and Obsession, a prequel e-novella

of dreams and rust

BY SARAH FINE

MARGARET K. MCELDERRY BOOKS

New York London Toronto Sydney New Delhi

MARGARET K. McELDERRY BOOKS

An imprint of Simon & Schuster Children's Publishing Division

1230 Avenue of the Americas, New York, New York 10020

MARGARET K. MCELDERRY BOOKS is a trademark of Simon & Schuster, Inc.

For information about special discounts for bulk purchases, please contact Simon & Schuster Special Sales at 1-866-506-1949 or business@simonandschuster.com.

The Simon & Schuster Speakers Bureau can bring authors to your live event. For more information or to book an event, contact the Simon & Schuster Speakers Bureau at 1-866-248-3049 or visit our website at www.simonspeakers.com.

Book design by Debra Sfetsios-Conover

The text for this book is set in ITC Baskerville.

Manufactured in the United States of America

10 9 8 7 6 5 4 3 2 1

Library of Congress Cataloging-in-Publication Data

Fine, Sarah.

Of dreams and rust / Sarah Fine.—First edition.

p. cm.

Sequel to: Of metal and wishes.

Summary: When the downtrodden Noor rebel in the West, Wen, overhearing a plan to crush the Noor with powerful war machines, leaves the ghostly Bo, now a boy determined to transform himself into a living machine, and journeys into the war zone to warn the Noor—and her great love, Melik.

ISBN 978-1-4424-8361-3 (hardcover)

ISBN 978-1-4424-8363-7 (eBook)

[1. War—Fiction. 2. Revolutions—Fiction. 3. Social classes—Fiction. 4. Love—Fiction. 5. Ghosts—Fiction.] I. Title.

PZ7.F495678Od 2015

[Fic]—dc23   2014030271

For Cathryn and Shizhou

of dreams and rust

Chapter One

IN THE LAST year I have come to understand the traitorous nature of skin. We cannot live without this barrier between our beating hearts and the outside world, yet it is the most fragile of things, as well as the most deceptive. My own, despite its golden undertones, cannot keep me warm. The memory of Melik's, the ruddy tan of earth under sun, leaves me aching in darkness. My father's, thin and buckling under the weight of his years and all the things he's lost, hides his silent strength.

And Bo's, so broken and torn, is woven from sheer betrayal. Stretched over his bones like the work of a clumsy tailor, carelessly patched, heedlessly sewn. I have come to know it almost as well as I do my own, and I hate it for its failure, for the painful story it tells. I hate it because, despite its weakness, it is somehow powerful enough to keep him from the world.

"Stop," he snaps, wrenching his forearm from my grasp. "You're making it worse."

I quickly rub my fingertips together, the rose hip oil slick between them. "It will keep the scar from growing stiff." I gentle my tone. "I'm sorry if I was pressing too hard."

Bo's machine hand, a work of mad, relentless genius, covers the scar on his arm, shielding it from me. His human skin is the same color as mine, but his machine parts glint silver beneath the lantern dangling from the rough rock ceiling of this chamber. Despite the fact that I have seen him without his mask, Bo always wears it when I visit. I am reflected in his half-metal face, my cheekbones and chin sharp, my forehead wide and distorted, my eyes dark. They, at least, tell the truth. The weariness and sorrow within them is as deep as the canyon that leads through the Western Hills.

Bo tilts his head. "You were far away just now. Again."

I lower my gaze to my fingers. I hurt him when I am not with him, but I seem to hurt him almost as much by being here, and I can't figure out how to change that. "Shall I continue?"

Bo blinks his brown eye. His ebony hair hangs over his forehead, part steel, part flesh, yet all smooth. "I'm sure Guiren will be missing you. It is almost time for the clinic to open."

"And I am sure you have many plans for today, all of which involve the use of this arm and these fingers, as well as both legs." I glance over at his long work table, strewn with metal body parts, a bicep here, a pectoral there, circuits for blood vessels, gears and springs and bearings waiting for Bo to give them purpose, to bring them to life. Usually I love hearing about his creations and inventions. When he talks about a new idea, his whole face lights up. Sometimes I come down here just to watch him work, a few hours on a quiet afternoon spent staring at his hands moving in concert while his face cradles the tiniest of contented smiles. I have even made peace with his metal spiders, for the most part. However, when Bo began designing himself a complete steel shell, when he started to fashion a machine arm to fit over his human one, and then a set of legs, I began to realize he was the creation this time.

Now the sight of them chills me to the bone.

"I have a few minutes before I must go," I say to him. "Let's make the most of it."

"All right." He sags a bit in his chair, its legs squeaking against the patterned metal panel that covers the floor. His machine arm arcs with precise grace to hang at his side. Sometimes it seems to move on its own, walking his skeletal fingers through a dance set to electrical pulses, transmitted by wires and circuits that wind like veins within the contours of his steel muscles. My own fingertips move hesitantly over the scar on his arm, the healed wound inflicted by his own fearsome spider creations as he rescued me and Melik from a mob—a trap that Bo himself had set for the rust-haired Noor boy who had claimed my heart. Bo's own heart would not allow him to see it through, though, and he paid for that mercy with blood. Four seasons have passed, but Bo's flesh has an unfailing, unforgiving memory.

"Any interestingly gory cases yesterday?" he asks as casually as he might inquire about the weather.

I smirk. "I am probably the only girl in the country who does not find that to be a repulsive and offensive question."

"You're the only girl in the country I talk to, so I guess I'm lucky." With his playful smile, he lifts some of the weight off my shoulders. It is magnetic, drawing the corners of my mouth up to match.

"Dr. Yixa is still put off by my eagerness to suture his patients' wounds. He makes the funniest faces whenever he witnesses me washing blood from my hands." I imitate it, lowering my eyebrows and grimacing, and Bo laughs. "But at this point he knows my stitches are neater and straighter than his own."

"Then I give him credit for being observant."

I wonder if Bo realizes how his simple faith in me melts away some of my own doubts.

"He should be grateful," Bo continues. "Gochan One was dangerous, but Gochan Two is as heartlessly deadly as the war machines it creates. He needed the help."

"Father and I were fortunate he did." After the destruction of Gochan One, Father and I thought we might have to leave in search of work, but Dr. Yixa, the chief physician and surgeon for the neighboring factory, discovered us caring for victims of the catastrophe, and he offered my father a position. My father refused to accept unless I could come along as his assistant.

"I was fortunate he did, too," Bo murmurs. "I thought I'd never see either of you again, and then Guiren found me."

I think of the little steel-and-wire girl that I keep tucked under my pillow, her hair short like mine was right after a spider sliced off my braid with its fangs, her body enfolded within the arms of a faceless, unknowable boy. Given how injured Bo was at the time, it must have hurt him to create her, to sneak her into the pocket of my dress. "You had sent me a message." He was giving me the chance to return to him—or to stay away. "I was happy that it helped us find you."

Bo's smile has not faded. "Not as happy as I was."

I'm not so sure about that. This morning, like every morning now, I woke to the light of the stars and moon winking dimly through my tiny window and the faint sound of my father's snoring coming from the next room. I pulled on my work dress and crept down the darkened stairways of Gochan Two, a sprawling beast that sleeps until the sun rises over the high factory fence. I slipped around the few traps, knowing well where they are and what they hold in store for trespassers.

Within the old mining tunnels and caves beneath this weapons factory, Bo is once again building himself a world.

Unlike his skin, his mind never fails him.

I followed his instructions, long since memorized, to find the hidden door that marks the entrance to his kingdom, merely the bones of what he plans to build someday. He escaped through these tunnels when he brought the Gochan One slaughterhouse down, burying a hundred men in a tomb of metal and brick and burned meat. And though he was wounded, he immediately began to weave his steel web around him. My father and

I helped. Bo is ours, and we could not let him go. And now I look forward to every morning, because in this hour I am more myself than I can be for the rest of the day. Bo knows my secrets, and whether he likes them or not, he seems to forgive me for having them. Knowing he looks forward to our time as well makes me determined to carve it into my day, no matter how early I must rise. It is an unspoken promise. It binds us to each other, out of mutual need.

And yet, lately, I feel like I am losing him, circuit by circuit.

Bo flinches again as my thumb follows the path of his jagged scar. "Must you always press right where it hurts the most? I don't see how it helps."

"Father says that if we do this every day, you'll be able to retain the mobility in your arm." I duck my head to make sure he is looking at me. "He also said that if you wear those mechanical frames around your arm and legs for too long, if you let them do the work of your body for you, you will lose strength in these muscles." I skim my palm over his forearm, a silent apology, but draw back quickly when he shivers.

Bo presses his lips together as he glares at his imperfect flesh. "Sometimes I wish I were made entirely of steel and wire," he says. "I often wish that, in fact."

"I don't." I continue to massage the rose hip oil into his arm, over the puckered, mottled pink and white of his scar and the light brown of his unmarked skin. "I like you this way."

He sighs. "When you are here, I like myself this way too," he says quietly. He draws himself up, setting his jaw.

6

"But you are not here most of the time. Including when you are sitting right in front of me."

The silence between us is alive with wishes, his and mine. We want pieces of each other that we will never have. Bo wishes I would stop missing Melik—and I wish Bo wanted to be human. If one of us could move, I believe the other could as well, but because neither of us can move, our hearts are frozen in place. And yet we give each other what we can.

"I am here now," I say. "And we have time to work on your leg—if you're willing? You said it was bothering you."

He frowns. "Give me a minute." His cheeks have darkened.

I fidget with my oil and cloth as he disappears behind a partition. His arm hums and fabric whispers as he pulls off his pants. We are about to do a delicate dance, one that sways between clinical and intimate. I never know, from moment to moment, if I want it or if I want to pull away, and I think Bo feels the same.

"I'm ready," he mumbles.

I rise from my chair and move around the partition, my skirt swishing around my ankles. Bo lies on his sleep pallet, his blanket pulled over his hips and his right leg. His left, the one savaged by a metal spider a year ago, is bare and goose-bumped. Bo's face is turned to the wall. He never looks at me when I do this.

"This scar looks a little better. Faded," I say as I sink to my knees beside him.

"I don't care what it looks like. I only care whether my leg is functional."

If that were truly the case, I don't think he would be trembling, but I don't call attention to it. I am careful with him. I always have been. Not because I am afraid he will lash out; he has never hurt me, and I think he would die from the pain of it if he did. No, I am more concerned with hurting him. If I cajole, if I hold back, if I craft my words just so, it makes it easier for Bo to stay with me, to stay himself. "Of course. I only meant that it looked stronger."

He laughs, just a hiss of breath from his nose. "I see right through you."

I pour a bit of rose hip oil into my palm and rub my hands together. "How so?"

"Do you really think I am so naive, Wen? You don't have to always say what I want to hear."

"I know."

He turns his head and looks at me. "Do you?" His human hand reaches across his body and touches mine. "How can I be your friend if you are always protecting me?"

I let him take my hand. I let him stroke my fingers. It feels both comforting and dangerous. "You always protect me. Why can't I do the same?"

His grip tightens. "Because it's not the same. I would protect you from anything that threatened you. Any man, any creature, any machine. And you, you protect me from . . . you, I suppose." He lets me go and then clenches his fist so hard his knuckles go pale. His metal fingers click, startling me. "It's the last thing I want to be protected from."

"That's not fair." I lay my warm palms on his bare thigh, over the thick, ropy scar. Bo's chest stills and his eyes close. "You know me better than anyone does."

He shakes his head. "Only the parts you allow me to see."

I press down a swell of frustration and begin to massage his leg, long downward strokes toward his knee and then upward to midthigh, as my father taught me. It will keep the muscles supple, the blood flowing, the skin from growing taut and angry. I am gentle at first, cautious. I watch my hands moving over his skin. I've memorized every flaw. It makes the perfect parts that much more exquisite, but as soon as that thought surfaces, I try to drown it. It would be utterly scandalous for me to be alone with a man, touching him like this with no one to supervise, but my father trusts us both. Bo is a patient right now, nothing more.

It is impossible to think of him as nothing more. But so is thinking of him any other way.

I remind myself to be like my father, to think like my father, and my movements harden. My hands become instruments, my thoughts technical . . . but with shamefully ragged edges. Bo clutches at his blanket with both hands. His face glitters with pinpoint beads of sweat. I'm hurting him, but Father said it would hurt if I did it right. What he didn't say: how my stomach would knot, how my eyes would burn, how my precision would be worn away by the desire to smooth back Bo's damp hair and kiss his forehead.

"You could take off your mask," I tell him after a few minutes. It must be uncomfortable when he sweats like this.

"No," he says in a choked voice. "I don't want to."

"I see only the parts you allow me to see," I say, a warped echo, an accusation that I for once do not hold back.

"How can you possibly think it's the same?" he whispers. "You hide beauty from me. The only thing I hide from you is ugliness." A tear suddenly slips free from the corner of his tightly closed eye, and he swipes it away as his face twists with anger and humiliation. I bow my head because my own tears are about to betray me as well.

Bo sits up abruptly. "I've had enough."

He says it so sharply that I freeze. For a moment there is only silence and stillness, but then he tips my chin up with his callused fingertips. I wonder if my eyes are red like his, if his chest is as tight as mine. His mouth opens, but his words are locked inside him. We stare at each other. I don't understand why this happens, why we make each other fall apart, why it can't be simple and easy. But as I look into Bo's face, half handsome and half monster, the space between us fills with all the things we do not say. The things we'll probably never say.

His hand falls away from me, landing in his lap like a dead weight. "I'll be out in a moment." His voice is rough, uneven.

I move quickly, eager to give him the privacy he needs so badly right now. While he gets dressed, I set a bun on a plate for him and start a pot of water heating on a small burner he keeps on his worktable. Once the coil flares red hot, I fill a large teapot with tea leaves and set out the strainer. "Someone saw you two nights ago," I say, longing to steer our conversation toward calmer waters, to occupy Bo's mind with the now, the real, the things he can control.

"Where?" he calls from behind the partition.

"Have you been to the construction site?"

His metal fingers click together, driven by the jolts from muscles in his shoulder, and he steps into the open, fully clothed once more. "I needed some tools."

"One of the foremen was still there. He told his crew to be on the lookout for you. One of them was injured by a beam yesterday and told us the story while we were splinting his arm. Some think you were just a thief, but others believe the foreman saw the Ghost."

Bo snorts. "'Just a thief.'" He comes over to stand next to me as I prepare our tea.

"It's safer for everyone if that's what they believe," I remind him.

"I'll be more careful," he mumbles. "I didn't expect anyone to be there so late."

"They have received orders to get the slaughterhouse running earlier."

His eye bores into mine. "You know why, don't you?"

"Feasting season, of course." My heart skips.

"No, because they want to make sure they have rations for our soldiers on top of the demand for meat during the feasting season. Gochan One supplied much of the beef for the central part of Itanya, and with the need to feed an army moving west, it is indispensable."

"We are not at war." It is a silly thing to say and I know it. We have been on the cusp of war for months. The western province of Yilat is churning with rebellion and revolution, and the sentiment is slowly creeping east.

Lost in thoughts of men with guns, I reach for the pot and whimper as my fingers skim over the burner.

Bo's machine hand moves quickly, like reflex. It snatches the pot away from me. "Let me do this. I never get burned." He flashes a grin that fades instantly. His impervious metal fingers pour the water over the little pile of tea leaves, then place the lid on the ceramic teapot. "You may be worrying over nothing, Wen." He looks at me out of the corner of his eye. "He may already be dead."

My throat aches, like he's closed those metal fingers around the stalk of my neck. "Melik is alive," I whisper. Right before he walked away from me to return to the west with his younger brother, Sinan, and all the men from his village, he promised me that I had not seen him for the last time. I believed him.

Bo rolls his eye. "You can't know that. It's been a year of fighting and bombing and turmoil in Yilat. The Noor are staking their claim on the west. And this time they have united with the lower-class Itanyai in that province." He slaps two teacups down and pours the bitter brew. "They are better equipped and organized than they have ever been. They want their own autonomous region." He fumbles with the strainer as he removes it from his cup, leaving a spray of sodden tea leaves across his meticulously neat worktable. "Don't tell me you believe your red Noor would sit idly by while his brethren fought for such a ridiculous goal. He was always full of similarly romantic, unrealistic sentiments. It very well could have gotten him killed, just like it almost did when he was here."

"What nearly got him killed when he was here was

the irrational hatred of the Noor." And the fact that Bo framed him, but I don't mention that. I never mention that, or how often I've had to forgive Bo for it, because every time I think of it, it leaves me hot with anger.

It's one of the things I hide from him. I doubt he would find it beautiful.

Bo turns his back on me and carries our cups to the table, where he sits down. "He was agitating for more rights for the workers. It made him an easy target." He puts my cup in its usual place and waits for me to join him.

I use my cloth to wipe his work surface. "You didn't know him, Bo." He won't even call Melik by his name.

"I watched him like I did everyone else." He grimaces. "More, even."

I stare at the floor. "I cannot think of him dead. No more than I could think of you that way."

"Do not compare us." Now even his voice is made of steel. "I am here. He is gone. Long. Gone."

To continue this conversation would be like stepping into one of his traps. I tuck my hands into the pockets of my skirt. "I need to go help my father. I will see you tomorrow morning."

Bo is silent as I walk past my steaming teacup and out of his chamber, as I stride through the tunnel toward the stairs. But just before I reach the door that opens to the world above, I hear a low curse followed by the sharp slam of metal onto metal.

I do not go back to see if he is all right.

Chapter Two

I CLIMB THE stairs and feel the vibrations of Gochan Two coming to life. By the time I exit the stairwell at the ground floor, the beast is awake, giving birth to war machines. The hiss of steam, the crash of the enormous metal presses, the whine of engines, the shouted orders from the foremen, all of it echoes through the hallway as I walk to the clinic. The sweat prickles on my upper lip and at my temples. When the factory floor is alive, the temperature inside Gochan Two soars. Outside the season of cold is beginning, but within these walls we cook year-round.

I round a corner and nearly collide with Boss Inyie, a broad-shouldered, round-bellied man with a scrubby mustache. He is still wearing his hat and is flushed from the cool air outside. His secretary, Sondi, a tall, bespectacled woman with streaks of gray in her hair, puts her arm out to protect him from my clumsiness. ". . . called a few minutes ago, Boss," she is saying. "I told him you would ring him back, but he said he would wait."

Boss Inyie hands her his hat. He doesn't even look at me. "It's about time," he says as he strides into his office. "Cancel my morning appointments."

Sondi looks over the rims of her glasses at me. "Shouldn't you be in the clinic?"

I am about to reply when I hear the word "Noor" spit from Boss Inyie's mouth like a curse. The door to his inner office slams. I tear my gaze from his doorway to look up at Sondi. "I-I—yes. Yes, I should."

Her eyes narrow. "I've heard about your sympathies. Onya told me all about them."

Onya, one of the secretaries from Gochan One who is now employed here, has not forgotten how I paid the Noor's debts last year. I wish she had. "Forgive me, Ms. Sondi, but Dr. Yixa is expecting me."

She lets out a dry chuckle. "Tell him to stay away from the liquor tonight. He needs to be at his best."

My brow furrows at her gleefully conspiratorial tone. "Any particular reason?"

Her eyes widen, full of false innocence. "Only that I am looking after the welfare of our hardworking Itanyai men, dear. Now, as you said, the doctor is expecting you."

I keep my head down and rush past her, eager to be back at the clinic. Generally, people at Gochan Two have been kind to me, either because they don't know that I feel differently about the Noor than most around here, or because they, too, recognize the Noor as something other than barbarians. I don't know which, because it is not something I talk about. My father told me to be absolutely silent about it, about Melik, about my time at Gochan One. We have so many secrets to keep.

Perhaps Sondi does too. I spend my walk to the rear of the factory pondering her words and the fact that Boss Inyie was talking about the Noor during his urgent phone call. When I enter the clinic, Dr. Yixa is already in his examination room with a patient. His rumbling voice easily penetrates the flimsy walls as he tells the worker that he can bind the back injury so he can return to the factory floor, but what the worker really needs is a week of bed rest. The injured man begs Dr. Yixa to bind it tightly and asks for opium.

"Opium on the factory floor?" The doctor lets out a thick, rolling laugh. "You need your brain on the floor, not just your muscles. No. You go home, you get opium. You want to work, I'll have Miss Wen make you some willow bark tea."

I grab a pot from the shelf and fill it with water, then start it heating on the stove. Dr. Yixa is fierce about his rules, and this one seems very smart. One moment of thoughtlessness can result in many deaths on the floor of Gochan Two, as I have seen repeatedly over the past year. Of course, a similar absence of thought could mean the difference between saving a man on the operating table and causing him to bleed to death, but Dr. Yixa seems to have no trouble guzzling sorghum liquor as if it were water.

By the time Dr. Yixa emerges with his patient—a stout man with huge arms, a deeply wrinkled brow, and a torso tightly wrapped with cotton bandages—I have the tea steeping. Dr. Yixa sniffs the air, his bulbous red nose twitching. When he exhales, the room fills with the scent of rice wine. He gives me a fatherly smile, revealing his cherry-red gums and missing front tooth. "Good morning, Miss Wen. Happy First Holiday Eve."

My stomach drops. I didn't wish Bo a good holiday. I walked away and said I'd see him tomorrow and didn't think at all. "Happy First Holiday Eve, Doctor."

He nods toward the steaming pot on the stove. "I see you've read my mind once again."

I bow my head. "Willow bark tea is useful and easily made."

"Pour this good man here a cup so he can go take up his place on the floor, will you?"

I pour a helping into a chipped cup, which I hand to the worker with a smile.

"Guiren's out tending to some cases of flu in the dorms," says Yixa as soon as he sees me glance toward the door to the cramped two-room space my father and I call our home. "We're quarantining early this year. Being strict. Glad I have the extra staff to make sure of it."

The factory worker slurps his tea and frowns. "Why? It'll only make it harder to complete our quota."

Dr. Yixa scowls. "You know what would make it even harder? If the entire factory staff was sick at once. Not to mention the fact that we've got soldiers on their way from the east. They'll come through the Ring and need to quarter in the town before they head over the hills, and we don't want them exposed to sickness. We're going to do our part to avoid that."

"Soldiers?" I say. "We've been hearing soldiers would come through for months, but they haven't."

"Ah, I suppose you haven't yet seen the news." He walks over to his cluttered wooden desk and scoops up a newspaper with his chapped hands. "Those Noor pigs have really done it this time."

My heart stutters. "What's happened?"

"They stormed Kegu. Imprisoned Yilat's provincial governor and his council. Opened the food stores and gave the emergency rations to whoever held out a hand. And now they're demanding recognition." He shakes his head, his overlarge ears growing pink with the affront.

"They want to rule themselves," I murmur. Somewhere over the Western Hills the Noor are attempting what Melik's father and other elders tried to do—and died for—so long ago. "And you think our government should not consider it?"

The factory worker gulps the rest of his tea and sets the cup down heavily on the table in front of me. A few remaining drops splash out of the cup and dot the back of my hand.

"They'd better not," he growls. "The rest of us would starve if the Noor got to decide who to sell the crops to. This drought has made some people forget that, but when the rains come, we'll all be sorry—and hungry— if we don't crush those Noor like the cockroaches they are."

My cheeks grow warm with anger. "They only want to own the land they work. Why shouldn't they?"

Both men look at me as if I have lost my mind. They exchange a glance, probably wondering whether to chastise me or dismiss me as a silly, ignorant girl. "Miss Wen," the doctor says kindly, speaking as if to a stubborn toddler, "everyone knows the Noor mind is closer to animal than human. They can be good workers if they're supervised properly, but left to their own devices, they're vengeful, petty, untrustworthy, and dumb. Would you want people like that in charge of half the good farmland in the country? No. You wouldn't. You'd want a savvy Itanyai." He grins and taps his temple.

The bandaged worker looks skeptical. "Good workers? Ha! Look what happened when they were brought to the slaughterhouse to work last year. They weren't here for more than a few weeks before they brought production to a halt. My brother worked the floor there." He mumbles a chant meant to appease dead ancestors, and I realize his brother was probably one of those killed when Gochan One came down. "The so-called official cause of the building collapse was structural instability, but I don't buy it for a second. You know they had something to do with it."

I don't know whether this is better than the rumors that the disaster was caused by the Ghost—or worse. I force a smile of submission onto my face. "Thank you both for explaining it to me," I say quietly.

Dr. Yixa puts his hand on the worker's shoulder. "Be careful today, and be glad tomorrow is a holiday. No celebrating tonight—go home and lie on a hot-water bottle if you want to keep your place on the floor."

The worker bows his thanks and leaves. When he's gone, Dr. Yixa turns to me, his nose even redder than before. "Don't let me hear you asking questions like that again," he says, low and rough. "Noor sympathizers are not welcome in this factory or in my clinic." He holds up his finger, his nail grimy. "Don't think I haven't heard about what went on at the meat factory. Whispers of scandal are louder than you think. I've overlooked it because Guiren is skilled and knows how to be discreet. I hoped you were made of the same stuff, but now I wonder."

"I'm sorry," I say, lowering my gaze so he knows I'm not being defiant. "I just don't understand why everyone hates them so much." A hatred that has intensified tenfold over the past year.

He snorts. "I like them just fine when they do as they're told and don't cause trouble. I thought they'd learned a lesson after the last time we had to put them down. They'd been quiet for a while." With a stifled belch he edges closer to his desk, where I know he keeps his liquor. He gives his bottom drawer a look of yearning before turning back to me. The understanding that he can't drink in front of me seems to fire his anger once more. His ears go scarlet.

"You realize how much we've done for the Noor over the years, Miss Wen? If it weren't for us, settling in the west and creating order, they'd still be ranging around like barbarians on horseback, half starved and all stupid." He's pacing now, a bit unsteadily. "But we gave them roads. We put government into place and police, too. We planted crops. We stored up for hard times instead of letting them squander the surpluses. We gave them the opportunity to do meaningful work instead of scavenging and fighting and overbreeding and killing each other. And once again they're repaying us with violence." He throws up his hands. "I suppose that's just their nature, though. They live in the moment and never think of the future. Sad, really."

"They are human beings, just like us," I say very softly.

Dr. Yixa lets out a laugh that drips with bitterness. "Just like us? Did you not hear what I've told you?" He grabs the paper from his desk and stomps over to me, then slaps it onto the table. The headline reads NOOR REBELS OVERRUN YILAT CAPITAL.

Below it there is another, smaller headline. WANTED: KNOWN REBELS is all it says. Beneath that are rows and rows of pictures, mostly artist's sketches, some photos. A few of them are Itanyai, but most of them are Noor. "Do they look human to you, Miss Wen?" asks Dr. Yixa. "Look at those faces. Look into their eyes. They are animals."

I stare at the pictures. Some of the men are listed by name, some by crime, some by description. These are the most dangerous, apparently, and they certainly look the part. Wild hair, dirty faces. The sketch artist has drawn them with their teeth bared.

At first I am almost frantic, scanning the page for any hint of a familiar face. I see none and slowly relax. Until I read the words beneath a face in the middle of the last row. THE RED ONE.

Like the others, the man in that picture wears a grimace that makes him look more beast than man. His thick hair is pulled away from his face. He looks foreign and strange. But there is something about the way the artist has drawn his eyes with only the lightest shading that fills me with deadly certainty. My fingers drift along the line of his jaw.

I remember what it felt like beneath my fingertips, rough and warm.

"Ugly sons of goats, aren't they? They'll get what's coming to them, Miss Wen, make no mistake."

"And what's coming to them?"

Dr. Yixa chuckles. "When our men march into Yilat, they'll hunt down and execute those troublemakers. Shoot on sight, if they get a chance."

I look into the eyes, pale gray in the artist's rendering. In real life they are jade green and full of keen intelligence . . . and sometimes fiery defiance. This paper does not say what he has done, and I'm not sure it matters. Somewhere, somehow, he has been noticed. Giddy happiness and utter dread twine tightly in my chest.

Melik, the boy who rules my dreams, is alive. He is also a rebel, marked for death.

I am thankful when my shift is over, because my concentration is fleeting at best today. Whenever I have a break, I find myself standing over the front page, staring down at the Red One's unfamiliar-yet-familiar face. And the longer I look, the more I wonder if it's actually Melik. Surely he and his brother are not the only Noor with rust-colored hair. I search my memories of Melik for something to confirm or dispute the accuracy of the drawing, but it is like trying to close my hands around a puff of smoke. Was his nose that long? Was his brow that wide? When I peer at it closely, I notice that the man in the drawing has a badly chipped tooth—is it a recent injury, or is this a different man?

Isn't that something I should know for sure?

Realizing that I have forgotten the details of Melik's face is like losing him all over again. The one thing I remember very well is the sight of him walking away from me after promising we would see each other again. Now that I have a window into what his life might have become, though, I have to wonder—does he bother to remember me at all?

I was only a few weeks in his life, with many days soaked in sorrow and grief and blood, both his and that of people he loved. We shared a few kisses, a handful of embraces, a fragile understanding floating in an ocean of want. For all I know, that ocean has dried up, leaving cracked earth and a broken promise. On the other hand, perhaps he is like me. Perhaps he can't forget. Is it possible that he carries those memories tucked inside his heart, beneath the long scar on his chest? Does he run his fingers along its length and remember the night I stitched him up? Is it possible that he dreams of me? Would it hurt him to think I'd forgotten him?

How on earth could he afford to spare me a thought, when his life, his people, and his freedom are at stake?

He will not leave my thoughts, though. Most days I can ask him to take a seat in the back, to stay quiet. Today he refuses. *I'm alive*, Melik whispers to me. *Just over the hills.*

It is almost as if someone has erased the hundred-mile stretch between here and there. Like I could walk my fingers over a map, striding over mountains to find him. But really it's a long day's train ride or a week of hiking, through dangerous passes known for rockslides and ambushes by bandits, to a lawless province that has fallen into chaos. People do not make the trip unless they must.

It is ridiculous even to contemplate.

What we lack in injuries and illness this afternoon, we make up for in gossip. At lunch the office girls whisper of war while the workers wipe the sweat from their brows and argue over whether the war machines they are building will be deployed. The thought steals my appetite, and I return to the clinic to find my father drinking willow bark tea and reading the paper. He looks up when I come in. "We have flu in some of the dorms."

"Dr. Yixa told me."

He nods. "You were with Bo this morning?"

"As always."

"I've just seen him. He's testing those metal frames again."

"Are you sure they'll weaken him?"

"Parts of him." Father sighs. "They make him feel safer, Wen. More powerful and in control. It is hard to blame him for wanting to feel that way."

"I don't blame him," I say. "I simply don't want him to become a machine."

Father chuckles and sips his tea. "He always thought like one."

"But he feels—"

My father stands up. "Yixa said he showed this to you this morning." He waves the paper.

From the exam room I can hear Yixa's muffled snores. "He seems certain the army will be sent to suppress the rebellion."

I hope my father will argue, but he nods instead. "When things go this far, the government cannot ignore the threat."

I bite my lip. "I heard something this morning. I was near Boss Inyie's office when he came in."

Father raises his eyebrows, and I continue. "He got an urgent call that he had been waiting for. And he canceled his morning appointments." I fold my arms over my stomach. "And I heard him mention the Noor."

My father, who is slight of build to begin with, suddenly looks even smaller. "That does not bode well for the Noor in the Yilat Province, then."

His words sharpen the teeth of the unspoken fear that has gnawed at me all day. I touch the paper. "Is that him, Father?"

My father folds the paper. "Whether it is or not, it tells you nothing."

I frown. "How can you say that? The men in those pictures are all condemned."

"And if there is a war, all the Noor are. The government will not be merciful, Wen, not with what they've done."

My eyes sting. "You say that so calmly."

"Would it make one bit of difference if I shouted?" He sets the paper on Yixa's desk. His narrow shoulders are slumped. "It is a hopeless situation." His eyes meet mine. "And I'm sorry that it hurts you. I'm sorry that you are still thinking about Melik, because it will only bring you more pain. It is best if you let him go."

"You don't know that I haven't," I say, lifting my chin.

Father stares at me for too many long seconds. "You say his name in your sleep."

I cover my mouth, my cheeks on fire with the humiliating knowledge that my father is aware of my dreams. I mumble something about needing some air, grab my overcoat from the hook by the door, and flee. Something is happening inside me. I thought I was headed toward a kind of peace, an understanding that Melik was gone paired with a never-ending hope that I would one day see him again, a place where I could think of him without so much pain and longing. Today has destroyed all of that.

With every moment I find more hints that something terrible is brewing. As I walk past the factory floor, it is still bustling with activity, though it was scheduled to close an hour ago. Despite having no good reason to do so, I cut through the administrative hallway, and my insides knot when I see the foremen from all three shifts crowding into Boss Inyie's office. Fearful someone will see me and guess that I am spying, I bow my head and hurry away.

Stone after stone of evidence is falling into place, and now the truth is as big and ominous as a mountain. I don't know exactly when. I don't know exactly how. But I do know this: Our war machines will be marching west very soon.

Chapter Three

FEELING AS IF I am suffocating, I leave the factory. At the compound gate the guard on duty—who must be a new hire, because I know all the staff by sight if not by name—hesitates when I tell him that I don't know when I'll be back. He scratches at the patchy beard on his cheek. "It would be best if you returned by midnight, sister," he says, conveying a respectfully polite kind of concern that I've rarely heard since moving from the Hill to the Gochan complex.

His gaze darts toward the factory entrance. On this day of all days workers should be flooding out of this place on a wave of eagerness and celebration, but the opposite is happening—men from the night and morning shifts are filing in, looking grim but determined. All of them are carrying rucksacks, as if they are going on a long journey.

The guard looks back at me. "The fireworks can be seen from our compound's square. You can come back early and watch them here."

I give him what I hope is a beguiling smile. "Because the streets are dangerous? I'll stick to the main thoroughfares."

His brows lower. "That's comforting to hear, but it's not why you should be back by the arrival of First Holiday," he says quietly, his lips barely moving.

I wish he would confirm for me what I already suspect, that he would be the one who drops the final stone into place, if only to release some of this burning, twisting anticipation. I lean forward a bit. "You are kind to worry about my reputation, brother."

He shifts uncomfortably. "You work here, I take it?"

I nod. "I assist in the medical clinic. I'm also Dr. Guiren's daughter."

"And you live on the compound. Not out in the Ring."

"Of course! Gochan Two has been my home for a year."

He folds his arms over his chest and peers about as if he's concerned someone will overhear. "I've been instructed to lock the gate at midnight," he whispers. "Anyone not inside will be unable to enter until they open again."

My eyes go wide. "In the morning?"

He shakes his head. "It's lockdown, sister. It will be longer than that."

I cover my mouth with my hand and try to look excited instead of horrified. "Something is happening, isn't it?"

He shakes his head. "I've already said too much."

He gestures toward the street. "Go have your fun, buy yourself a sweet, and return early if you know what's good for you."

I thank him in a chirpy, overly cheerful voice and leave the compound with my fists balled in my skirt. I walk through the Ring on sidewalks already crowded with vendors and First Holiday celebrants. It's all bright and festive and normal, like it has been every year since I was a child. There is a bounce to each stride, a smile on every face. A mother and a father walk by, each clutching a hand of the small boy between them, and his cheeks are round and fat and pink with happiness. I stare longer than is polite, clinging to my wish that things were really this way, that the world were full of peace and jubilation and nothing else, that the shadow of war had not descended. As I look at that lovely little family, it is almost possible to believe.

But then I make my way past fences plastered with anti-Noor slogans, patriotic phrases, and more wanted posters. These are a step beyond anything I have seen so far. In every image the Noor are drawn as hairy beast-men with overhanging foreheads, too-wide shoulders, and massive feet. There is one poster of a valiant and handsome Itanyai soldier, his black hair perfect, his eyes dark and intense, bravely facing down a horde of Noor on horseback. Another shows a Noor standing beside a burning, ruined bean field, grinning like a monster, his huge, jagged teeth protruding from his mouth. These are pictures meant to spread fear and anger, to spark a fire in the blood. It is easy enough to do—with food prices rising every day and with shortages of basic staples affecting most of the country, we all want to blame something for our suffering. Of course, the real culprit is the drought, not the Noor. But perhaps the government believes the people won't turn on it if it provides another target for our helpless, hungry rage—one that can be oppressed and killed.

Before long it is too much. My flimsy, silly wishes have been demolished. My heart is beating too hard. Melik is too loud in my thoughts. My eyes are burning with tears that it isn't safe to shed.

I retreat back to the factory, waving conspicuously as I enter to show the guard I listened to his guidance. Instead of returning to the clinic, though, I climb the stairs all the way to the roof of Gochan Two. I hover at the edge, looking down on the empty factory square. The heat and noise from the factory floor have not stopped. I wonder what the workers are feeling, if they're resentful or content. Usually, everyone is eager to venture into the Ring on this night, and until a year ago, so was I.

But last year I spent First Holiday Eve with my red Noor, sitting on a cold concrete floor in a dank room, happier than I have ever been as I watched fireworks pop beyond a dirty windowpane, as my eyes traced Melik's profile, the slope of his nose, the smile on his lips. It was a pure moment when anything seemed possible.

Now I feel the opposite. My thin fingers curl over bricks, too weak to bend things into the shape I wish them to be.

"You remembered," Bo says softly from behind me. "I was sure you wouldn't."

I whirl around to see him standing near the flaming

smokestack that looms high above Gochan Two, a fragile smile playing across his lips. My stomach lurches. Both of Bo's arms are too long for his body. His remaining flesh-and-bone arm is encased within a frame of steel and wire. He looks down, and his hands rise for his examination, palms up. "I'm testing them," he says. "What do you think?"

I think he looks more like a monster than he ever has. "You must have worked very hard today."

He stands up a little straighter. "I did. And I thought I'd be watching the fireworks alone, but you're here. This day is ending even better than it started."

I turn back to the Ring. The sun is setting over the Western Hills, lending the smoky haze over the town a golden glow. "My day was not so good."

Bo joins me near the low wall that rings the roof. "Was Yixa cruel to you?" His voice is sharp, and suddenly I fear for the old surgeon.

"No. I've told you—he's always kind."

"He drinks too much."

"He did nothing to hurt me." I close my eyes. "The cruelest thing he did was to show me a newspaper. The rebels have taken Kegu."

"I heard."

Bo hears everything. Like in Gochan One, he has taken advantage of the antiquated piping system to watch and eavesdrop on nearly everyone in Gochan Two.

When he looks down at me, his metal mask reflects the lights of the Ring as they flicker on to beat back the encroaching darkness. "I heard something else today, actually. Something top secret."

Nausea rolls over me. "I think I know what it is. But tell me."

He sounds excited as he confirms all my fears. "Boss Inyie received a large order from the national army this morning. Battle machines and a carrier as well. He is ecstatic. War means money."

I stare at him. "War means suffering and death."

Bo shrugs. "It means the war machines will have their day. I've always wanted to see one in action."

"Are you saying that just to upset me?" I cry.

He shakes his head, looking puzzled at my reaction. "I'm saying it because it's true."

I point toward the compound gate. "It's going to be locked at midnight. The guard warned me."

Bo looks unsurprised. "And from now on Gochan Two will not close. Not until they have fully equipped the national forces. They are calling in the weekend staff and hiring extra men on the pretense that they are building a new civilian transport machine. Boss Inyie wants to house the entire staff here and close the compound to keep the secret from spreading. New hires will be able to come in, but no one will be able to leave."

That explains why all the men were lugging rucksacks. My stomach feels hollow. "The army is planning an invasion." It's really happening. My father was right—when the rebels took Kegu, the government decided to take action.

"Very soon," Bo says. "Apparently, several battalions of troops will arrive within the week. We are the gateway to the western province."

"No," I breathe. "So many will die."

Bo's metal hands flex as his excitement is transmitted through his muscles. "They'll send an advance force of war machines to decimate the resistance. The machines can move through the hills quickly and do not need roads or tracks. They'll catch the rebels by surprise."

Melik's village is nestled at the opening of the canyon. "They will kill more than rebels."

Bo chuckles. "I believe that is the idea."

I step away from him, my whole body shaking.

Bo does not notice. He is gazing at the hills. "I wish I could pilot a war machine. I have dreamed of such a thing for years. I've studied their designs. I understand them very well, what they can do. I could—"

"Can you stop them, Bo?" The idea occurs to me all at once. If anyone can prevent this invasion of metal monsters, it is the Ghost. "Can you sabotage the floor? Shut it down?"

His eyebrows rise. "Why would I ever want to do that?"

He knows why. But if I say Melik's name out loud, I know it will hurt him. Besides, Melik is not the only one I'm worried about. "Because I am asking you to, Bo. Because it would save lives."

"Whose lives, Wen?" His tone sharpens. "The war machines will crush the rebellion before the bulk of the army even arrives. Think of the lives that will save."

"At the expense of so many others."

"But those are Noor. Do you realize you're asking me to betray our people? Our entire country?"

"You speak as if the Noor are not a part of our country."

"It's called Itanya for a reason," he says coldly.

"I have to go," I say in a choked voice.

Bo's brow furrows. "Why? The fireworks haven't started yet." All at once he seems so childlike, easily diverted by the things that bring him delight. But as his gaze skims over my face, his expression hardens. "As always, your only thoughts are of that foolish Noor boy who walked away from you."

My bottom lip trembles. "That's not true. Or fair."

Bo's jaw ridges with tension, and he leans forward. "He deserves everything he gets," he hisses suddenly.

I shake my head, imagining children playing in the shadow of the hills, looking up to see their death descending upon them. I picture their mothers trying in vain to protect them. I remember the pain in Melik's eyes as he told me about the last time the war machines came through the canyon. "This is about more than that, and more than him."

Bo's mechanical fists clench. "The red Noor made his choice. They all did."

"What would you do if you were in his place?" I ask, my voice cracking. "Would you break, Bo? Have you ever broken? Can you blame him for refusing to surrender?"

"I blame him for exactly one thing," he says, "and as for the rest, I don't care."

"Then you are as unfeeling as you look," I snap, gesturing at his mechanical arms.

"Or perhaps I feel more than you could ever guess, whether I want to or not!" he shouts, then turns away quickly, grimacing, his metal fingers clicking. "Either way, it doesn't change a thing. This is bigger than you or me or one stupid Noor, Wen. It's silly for us to argue about it."

"Because I can't do anything to stop it," I say. And because Bo won't do anything to stop it.

"Precisely."

I look down at my hands, small and weak, flesh and bone, and then I look at Bo's, powerful and merciless, steel and wire. "Maybe I should try."

His eye goes wide. "You're not serious." He takes a step forward, his mechanical hands rising, and I flinch back. He winces and his machine fingers rise to his opposite shoulder, twisting and pressing in a precise sequence of steps. The metal frame surrounding his human arm slides to the ground with a clatter. His warm fingertips caress my cheek a moment later. I am shocked by the intimacy of it, and by the knowledge that Bo understood the one thing he could do to bring me closer.

He gives me a small, sad smile. "I'm sorry for everything, for all I've said, for the war, for the orders that have already been given. I'm sorry for what's going to happen. I'm sorry for being cold. All of it."

His regret is not enough to soothe me because it changes nothing. Determination is wrapping itself around my limbs, winding its way along my bones, my veins, my muscles. Maybe I should try. How can I not? How can I live with myself if I sit idly by while those machines tear through villages full of Noor whose only crime is living and dreaming and craving the same rights that I have always taken for granted? This is not about Melik, not really. This is about Sinan, Melik's little brother, and his mother and his younger, more vulnerable self. No one was there, all those years ago, to warn them. No one was there to whisper, "Run, hide, get to safety."

Bo cups my cheek and strokes his thumb over my skin. "Say something, Wen. Say you forgive me."

"I forgive you," I whisper. "I am sorry I asked you to commit treason. It was very wrong of me."

His eye closes, dark lashes long. "You scared me."

I am scaring myself. "I didn't mean to." But I am going to do it again, because my thoughts are filled with treason and betrayal. Right now I wish I were not Itanyai. I was raised to be proud of my people, of my part in this great culture, but now I am nothing but ashamed. Because I was raised to believe something else, too: that compassion is golden, that it is best to preserve life, to ease suffering, to value mercy above all else and others above myself. My father was my most diligent teacher. If Bo knew my thoughts, though, and if he told Father, the two of them would prevent me from doing what I think I must. No matter how much compassion he has, my father is still a father. He would not allow me to leave, which means he cannot know.

Above our heads there is a deep pop as the first firework goes off. It paints Bo's metal face pink and yellow, the soft shades of a spring flower. "Stay with me for the fireworks?" he asks, his voice low.

He was wrong when he said I could not guess what he feels; I know how deeply it runs. It is the catch in his breath, the shadow in his eyes, the twitch at the corner of his mouth. I know he wants to touch me, to have my whole heart. Maybe he knows he could have, if things had been different. Maybe he even senses that he has a part of it already. And that part of me aches, knowing that tomorrow he will realize I was lying, when I murmur, "Yes. I will stay."

I take his hand and I lace my fingers with his. It's my final gift to him. Because I feel it too, a wish that things were simple, a wish to save a piece of Bo that he himself is trying to kill, a wish that this were enough for both of us.

I lay my head on his shoulder and smell his skin, soap and sweat and machine oil. We turn our faces to the sky and accept the deep, smoky kiss of the night air. His thumb strokes the back of my hand. As the fireworks stretch fingers of light across the sky, I set aside my wishes and sink into dreams. Can I save a single life? Can I do anything at all? Am I stupid for considering this?

It is the loneliest of feelings, but it is warm nonetheless. I think of Bo, how even when his body was torn and splintered, he did not give up. And how Melik, even when the whole of our nation told him he was worthless, no better than an animal, stood straight and demanded to be dealt with as a man. And how my father, even my quiet, meek father, devoted all he had to his patients, with little thought for himself, who even now eats a tad less than he should just to be able to afford medicine for those who need it.

And me . . . what have I ever risked? What have I sacrificed? What have I ever done but allow others to stand between me and the danger?

Yes, I am a girl. One with no special skill or talent or power. But all I have to be is a message carrier. All I need to do is tell what I know to someone who can take action. And if I don't try, I think I will break—and that would be exactly what I deserved.

So I clutch Bo's hand and feel him squeeze mine. I draw breath and feel my heart beat. I make a mental list of things I must take. I recall the whistle of the train, the one that leaves for the west late in the night. And I think of the people I could save, people who do not look like me, who do not speak my language, but who love and hate just the same. I imagine what could happen to me, and to them, if I fail. And I tremble with fear.

But then I remember a rust-haired boy, and his smile, and his eyes, and his softly spoken words.

There is nothing wrong with being scared. It only means that something important is at stake.

Judging by the terror coursing through my veins, I know that warning the Noor of the impending invasion is more important than anything I will ever do.

Chapter Four

WHEN THE FINAL fireworks have exploded over the Ring and fallen in cinders and ash to the ground, Bo turns to me. My hand is still in his. I am afraid to let go, because it means we are over. I shiver as the wind gusts my hair, which has grown past my shoulders once again. Bo's eye follows the movements of my fingers as I tuck stray locks behind my ear.

"Last year I stood on the roof of Gochan One, and I watched you come out of his dorm," he says quietly.

I swallow hard. "I know."

"I had been imagining that you might choose me, that you would come to the roof and that I would reveal myself to you. But when I saw you there, I knew you had made a different choice."

I bow my head. His machine hand rises and with the

slightest brush of his steel fingers nudges my chin up. He gives me the most painfully hopeful of smiles. "But tonight you chose me," he whispers.

I cannot stand it. I don't want to leave Bo. I don't want to hurt him. I don't want to lose what we have, and in leaving I am setting it afire, burning it to nothing. I release his hand and step into him, throwing my arms around his waist and pressing my head to his chest. I listen to the heart that I am going to break. It beats furiously against my ear like a caged bird. If I could, I would tell him everything. But like my father, he would never let me go. "You are dear to me," I say, choking on my tears. Because I do not know what the future holds for me now that I have made this decision, so I must live from moment to moment. Each second may be the last one of its kind. Like this one, as his human arm wraps over my back, as his fingers stroke my hair, as he leans his head on mine.

"You are the only thing to me," he replies. "Wen . . . I—"

"I must go," I blurt out, and then I stand on my tiptoes and kiss his cheeks, first the smooth perfection of his metal mask and then the warm softness of his skin. "It's so late."

"Of course," he murmurs. "Of course." Disappointment and longing weigh down every syllable, and each sinks into my aching heart. "Sleep well."

I press my forehead against his chest one more time, inhaling his familiar human-machine scent, and then I walk quickly for the stairwell. I do not look back. Bo will be hurt when he finds out I am gone, but he will be alive and safe. Melik, on the other hand, will die along with countless others if I don't warn them.

I return to the clinic. Despite the thunder of noises from a factory floor that is usually silent at this time of night, my father is deeply asleep, done in by another day of tireless work. I stand over his sleeping pallet, watching his lined face lit by the soft glow of holiday lights filtering through the window. I used to think he was fragile, but now I know him to be stronger than he looks. He has never hesitated to make sacrifices for people who need care, who need medicine, who need compassion. He has never turned away from a soul he could help. There have been times when I thought he was foolish, spending his money and his time on people he barely knew, but now I understand. Now I am proud to be his daughter, and I can only hope I am strong enough to live up to his example.

He and Bo will have each other when I am gone, and I am glad.

I pack a satchel with an extra pair of shoes, a shawl, and a few hard biscuits. I wrap one of my father's scalpels in a cloth and tuck it into the pocket of my overcoat. Then I creep into the clinic and open the bottom drawer of Dr. Yixa's wooden desk. I feel along the top until I find the paper sack tucked into the wooden frame. This is the stash of money Yixa uses to buy his alcohol. He collects fees from the workers for extra things, like notes excusing them from work or allowing them to return even though they are still injured. He tucks each coin away, then dips into this treasure trove to purchase the rice wine and sorghum liquor that steadies his hands and keeps him on his feet.

I don't steal all of it. Only enough for a round-trip ticket to Kegu and several meals. I am going to try to come back, though I know there is a very real chance I may never be able to return. My hands shake as I stuff the coins into the lining of my satchel. For a moment I sit on the floor, paralyzed by the pull of inaction. How easy it would be to put this money back and crawl under my blanket. How easy it would be to lie warm in my bed.

But at the same time, how impossible.

I pull up the hood of my overcoat and slide on my leather boots. Then I slip out of the clinic and into the hallway, any sound I make cloaked by the incessant clamor from the floor. I slide my hand along the wall, the vibrations rattling my bones. On the other side men shining with sweat are attaching the enormous legs, calibrating the guns, oiling the hinges and gears, preparing to unleash a nightmare on the west. I am almost running by the time I reach the end of the hall and duck out a side exit, but not before checking the clock on the wall.

It is twenty minutes to midnight. The guard is still in position by the gate, but the sidewalks just beyond it are packed with people, some dragging themselves home now that the fireworks are over, some just getting started in their celebration. Instead of walking straight through the square and approaching the gates head-on, I loop around by the compound fence and follow it until I am only a few yards from the open gate—and the guard. Given the concern he showed for me earlier, I cannot believe he would let me stroll out of the compound without trying to stop me.

He is chatting with passersby, though his attention keeps drifting toward the pink-light salon just across the street.

They are doing a bustling business tonight. Opium fumes drift from the salon's open windows, and musicians entertain the drunken patrons as they wait outside.

I hover in the shadow of the gate, waiting for my moment. The guard is not entirely distracted. Despite his friendly smile and wandering eye, his posture is tense. I am sure he is counting down the minutes until he locks us all in. I peer through the fence at the citizens, awaiting the right group for my purposes. A shiver passes through me as the guard checks his pocket watch once more. But then I see my opportunity—a group of girls about my age, all wearing overcoats with hoods and giggling as they head toward the Hill, where the middle-class families live. They look finer than I do. The hems of their dresses aren't frayed, and their coats are not threadbare like mine. I edge toward the gateway, feverishly hoping the guard won't notice such details.

Right as the girls pass, I take a sudden side step and tuck myself in behind them. The guard senses movement and turns to look, but I am wearing my hood and am indistinguishable from the others as we pass him. Nearly faint with relief, I break free of Gochan Two. I am on my way.

No one pays me any mind as I walk past the quiet hulk of Gochan Three, the textile mill and clothing factory. I turn right when I reach the corner, leaving the Ring behind and heading for the train station. I am not the only one. To my surprise, the platform is crowded: men in bulky gray overcoats with their hats pulled low over their ears and their breaths puffing out like smoke from between their lips, a few grandmas in heavy shawls, a few families with small children in tow, and a few young women looking chilled and pinched in the night air. I find it oddly comforting. I look just like them in my brown work dress and plain wool overcoat.

The old man in the ticket booth frowns at me when I ask for passage to Kegu. "Why you going all the way there?" he barks. "Don't you know it's overrun with rebel dogs? No one's going that far, my girl. Farthest anyone else is going is Vuda, before the crossover into Yilat."

My fingers clamp hard over the straps of my satchel. "Yes, sir, but my family needs me."

He squints at me through smudged glasses. "You should stay in the Ring. Dangerous time, this is."

I pluck my coins from my bag and slide them beneath the glass partition, including an extra bronze penny to grease the gears in this transaction. "My mother is ill," I say. "She has a cancer, and I'm afraid she doesn't have much longer on this earth."

"Oh." He blinks down at the extra coin, then slides it back over to me. "All the best to you, then," he says, his voice suddenly hoarse. "Family's important."

I mumble my thanks and take back the tiny bribe that he rejected, embarrassed that I insulted him by offering it in the first place. Ticket in hand, I join the people on the platform, standing near a clump of old ladies and tucking my hands into the pockets of my overcoat, wishing I owned gloves.

The platform is abuzz with gossip, mostly about the barbaric Noor and their intentions to come to the east and kill us all. The young women discuss it in low tones, the old women more loudly. I am relieved when the steam engine finally shrieks and roars into the station, drowning out their voices. The conductor catches my arm as I head for the rear of the train. "Up front," he says gruffly. "Women up front."

I obey him, following the factory girls up the steel steps and into the car. I find myself a seat, a hard wooden bench, really, and stare out the window at the Ring, still within reach. I could change my mind now. I could jump off and scamper down the steps. I could sneak back into the factory and the clinic and no one would be the wiser.

But as the train jolts into motion, I realize it is too late. I have made my choice. It feels like my chest is caught in a metal press, squeezed flat under the overwhelming pressure of my sorrow and fear. I've left my father and Bo behind. I left no note, no hint of where I've run to.

They cannot reach me. They cannot help me or save me or stop me. I have done it.

I am on my own, and I need to make a plan. I have to tell someone who matters, someone who can do something with the information I possess, so my first idea is to go straight to the municipal complex in Kegu and ask to speak to whoever's in charge.

When I think through it like that, it seems so incredibly foolish. But what is the alternative? It is not as if I can trust a letter to get there, and a telegram can be intercepted too. And it is not as if I know any rebels.

Well. I might know one. But I haven't spoken to him in a year, and I have no idea where he is, no way to contact him.

"May I sit here?"

I look up to see a girl, about my age, with pink, cold-kissed cheeks and bright eyes. Her black hair is parted in the middle and braided, and her shirt and slacks tell me she probably works at Gochan Three. "Certainly," I say, moving my satchel off the bench to make room for her.

"My name is Anji," she says, settling onto the bench with her large cloth bag at her feet.

"Wen," I say. "It's nice to meet you."

"Where are you going?" she asks. "I'm headed to Vuda for the holiday. My family lives in Lavie. Easy enough to walk."

"I'm going to Kegu," I say. "My family is there."

Her eyes widen. "They should be coming to you, not the other way around. It's so dangerous there!"

"My mother is ill. She cannot travel." Lying is becoming second nature, it seems, because my voice does not even shake.

"But you are all alone? How can your family allow you to do such a thing?" Anji looks horrified, and it makes my heart thump.

"I suppose the news out of Kegu has been rather alarming."

She lets out a laugh. "I hope your father or brothers are meeting you at the station. Otherwise, you could be plucked right off the street. I heard there are roaming bands of rebels just looking for young girls to kidnap."

I suspect some of those stories are not quite true. I grew up on tales of the savage Noor, and then I met some of those men, who turned out to be just that—men. But

I am not about to have that argument with Anji. "Oh, of course. My brothers will be waiting for me."

Anji relaxes and leaves me to my thoughts for a long while. The train chugs upward, along a high pass that will carry us west. Above us loom the northern peaks of the Western Hills, and to our south is the canyon that winds through them, a split in the land through which men and machines can walk to get from the Ring directly to the border villages of the Yilat Province. The train tracks stick to the northern foothills, and to my right, down the rocky slope, stretches the grasslands.

I have never been this far north and west before. My nose skims the window glass as I squint in the early dawn. Most women in the car with me are napping fitfully, their heads resting on their shawls and cloth bags, but I am wide awake as the sun rises slowly behind us, lighting the way. My throat aches as the golden light glints off a bend in the track. My father will be waking now, and will probably assume I am with Bo, since I start most mornings in his underground kingdom. And Bo will be awake too, wondering when my footsteps will echo through the tunnel.

I push them out of my thoughts as my eyes begin to burn. I think of what I have to say to the rebels. They need to prepare for those war machines to stride through the canyon, before they spill into Yilat and destroy everything in their path. Lost in those fears and my own memories, I drift through the next few hours.

The train is just pulling out of Ganluo, merely a depot in a small hillside village, when Anji pokes me in the shoulder. "Vuda is the next stop, but it's almost an hour away still. Are you hungry? Will you come to the dining car with me?"

My stomach growls in response. "Let's go."

We sway down the aisle, rocked by the train as it rounds a curve and heads higher into the hills. There's a sudden jolt, and I nearly topple into an elderly woman. Her knitting needles stab into my side. I apologize and keep walking, rubbing the sore spot over my ribs. When we get to the space between the cars, the conductor frowns. "The men are having their breakfast," he says.

"Well, we're hungry too," says Anji, putting her hands on her hips, "and our money is as good as theirs."

The sliding door to the dining car clatters and shrieks as it opens. A young man with his cap tilted cheekily to one side grins at us. "You are welcome here, ladies." When he sees the look on the conductor's face, he slaps the man on the shoulder. "We'll be on our best behavior, but you can't blame us for wanting to bide time with pretty girls, can you?"

The conductor, staring at the fellow's off-kilter cap with sharp disapproval, says, "I'm responsible for their safe passage."

The grin slides off the young man's face. "Then I accept the responsibility as my own. I promise you, no one will lay a finger on them." He looks as if he could make sure of it—his shoulder muscles are straining at the fabric of his coat. He is quite bulky, and as I look into the dining car at the young men lounging on the benches, dining on dumplings and sipping on tea, I realize all of them are.

The young man turns his gaze on me. "I'm Leye," he says, bowing.

Anji and I curtsy and introduce ourselves. Leye offers his hand and helps us step over the coupling and into the dining car, where every head turns as we enter. I am so used to viewing myself in the reflection of Bo's metal face that I wonder what exactly these boys are seeing. Because they are boys, really, or little more than that. They can't be but a few years older than I am, and they are all clean shaven and raw looking. "Where are all of you going?" I ask.

"Oh, Vuda. There is a new mill there that needs workers."

Anji rakes her gaze over them. "There is work in the Ring."

Leye's cheeks turn ruddy. "Ah, there is better pay in Vuda, or so I hear."

"But haven't you already been hired?" I ask. "You're all wearing the same clothing."

Leye clears his throat as he glances at the other boys, all clad in gray trousers, black boots, thick gray overcoats buttoned up, bulky over the layers underneath. It is as if they are wearing their entire wardrobes on their backs. The smell of sweat is heavy and musky. "Yes. Yes, we all have jobs waiting for us."

Anji arches her eyebrow. "Nice of them to send you work clothes."

Leye gives her a charming smile. "And a bit of advance pay. May I buy you a bun?"

I move up the aisle ahead of them and ask the attendant for some tea, inhaling its astringent fumes gratefully. A young man who introduces himself as Musa moves over and offers me a seat, and I take it as Anji and Leye order their food.

SARAH FINE

"Do you have family in Vuda?" Musa asks before blowing steam off his dumpling.

"Oh, she's not getting off in Vuda. She's going all the way to Kegu," says Anji, bumping her hip against mine as she sits down with a sweet bun.

Musa turns to me, his broad back against the window of the car. He is a handsome boy, the kind my friend Vie would fawn over, with smooth skin and high cheekbones. "You cannot do that."

"My mother is sick. I must."

But Musa shakes his head. "Absolutely not."

"I'm sorry," I say, smiling at his concern, "but I think I am old enough to decide."

Musa angrily beckons to Leye. "Did you know there are people on this train headed to Kegu?"

Leye frowns, an expression that looks odd on his face, which seems made for smiling. He rubs at the back of his neck. "Miss Wen, we strongly advise you to get off in Vuda."

"Why, so you can take her for a walk, maybe buy her a drink?" says Anji, tart as a lemon.

"No," says Leye, all serious now. His black brows knit in concern. "So you will not die."

"I've heard the warnings," I say, "and I understand it is dangerous. But I suspect they are exaggerated."

Musa chuckles. "Maybe they are. That's not why we're concerned."

Leye's hand drops from his neck as he exchanges a hard gaze with Musa, who nods. Both boys reach up and unbutton the top few buttons of their coats, revealing the insignia of the national army. "We are not going to

50

Vuda," Musa says quietly, leaning so close that I smell the garlic and pork on his breath, that I see the faint red rash on his jaw where he shaved a bit too zealously. "We're going to Kegu. All of us. And we're going to take back the capital."

"Oh my," says Anji, looking them over as my heart flutters painfully. "So you are soldiers."

Leye nods. "The rebels won't expect us to come this way." He lifts his coat, and I see why he looks so bulky. His rifle and knife are strapped to his body. "The conductor knows. There are two trains behind us as well."

"And we are cover for you," I say quietly. "Because this is a civilian train."

Musa has the good grace to look ashamed. "You are in no danger now. Especially if you get off in Vuda."

I look over his shoulder at the craggy mountainside hanging above us. We are headed into a pass carved between two high hills. "How far is it now?" My mind is spinning. Judging by what the ticket seller said, I am the only person apart from these soldiers who is going to Kegu, and now these boys know that. Can I make it to the capital and slip away to warn the rebels? Will I have to get off in Vuda and figure out how to travel the rest of the way? Will there be any other civilian trains, or has the military commandeered the rail line?

"We're nearly at the peak of our journey," Leye tells me, and from the way Musa rolls his eyes, I can tell this is something Leye is particularly interested in. "We are a mile from the highest altitude we will reach, and after that we'll descend into the valley where Vuda lies. As the crow flies, we are not far from Yilat. Maybe thirty miles or so—if you want to trek over the high passes or descend to walk through the long canyon. But by train, once we leave Vuda, we skirt the mountains and enter Yilat from the northeast." He touches my shoulder and winks. "Without civilians."

I bite my lip and look ahead, at the high pass. There is snow crusted on either side of the rails. It's odd, this soft beauty next to the hard metal snake of the rail. I wonder—

The world roars and a burst of fire flashes before my eyes. The entire dining car jerks and squeals, then flies up into the air, spinning like a child's toy. I am crushed and tossed, turned upside down and inside out, punched and jabbed and smashed. As the lights go out and everything breaks and flies apart, my ears fill with pleas and shouts and screams, some of which are surely my own.

Chapter Five

WHEN THE WORLD stops moving, I find myself staring up, not at the ceiling, but at the floor. On either side of me are shattered windows and bodies, bleeding and thrashing, groaning and crying. A hand clutches at my sleeve. Anji, bleeding from a deep gash on the side of her head, pulls herself closer. "Help me," she says in a rasping voice.

Within this dining car, amidst the spilled dumplings and overturned teacups and napkins that flutter like flags of surrender, some of the soldiers are pushing themselves to their knees, helping their brothers do the same. Others lie still and broken. I grab one of the napkins and press it to the side of Anji's face. "Hold it there," I say, hoarse and panting.

Someone grabs my hand. It's Leye, his wide, friendly

face a mask of pain. He's lying next to me, with some of his comrades piled on top of his legs. "Are you all right?" he asks.

I do a quick inventory. My head hurts, but I am thinking, though not beyond the moment. My chest aches, but I can breathe, and my heart is beating fiercely. My ears are ringing as sharply as a shift whistle, but I heard what Leye asked. My limbs feel as if they have been pulled out of joint, but all of them are still attached, and I can move them. And my lips are buzzing with numbness and cold, but I can speak. "I'm fine. What happened?"

He slowly sits up, hissing as he tries to move the other men off him. "Derailment."

"There was an explosion," says Musa. "Could be an ambush."

I glance over to see him on his feet. He moves carefully over to Leye and lifts the bodies of unconscious and dead friends to free his comrade's legs. I move in the direction of a trickle of cold air, thinking to escape that way, but only a narrow gap remains between the crushed window frame and the roof of the car. Beyond the wreckage there is a wall of rock, some twisted rail, scattered debris, a few bodies, and a lot of smoke.

"How could this be an ambush?" Leye asks as Musa frees his legs. "We're not even in Yilat yet."

Musa shrugs, slinging his rifle onto his back. "Maybe it was an engine fire. Or maybe there was something on the rails? Colonel Boren was in the last car. We need to get everyone out, take roll, and get his orders. Maybe we can radio for help. There is supposed to be another train five hours behind ours."

Leye nods, still holding my hand. I recognize the sweaty desperation in his grip—he is hurting and doesn't want to cry out. "And the girls?"

Musa impatiently wipes a trickle of blood from his short ebony hair and searches the ground for his cap. He grabs the nearest one and jams it onto his head. "We don't know how the other cars fared. We had one car of civilians and four carrying our men. First thing we have to do is get out."

He wraps his arm around Anji and pulls her up. She leans on him gratefully, her slender fingers bunched in his coat. Her skin is pale, almost gray, beneath the mask of blood. "You're going to be just fine, sister," he says, his voice gentle. "Can you walk?"

She nods, but her grip on him doesn't loosen. Musa looks down at Leye, who has pushed himself up to a sitting position. "Can you walk?" he asks his friend.

Leye grits his teeth as he moves his left foot. "It may be broken."

"I'll help you," I say, getting clumsily to my feet, wrenching my overcoat and skirt from between two limp bodies. The upside-down car rocks as the weight of all its surviving occupants shifts this way and that. I have a brief flash of fear, picturing us rolling down the side of the mountain, but I push it away. I let Leye lean on me as he stands up, keeping the pressure off his left foot. I put my arm around his waist. We are standing in space of the aisle, the backs of the bench seats crowding our shoulders, several unmoving bodies complicating our path to the exit. I try not to think too hard about how many of those slack, bloody faces were smiling a few minutes ago.

"Let's move out and see if we can't get these girls with the other civilians, and then we can find the colonel and get our orders," says Musa. He leads Anji through the cluttered mess, careful not to tread on limbs or bellies. We have to step around one fellow, obviously dead, whose body is caught between two benches that were crushed together. I turn my face away, but when we edge past his hanging head and arms, my stomach clenches. The exit is blocked by a grisly tangle of steel and flesh. "We'll have to crawl out the window," Musa says, gesturing to a few of his comrades who are moving toward us. "This one is the only opening that's big enough."

I help Leye lower himself onto a relatively clear patch of the metal ceiling before joining him. Musa guides Anji down too. The window frame here didn't buckle, and we'll be able to crawl out. Musa calls to the others, "Whoever can walk, we need you to help the wounded out and get them clear of the wreckage." He sounds strong and assured, even as a stubborn trickle of blood escapes from beneath his cap. Like Anji, he's hit his head, but he is paying it no mind at all. He puts his arm around Anji. She is crying, tears streaking through the blood on her cheeks. "You stay with me, okay?" he says, giving her a smile.

"Okay," she whispers.

He strokes a tear from the corner of her mouth and holds her waist as she crawls out through the window, following close behind her. As the others scramble past us, I look over at Leye. Lines of strain bracket his mouth. "We have to find a way to get to lower altitude," he says, watching the fog of the soldiers' breath. "We'll freeze if we're caught out in the open."

"We'll think warm thoughts," I say, trying to resurrect his smile. I need him to give me that, just like Musa smiled at Anji. Somehow, when things are shattered, one curve of the mouth can calm a thousand fears. But Leye can only wince and nod. "Shall we go?" I ask.

We are the last in the car, or at least, the last who can move. Leye is bracing himself to inch forward on hands and knees when the air is filled with a *crack-crack-crack*. Near, far, piercing and echoing. Leye's eyes go wide, and I turn back to the window in time to see Musa fall with Anji in his arms. The others shout and reach for their rifles, but their blood mists the frosty air and they fall with crimson flowers blossoming on their chests and legs and faces and backs. I blink, unable to understand what I am seeing. I am huddled in this metal bubble as the people outside are cut down by an unseen force. My brain tells me we are under attack, but still I cannot comprehend.

Musa is staring at the sky, his reassuring smile gone.

Anji's head is on his chest. She is not crying anymore.

"No, no, no," Leye mutters, his voice breaking and hitching. The thick barrel of his rifle skims my shoulder as he yanks it from his coat. Beyond the window the soldiers who escaped the train have all been hit, though some of them are still alive. A few are trying to crawl back to our dining car. One of them looks right at me, his dark eyes full of pleading. My own eyes burn as I read his silent scream—he doesn't want to die. It is wrong for him to die. He is barely a man. He has so much left to do.

But as I lunge, my hand outstretched, thoughtlessly desperate to get to him, Leye throws himself on top of me. "You can't," he huffs, crushing me to the metal ceiling.

A second later the boy outside is snuffed out, the bullets jerking his body to the side. I realize Leye is holding me down before I understand that I am fighting him. We both freeze as several men walk into our field of vision, their fingers on the triggers of their rifles. There are at least twenty of them. Their brown caps are low, and they are a scruffy bunch. Dirty faces, scraggly beards, filthy, torn jackets. But even so, they are unmistakable.

Leye curses. "The Noor," he whispers, sitting up and dragging me deeper into the car. "How did they know? This is a civilian train!"

From outside there are a few more shots, one at a time instead of the rapid-fire clatter from before. "The bastards are killing the wounded." Leye's voice is high-pitched with terror and rage as he tries to maneuver us toward the back of the dining car, away from the windows.

My breaths come too fast and I am dizzy. My fingertips tingle and spots sparkle in my vision like snowflakes in the sun. The Noor. They killed Musa and Anji. They did something to the train. They are just outside, shooting wounded men.

Together, Leye and I wedge ourselves against the wall where the kitchen was, cutting our palms on broken pottery and glass. "Wen, I'm sorry," he whispers.

"No," I mouth. "I am."

Disbelief laces my thoughts. I wanted to find the Noor, and so I have. I decided to betray my own people, and so I could. Right now. My heart is beating so hard that I cannot find space between the beats. I lean into Leye, who has tears running down his face as he tries to get his rifle loaded. But his hands are shaking too hard to allow him to fit the cartridge into the weapon. "If you point that at them, they will shoot you," I say. And me, too. Look what they did to Anji.

"I'm not a coward," Leye snaps, spittle flying from his lips. He wipes at his streaming nose and eyes with jerky, wrenching movements before returning his hands to his weapon.

Metal creaks and glass crunches as one of the Noor raiders slides into our car and stands in the aisle space. He is so tall that his head is level with the legs of the bench seats. He says something in Noor, his tone singsong, as he slowly walks up the length of the car, searching for survivors to kill, perhaps. I hold my breath and stay very still, but Leye jerks at the bullet cartridge, and it clatters to the floor. The Noor ducks around the hanging body in the aisle and sees us. He raises his weapon.

I put my hands up, and the Noor's mud-colored eyes dart back and forth between me and Leye, who is now trying to draw his bayonet. The Noor sneers and aims, squeezing one eye shut and pressing his cheek to the rifle, peering at us through the sight. And I can't. I can't let him shoot this boy in front of me. I lean forward on my hands, blocking his way to Leye, and say one of the very few Noor phrases that I know, the first one that comes to mind: *"Yorh zhaosteyardie."*

It means "I want to help."

The Noor's brow furrows and he raises his head from his rifle sight. He jabbers at me in Noor, questions I don't understand.

I say, "Please." I put my hand on my heart and extend my palm to him, which makes him blink with surprise. I grab Leye's bullet cartridge and throw it toward the Noor's feet as Leye curses again.

"What are you doing?" he cries, lunging forward. I knock his injured foot to the side, and he screams with the sudden agony.

I squeeze my eyes shut. "I'm trying to keep us alive," I say. "I'm so sorry, Leye."

The Noor comes closer and pockets the bullet cartridge, never taking his eyes off me and the soldier I am shielding. He fires a few more questions at me, and all I can do is shake my head and repeat the Noor phrases I know, even though they are meaningless in this situation.

"I have tea. I have medicine. I want to help. I will not hurt you."

I say them over and over again, offering him my heart, my gratitude, my open palm, all useless nonsense. The Noor kneels, shaking his head as if he wonders why he's not shooting me, and calls out one of the shattered windows. He says a word I know—"*kuchuksivengi*"—the Noor word for "Itanyai," which my father once told me translates as "small, dark-haired people." The Noor turns back to me and says something else, but I shake my head. This is hopeless.

He points to his mouth and moves it without making a sound. He points to me, then jerks his thumb behind him. Boots crunch over stones just outside the car.

Leye clutches at my arm. "What are you saying?"

"I barely know," I tell him as another Noor raider

crawls into the car. He is tall too, and his shoulders are wide enough that he must turn his body to negotiate the narrow space between the benches.

The newcomer keeps his head down as he navigates through the debris. He uses the barrel of his weapon to poke at a few of the broken bodies, as if to verify that they are not a threat. He asks a question in Noor, and my stomach tightens. The first Noor laughs and replies, repeating the phrases I said, but slow and childlike, mispronouncing words like I did. In that singsong voice he says "I have medicine," then chuckles.

The newcomer stops abruptly and repeats the phrase correctly, every syllable as sharp as a rifle shot and full of questioning demand. His voice . . .

The Noor closest to us says yes as his companion quickly ducks around the hanging soldier's body. My heart stops when the newcomer raises his head. His skin is ruddy and chapped from the chill wind. His cheeks are covered in thick red gold stubble. I stare into his pale jade eyes. "Melik."

Chapter Six

MELIK'S MOUTH OPENS and closes a few times, the motion stiff with shock. And then he finds his voice again. "What are you doing here?" he shouts.

His tone is so rough that it wears away my joy in the space of a moment. "I—"

Behind me Leye shifts suddenly, and both Melik and the other Noor raise their weapons.

"Put that down," Melik says to Leye, deadly quiet. "You are endangering the girl."

I look over my shoulder to see Leye clutching his bayonet. "You're going to kill us both anyway," he says to the Noor, his eyes glittering with pain and hatred. "Like you killed everyone outside."

The other Noor asks Melik a question, and he answers. I think he's translating what we say. "If you surrender, we will not kill you," Melik says. I turn back and look into pale eyes brimming with questions and anger. "Do it for her if not for yourself," he says to Leye.

The bayonet clatters to the floor, and the other Noor reaches forward and snatches it. And then he grabs me by the arm and wrenches me to my feet.

"Bajram," Melik snaps. He puts his hand out, gesturing at his comrade to hand me over.

Bajram tilts his head and says no, followed by several other things I have no hope of understanding. Melik's mouth twists with frustration as he argues with the young man, their voices getting louder by the second. But finally Bajram says something that knocks Melik back a step. Melik's eyes meet mine for a moment before he looks away. He steps around me to yank Leye up.

The Noor drag us the length of the destroyed dining car, and with each step my blood sings with fear. Was Melik lying? Are they about to shoot us? I twist in Bajram's grip, trying to look back at Melik, but my captor's fingers sink into the folds of my overcoat. I want to call out to Melik, to beg him to explain what is happening, but I fear that one wrong word will mean death not only for me, but for Leye. Bajram keeps a tight grasp on my waist as we crawl through the shattered dining car window and into the cold, smoky mountain air. The sun is high over the grasslands now, washing out the brown and white rock of the hills, illuminating a scene of carnage.

I have seen many terrible things in my life. I have witnessed metal spiders swarming onto the killing floor and feasting on the flesh of the slaughterhouse workers.

I have seen torn skin and exposed bones. I have heard cries of agony.

And still, this is much worse. The engine and the passenger car at the front, the one that held the only civilians on the train, the place where I had been sitting until a few minutes before the attack . . . they are a twisted, blazing inferno. As I look around, I see none of those old ladies, none of the factory girls, none of the families. I can only assume they were trapped inside. There is no rescue effort, no attempt to put out the fire. The Noor raiders, their guns slung over their shoulders, walk among the dead soldiers, removing rifles and bayonet blades to pile near the rock wall.

Bajram drags me past Musa and Anji. Except for the blood, they look for all the world like lovers. Behind us I hear the shuffle of Leye and Melik, and Leye's stifled moans as he tries to walk on his broken foot. We weave our way through a maze of dead young men, gray uniforms stained with their heart's blood.

What is the price for giving my secret knowledge to the rebels? More dead Itanyai boys?

But weren't these dead boys on their way to Kegu to do the same to the Noor?

Bajram shoves me around a bend, and now I see what happened to the rear of the train. One of the cars was knocked from the rails and rolled down the long incline. Bodies and debris litter the rock field below us. But the other car is still on the track—there are survivors, and some of them are huddled, injured and bleeding, gray faced and silent, against a few big boulders, guarded by more Noor raiders. Bajram pulls me to the end of the line and points to the ground.

"Sit," says Melik quietly, guiding Leye down. I obey, pulling my knees to my chest, huddling within my skirt and coat, wishing I could disappear entirely. Melik and Bajram converse for a few moments before Bajram jogs toward a knot of raiders near the last car in the train. They are gathered around a body, and I find myself wondering if it is the Itanyai colonel.

Melik squats in front of me. He looks like he has aged five years at least since I saw him last, with lines around his mouth and the thick growth of his beard to hide his youth. His teeth, however, are not chipped like I saw in the wanted poster. Now that I see him up close, I know he is not the Red One. I doubt that would matter to an Itanyai soldier, though, especially now.

"Why are you here?" he whispers harshly. "This was a military train."

"No, it wasn't," I say. I glance at Leye, who is nearly green with the pain from his foot. Despite the cold, he is sweating. "The first car was full of grannies and factory girls." My throat is so tight I can barely speak. "There were children, too."

Some of the color drains from Melik's face. "That can't be true."

"Why would you care?" Leye spits out. "You pigs shot an unarmed woman not twenty minutes ago." He gestures to where Anji lies on Musa's chest.

Melik stands up, towering over both of us. "And why would you care? Itanyai." He says it like a curse and makes a quick, dismissive gesture that feels like a slap. "How you love to trample on the vulnerable. Using women and children to disguise your intentions." His lip curls in disgust.

"They were all getting off at the next station," says Leye from between clenched teeth. "But you killed all of them first. Don't try to blame this atrocity on us."

Melik grimaces and turns away for a moment before glaring down at me again. "You were traveling to Vuda?"

"No, she was trying to get to Kegu, but we wouldn't have let her." Leye swallows, looking on the verge of vomiting.

Melik doesn't appear to hear a word Leye says after "Kegu." He is too busy staring into my eyes, his brow furrowed under the brim of his dirty cap. "Is that true?" he asks me, a million other unasked questions clouding his expression.

I nod.

He sinks to his knees in front of me. "Why?" he whispers.

Leye groans. "Her family lives there, you idiot."

Melik's eyes narrow. He knows very well that's not true.

I bow my head. I have to find a way of offering this message without putting Leye and the others in danger, and I don't know how. My mind spins with possibilities. Could I offer to tell them in exchange for the prisoners' freedom? Is there any way to do that and still keep all of the Itanyai soldiers from knowing I am a traitor?

A deep, rumbling voice calls out in Noor, and Melik jumps to his feet and salutes with his hand over his chest. A thick-bodied man with a long, silver-streaked brown beard strides toward us with Bajram at his side. Bajram gestures at us and then at Melik, who speaks in Noor, making more slicing, rapid-fire gestures as he does. As the older man listens, he slowly draws a revolver from his belt.

At the metallic click Leye takes my hand. His dark eyes are riveted on the weapon. That he feels empowered to touch me without a reason tells me that he thinks it is the last thing he will do. Melik points at Leye and continues to speak the harsh, back-of-the-throat language, one that suddenly sounds ugly and cruel. The air is hazy with smoke from the destroyed railcars, and the wind is heavy with the scent of burned meat. I don't want to think about what it really is.

The older man points his revolver at Leye. Melik looks down at us, and I don't think I am imagining the concern in his eyes. "Commander Kudret wants to know if there are other trains of soldiers coming behind this one," he says. "He wants to know the timetable for the invasion."

Leye looks at his fellow soldiers, nearly a dozen in all, and shakes his head. "I won't talk," he says, his voice strained.

The commander swings his gun to the left, and suddenly I am staring down its barrel. Melik begins to speak very quickly, gesturing at me and then at Anji. He points to the fire that still burns within the first derailed car. The commander frowns as he sees Anji and the carnage beyond. He lowers his gun and speaks sharply to Melik and Bajram, neither of whom look happy. He beckons to a few other raiders and then walks down the line of prisoners, pointing to the ones who seem most healthy and fit. Then he walks away, shouting and waving his arms, gesturing at the hills.

"We are leaving now," says Melik, his expression smoothing over. "The pass is blocked and the rails are destroyed. No more trains will get through. We are returning to Kegu so the general can speak to a few of you."

"You're going to torture us, you mean," calls out a soldier at the end of the bedraggled line.

Melik's gaze settles on him. "You have three days of hiking ahead of you, during which you may wish to think about what information each of you can use to save your own life."

A few more raiders jog over with a length of hemp rope. They yank the selected soldiers out of the line and bind them to one another, with the rope around their necks. Melik shudders and rubs at his throat as he watches. For a moment I see the hulking shadow of memory in his haunted eyes, and I know he is reliving the mob, the noose, the minutes he spent dying. But when two of the Itanyai soldiers begin to speak in low tones to each other, he snaps back to the present and shouts, "No talking! You will have plenty of time to talk when we reach Kegu."

"What about the rest of us?" Leye's fingers are still tight over mine, and Melik's gaze drops to our joined hands. I cannot tell what he is thinking. After so many nights of dreaming of him, it is strange to be this close, especially because in those dreams I felt nearer to his heart than I do now.

"Those too injured to hike are staying," he says to Leye, giving a sidelong glance to Bajram.

Leye scowls, as do the other six who are too wounded to walk. "We'll freeze to death."

Melik gives him a ghostly smile. "I'm certain that won't

happen." He takes a step forward and offers me his hand.

I stare at it for a moment before taking it. His callused fingers enclose mine, and I shut my eyes, dazed by the touch I have wanted to feel for so long, wondering if perhaps the distance between now and the past is too far to bridge. He pulls me to my feet and immediately lets go of my hand.

"Are you injured? Can you hike?" He yanks my skirt just high enough to see that I am wearing boots, then drops it again. "You're fine. You'll be just fine. You can hike," he mutters. He says something in Noor to Bajram, who arches his eyebrow and looks at the hem of my dusty, blood-streaked skirt.

"I can hike." My legs are aching, my head is aching, my heart is aching. When I imagined carrying my message to Kegu, I did not think it would happen like this.

Leye's voice breaks as he says, "This girl is innocent. You should leave her here with us."

Melik's expression is blank as he turns back to Leye. "Commander Kudret says she must come with us."

Melik pokes at my shoulder and gestures for me to stand behind the line of bound soldiers. When one of the Noor raiders lifts the end of the rope and comes toward me, Melik snaps at him. The fellow drops the rope, and I sigh in relief. At least I will not be wearing a noose as I stumble over rocks and shiver in the cold.

I look over my shoulder at Leye.

"You'll be all right, Miss Wen," he says to me. "Maybe they will let you see your family."

I can tell from the strained sound of his voice that he does not believe I will be all right, but he does not want me to be scared. "Thank you," I say. "When help arrives, tell them to splint your foot and then take you to a doctor to make sure the bones set properly."

He smiles, and it is laced with pain but also sweetness. "It was nice traveling with you, if only for a short time."

Melik takes my arm and gestures after the other soldiers, who have started to trudge at gunpoint along a trail that zigzags up the hill. A line of Noor raiders is ahead of them, and my gaze traces the row of men until I see the ones at the front slipping into a narrow pass just beneath the summit. I turn back to Leye. "It was nice," I say.

He waves to me. "Please be careful."

He smiles once more before Melik mutters that we have to leave. I follow the prisoners, stepping gingerly along the narrow path, trailed by another line of raiders behind me and Melik. They talk in low tones, gesturing quick and sharp, eyes darting all around, as if they are afraid of an ambush too. The higher we get, the better I can see the wreckage of the train scattered along the twisted rail. The smoke billows high into the sky, and I am sure this is what is making the Noor anxious. People will see it. They will send the authorities. It makes me happy for Leye and the other wounded, but also scared—who will be chasing us, and will I be cut down like Anji was, one of the unlucky?

It takes us only a few minutes to reach the narrow pass below the crest of the hill, but by then I am huffing, my breath fogging, too warm even in this frosty air. My fingers are stiff with cold, and I shove them into the pockets of my overcoat, the one on the left side already stuffed with my father's cloth-wrapped scalpel. My fingers curl over the bundle, and in it I take a measure of comfort. I'm not entirely defenseless, but I will have to be smart about how I use this, my only weapon and tool.

The trussed soldiers plod along, occasionally stumbling, while their Noor captors maintain a tight grip on the ropes that keep them under control. We enter the pass, a long, narrow trail bounded on either side by sheer cliff faces. As soon as I step into it, a shot rings out down below. The Itanyai soldiers in front of me look around in alarm as we hear another, then another. Their eyes are wide with horror.

It takes me a moment and one shot longer, but the jagged puzzle pieces slip into place and I realize what is happening.

I cry out and spin around as the cracks fall silent, colliding with Melik as he steps forward.

"No, Wen," he says quietly, taking me by the arms. "Keep walking. Keep walking." His grip on me is as hard as the rocks enclosing us.

"They're shooting them, Melik! Leye and the other . . ." Then I catch the look on his face. "You knew. You knew! You told him he would not be killed if he surrendered, and—"

"They could not walk," he replies in a tightly controlled voice. "Commander Kudret gave his orders."

My tears, absent until now, spring forth, flooding my eyes and spilling onto my cheeks. I kick at Melik's shins and slap at his chest, stupidly trying to get back to Leye, even though I know it is too late and he will never smile again. "They were just boys!" I scream, the savagery of the day ripping the sound from my throat.

"No," Melik says, standing solid and immobile as I pound on him with all my might. "They were soldiers."

71

"How could you be a part of this?" I sob, grabbing handfuls of his shirt over the spot I so carefully stitched up all those months ago, when I prayed that he wouldn't die, when I was willing to risk anything to save him. "I believed you to be so much better than that. How could you not say one word to prevent it?"

"What do you think those soldiers would have done to us if they had had the chance?" he shouts. "You've witnessed what they're willing to do to people like me!" Melik gives me a shake that rattles my bones. "This is a war, Wen."

I stop fighting him, anger running quiet and poisonous through my veins. "And you are a soldier too."

His mouth forms a taut gray line, and he nods.

I look up into his eyes, eerie and pale and giving nothing away. "If your commander gives orders for my death, will you pull the trigger yourself, or will you ask someone else to do the job?"

He lets me go and steps back, his nostrils flaring as he sucks in a sharp breath. Someone behind him mutters a question.

"*Susmaye!*" Melik barks, and the raider's mouth snaps shut. I stand there, waiting for him to answer my question. Waiting for him to say he would not kill me, that he would never allow anyone to hurt me, that he does not want to be a part of this at all.

But instead he points at the trail. "We are falling behind," he says, cold and calm again. "Start walking."

Chapter Seven

SOMETIME IN THE last several hours I tore my dress on a sharp stone, and it is the one thing that went right today. I pull at the tattered fabric as I huddle near the fire, my face warm and my spine tingling as the wind places cold kisses on the back of my neck. When we arrived at this ridge, there were more Noor waiting. There appear to be at least a hundred of them, and they have a few packhorses to carry supplies. Several of the rebels are women, as dirty faced and ragged as the men, but also as sturdy and determined-looking.

I recognize at least two of the rebels as men from Melik's village, men who worked at the factory last year. One of them is the man who wiped blood from my face and hands after finding me in the lower levels of Gochan One with Ugur, who had been killed by one of Bo's spiders. Baris, I think his name is. He is short for a Noor, but built strong like a bull, and he and Melik embraced when they met on the ridge. Now all the Noor have separated into camps, and their fires, fed by scraggly brush, dot the ridge.

I tear one long strip from my skirt, then another, then another. Above us the stars glitter like chips of ice. My head throbs with the effort of blocking out memories that could bring me down, but I will not let myself collapse and give up. I am best when I am working, so I will work. By the time I am finished, the hem of my skirt is three inches higher than it should be. Ordinarily, that would be quite shameful, but I am wearing long boots and my overcoat, so nothing is revealed.

I get to my feet and slowly approach Bajram. He is guarding us while the others, Melik included, eat dried beef and hard biscuits with their commander. They are clustered on the boulders just up the ridge, where they have built their own fire. They no longer seem to have a fear of detection—we are deep in the hills, with a clear view of the slope below us and the path on either side. From the dramatic gestures and loud laughs, I suspect they are drinking more than water.

Bajram's brow furrows when I hold up the strips of my dress and wave them under his nose. He has hollow cheeks and a soft-looking mouth that he has tried to hide with a scraggly beard, and up close it is clear to me that he is Melik's age, maybe younger. He looks down at my shortened skirt peeking out from the folds of my overcoat, and then at the scraps in my hands. He steps away from me cautiously, as if he believes my behavior is part of a bizarre Itanyai mating ritual.

"Bandages," I say, then point at the bedraggled group of young prisoners, some of whom are dozing with their heads on their knees. Their comrades sit around them, shoulder to shoulder, but we are Itanyai, and Itanyai men do not lean on one another. I run my fingers along my throat and then point to them again, saying I want to help in clumsy Noor. *"Yorh zhaosteyardie."*

Bajram gestures with the nose of his rifle. "Go."

I place my hand over my heart and turn my palm to him, and he rolls his eyes and mutters something in Noor. Biting my lip, I inch past him and kneel next to the nearest soldier, who has blood crusted in his ears and the rims of his nostrils. He stares into the fire as if it is the only thing he is aware of. We are in the open, sitting on a mountainside at the edge of the massive, deep canyon that connects the Ring to Melik's village, linking the west to the east. It is a grand sight, lit by stars and moon, brightened by cold, but the young man next to me is focused on the flames. "How are you?" I ask softly, and he flinches.

Slowly his gaze slides up to mine. "I told my father I would be back before Third Holiday," he says. "I promised him that we would feast together."

"And maybe you will." I settle in next to him. The flesh of his throat is chafed and raw from the rough pull of the rope. Now that we aren't walking, the Noor raiders have bound the soldiers' feet and hands instead. "I can bandage your throat for you."

"Who are you, sister? Why do you talk to the Red One as if you know him?" he asks, confirming that although Melik is not the man on the poster, it hardly matters. The title fits, after all.

My fist closes over the thin brown strips of cloth. Now it is my turn to gaze at the fire. "I did know him once," I murmur. "We worked at the same factory last year."

I could say so much more. I could tell him what Melik and I started to build together, and how the last year wore it away, how this morning destroyed it entirely. I could explain how Melik was gentle, how he protected me. I could admit that my desire to protect him and his people is the reason I am probably going to die. I could tell him how my heart is aching, and how Melik's has turned to stone. All of those laments and confessions are on the tip of my tongue, but it does no good to say them aloud. It might even do harm. I blink and look at the soldier. "My name is Wen, and my father is a doctor. Let me bind the wound?"

The soldier, with a lean body and eyes heavy with fatigue, says, "I'm Shimian." He nods toward his fellows. "And that's Yino, Mabian, Senza, and Lidim."

The others nod and mumble their hellos, devoid of the bravado and flirtation of this morning. "Do you have a family, Miss Wen?" asks the one named Mabian, who has a gash above his eyebrow and dried blood striping the right side of his face.

"Just my father now." And Bo. I have come to think of him and my father as the places I call home.

"He will be missing you," says Mabian.

I swallow back the pain of missing them both and nearly choke on the sadness I know I have caused them. "If my father were here," I say, my voice breaking, "he would tell me to get to work and take care of my patients."

I tilt Shimian's head to the side and examine the abraded skin of his throat. It is brownish red with dust and grime.

"Bajram?" I call, and our guard takes a step closer, his finger twitching toward the trigger of his rifle. I point to his canteen and say, "Please," then pinch my fingers together. Just a little water is all I ask.

He shakes his head.

The soldier at the far end of the line of five, the one named Lidim, lets out a snort. "If you think that Noor is going to offer his precious water so that you can clean our Itanyai wounds, you are very naive."

I suppose I am. I glance at the knot of men with Commander Kudret. Melik is a shade taller than the others, easy to spot even when he is wearing a cap over his rust-colored hair. He is gesturing wildly, speaking loudly. His face is lit by the firelight, his smile bright as he entertains the group. He never once looks my way. I thought I understood him. I thought I knew who the Noor were. How wrong I was.

Without water to clean the wounds and ointment to soothe them, there is little to do but cover them and hope the scraps of my dress will protect these boys' necks from the merciless chafe of the rope. Shimian holds still while I gently wrap the fabric around his neck and tie it tight enough to remain in place, but not tight enough to hurt him. He thanks me.

Next to him is Yino, whose eyebrows are thick, with little separation between them. "They're going to kill us," he whispers in my ear as I wrap the strip of cotton around his throat. "Your kindness is wasted on dead men."

I pause, looking into his eyes. The flames dance in his dark pupils. "Have some hope, brother."

"Hope is a luxury I cannot afford right now." He shifts awkwardly, wincing as his wrists rub against the blood-spotted rope tightly wound around them.

A familiar voice startles me, and the soldiers go still. Melik is standing next to Bajram, handing him his own canteen. Bajram grins and takes a long swig, then coughs while Melik laughs and slaps him on the back. Melik gestures at us and Bajram nods.

For the first time since this morning Melik's eyes meet mine, but only briefly, like I am exactly as interesting as one of the billions of pebbles and boulders that surround us. He strides over to us and drops a bag at Shimian's feet. "Your rations," he says. "You have a long hike ahead of you."

"How kind of you," says Yino, his voice ragged with hate.

"Would you be kind to me, soldier, if I were in your place?" Melik asks softly. He leans down to look into Yino's eyes, but the soldier stares at the ground. Melik glares at the top of Yino's bowed head. "Would you like me to answer that question for you?"

Melik is close enough to touch, but I shrink away from him. I have heard this bright, overfriendly tone before. I have seen that fire in his eyes. This is how he looks when he wants to kill.

"Thank you," I say quietly. "We are all hungry."

His gaze snaps to mine, and I am paralyzed by its intensity. "You're welcome."

He stands up, pivots on his heel, and strides back

toward the other raiders, pausing only to wave away Bajram when he tries to return Melik's canteen. Bajram grins and lifts the canteen in Melik's direction before taking another long drink. I watch Melik, the Red One by default, the warrior by choice, return to his commander and comrades, and then focus my attention on the bag he left us, opening it to see that there are several hard biscuits and sticks of dried beef inside.

"We can eat after I bandage you," I say, trying to infuse my voice with a bit of cheerfulness.

"Do you know where we are?" whispers Lidim as I move to Mabian, the one who badly needs his head wound stitched. If I had the right tools, I could sew him up, good as new.

"The Red One said it was three days of hiking, and we've just completed one," says Senza. "When we derailed, we were about to descend into the Vuda valley, and we've been walking on a southwest path as opposed to due west in order to get to this part of the canyon." He squints as if he's doing calculations in his head. "I suspect we are perhaps three or four days hiking from the Ring."

Lidim leans away from Senza, scowling. "You say it like it is nothing at all."

"No, I state it as a fact," says Senza, still keeping his voice barely above a whisper. "And here is another—these pigs are feeding us and keeping us alive because they want to do two things. One, to drag us in humiliation through the streets of Kegu, to tout their victory over the army. And two, to torture us for information. Once they've done that, whether we break or not, they will kill us."

"Those are not facts," I say.

Mabian raises his bound hands. "Here are some for you, sister. These Noor destroyed a railcar full of helpless women and children without a wisp of remorse. They slaughtered all our soldiers. They shot the wounded. They let the survivors believe they would be spared, only to execute them moments later."

And Melik was part of all of it, the lie, the betrayal, the slaughter. I sit back, the fire heating my skin as I take in each Itanyai face, dark eyes full of fear, ankles and wrists bound. Mabian and Senza are probably right. These boys will not be allowed to live—and they will not be allowed to die until they have suffered greatly. As Melik pointed out, though, if he were in their place, they would, I have no doubt, be happy to offer him and his comrades the same fate.

Who deserves my loyalty? The Noor I came here to protect or the Itanyai who are now at their mercy?

Right now I will let neither rule my heart. Instead I will be led by something deeper and dearer to me than those labels, this war, and my own fear: conscience.

My hand creeps into my pocket and closes around the cloth-wrapped scalpel. "If you had the chance to escape, however risky and remote," I whisper, "would you take it?"

Mabian watches the movement of my hand in my pocket. "We will face death again and again if there is a chance to live."

The others nod. No hesitation.

I look toward Bajram, who is busy eating his rations, his jaw working furiously to grind the dried meat. He takes another sip from Melik's canteen to wash the food down. He is not paying us any mind at the moment. I shift my attention to the nearest rebels, who are gathered around their fire. Melik is giving a speech, his voice echoing off the stones above us, and the rebels' gazes are fixed on him. I pull the cloth-wrapped scalpel from my pocket and pull at the fabric until the mercilessly sharp blade pokes through. "Hold your wrists close to your neck," I tell Mabian.

He obeys, and I lean over him, pretending to wrap his neck while I saw through the ropes instead. I work as quickly as I can without slicing his fingers off or jabbing his throat. The others huddle closer, forming a semicircle around me.

A few minutes later Mabian, Senza, and Lidim have wrapped throats and free hands. They keep the ropes looped over their wrists, though, so it looks like they are still bound.

"We'll leave when they're asleep," Mabian whispers. "If we can get down the slope and into the canyon, it will be hard for them to find us."

"They know the hills better than we do," says Senza.

"That is true," I say. "Some of them are from a village at the western mouth of the canyon. They grew up climbing these peaks and passes."

"Which is why we must get a few hours' start on them," says Lidim. He nods at the bag of rations. "That stupid Noor may have given us enough food to survive until we get home."

"*Cuz*," barks Bajram, startling all of us. "*Muraye*. Come." When I look over my shoulder, he is beckoning me away from the soldiers.

I press the scalpel into Lidim's hand. His fingers close around mine. "Come with us," he breathes.

Confusion floods my thoughts. Do I want to escape? Do I still want to tell the Noor about the war machines and betray my people? Can I do any good at all if I stay? Isn't that the only reason I came? "I'd slow you down," I whisper.

"We would not leave you behind, sister," says Mabian. "We would take care of you."

"The rations will last longer if there are five, not six," I murmur.

"*Cuz!*" snaps Bajram. His footsteps crunch on the rocks beneath his soles.

I stand up and meet Mabian's eyes. "It's all right. Go," I mouth as Bajram grabs my arm and yanks me away from the soldiers, who bow their heads and look properly cowed. Shimian lifts his bound wrists so that they are clearly visible in the light, as if to show Bajram that the soldiers are still helpless.

Bajram drags me away from the fire and dumps me onto a rock near where he was sitting, then plops down next to me and sets his rifle at his side before returning to his rations and drink. He's probably quite frustrated at being singled out to guard the prisoners while his friends talk and laugh and discuss strategy, or whatever it is they are babbling about with the commander. Melik probably took pity on him and brought him food and drink as consolation.

Bajram ignores me while I shiver, but when I inch closer to the fire, he barks at me again. I tuck my hands into my coat and curl on my side. On the other side of the fire the Itanyai soldiers stare back at me. They are still and steady, but I know that they are probably only waiting for the rebels to fall asleep so they can saw the ropes around their ankles.

Bajram leans his head back against a boulder and sighs. He upends the canteen, pouring the last few drops of liquid onto his tongue. I blow into my cupped fingers, shuddering with cold, wondering if I'll be able to creep closer to the fire if Bajram falls asleep. Voices drift toward me on the frosty breeze, and one of them is Melik's, powerful and riveting. No matter what language he speaks, it makes people want to listen.

I close my eyes and remember the last time I was this cold.

I was in his arms. He was whispering in my ear, in Itanyai, in Noor, and it didn't matter which because I believed I understood. It was a moment both impossibly dire and unbearably sweet. The memory rises up and coils around my throat, choking me. The pain seeps into my chest, squeezing the breath from my lungs in a low sob. I pull my knees even tighter to my body, trying to hold in the noise, the sorrow. I quake with the loss of all my grand ideas, of all my faith in the Noor and their goodness, of all my belief in Melik and his promises . . . and his affection for me. I try to grab ahold of the reasons I'm here, allegiances that go beyond two simple extremes, principles that are strong enough to get me through this, but I'm too weak to catch and keep them close.

The drift from consciousness into dreams is seamless and painless. I slowly go numb, and my head begins to buzz, and then I am in Bo's metal world, my face reflected a thousand times in the hammered metal panels and in his steel mask. "You are the only thing to me," he says.

He reaches up to remove his mask. But when it falls away and reveals the other half of his face, it isn't his at all. The eye is jade, and the jaw is squared and rough with red gold stubble.

I startle awake, foggy and half delirious, and see that I am much closer to the fire. My head is resting on a folded cap. A thick jacket that smells of sweat and smoke has been laid over me. Bajram is behind me, staring at the fire, his eyelids drooping. The Itanyai soldiers are still sitting on the other side of it. Mabian nods at me and gives me a small smile. Weighed down with fatigue and the relief of warmth, my head sinks onto the cap, and my dreams claim me once again.

The next time I am jolted awake, it is with a fierce kick in my side. I cry out and open my eyes. The sky is purple with the slow ooze of dawn. The fire is out.

And Bajram is pressing the muzzle of his rifle to my forehead.

He shouts at me in Noor and his finger contracts over the trigger.

I close my eyes and prepare to dream forever.

There's a yelp and the thud of one body colliding with another. The pressure of the rifle disappears and I bolt upright, my heart beating heavy and frantic against my ribs.

The Itanyai soldiers are gone.

The Noor are shouting among themselves and pointing down the slope.

And Melik is wrestling with Bajram a few feet away from where I sit. Several other Noor sprint over and grab the two of them, separating them. Melik is yelling. He's no longer wearing his cap, and his rust-colored hair flies around his face as he struggles to free himself. After a minute Bajram raises his arms in surrender, and he and Melik are released. Bajram promptly leans against a boulder and vomits all over the stones.

I expect Melik to dust himself off. To take a breath. To walk away. Instead he comes straight for me. He yanks me up by the arms and shakes me. "How could you be this stupid?" His voice is choked, half growl, half plea. "Tell me!" he roars in my face.

"Did they get away?" I manage to ask, trying to catch my breath.

He makes an agonized sound in his throat. "Why did you do this?"

"I had to try," I say, hissing with pain as he squeezes my arms. "I couldn't sit back and let them die."

He pulls me onto my toes and leans so close that our noses touch. "Why didn't you go with them?" he whispers, pressing his forehead to mine hard enough to hurt.

"What?" I squeak.

His eyes are bright and bloodshot, filled with betrayal. "Why didn't you escape when you had the chance?"

That question is far too confusing to answer, as is the fact that he is asking it at all. "Did your commander order you to interrogate me, Melik?"

He grinds his teeth. "You have no idea what you've done. The commander has ordered us to recapture the prisoners by noon. And if we do not, we are proceeding to Kegu without them."

So the five Itanyai boys have a fighting chance. Maybe they can make it. Maybe they won't starve or freeze or fall prey to bandits. Maybe they will make it back to the

Ring. Even if they don't, though, they have escaped being dragged through the streets of Kegu, being tortured by the Noor, being executed. With my help they have chosen their fate.

Melik must see the spark of defiant hope in my eyes, because he shakes me again. "You still don't understand." He lets me go abruptly, panting. His gaze is bottomless and unreadable. He scoops his cap from the ground and jams it onto his head, then grabs his coat. For a bare moment I feel the pang of knowing that his cap was my pillow and his coat was my blanket, and perhaps he was the one who moved me closer to the fire.

But then he yanks the jacket on, snatches a rifle from atop a rock ledge, and slings it over his shoulder. "If we don't recapture the prisoners, the commander says you will take their place."

He beckons for Baris to follow him and strides away, headed for the trail that leads into the canyon.

Chapter Eight

I HUDDLE NEAR the dying embers of the fire while Bajram and two other Noor guard me. Melik and Baris disappeared into the canyon hours ago, along with several other pairs of rebels, all in search of the escaped prisoners. But now that the sun is rising high, the searchers are trickling back into camp, dusty and grim. Each time a pair of them returns empty-handed, I twist in a storm of terror and defiance. If the Itanyai are found, I might be spared. If they are not, I am doomed.

I don't have it in me to wish for their death, though. Like them, I made my choice.

Commander Kudret orders his men to pack up the camp, and all along the ridge there is bustling activity as the rebels prepare to continue the march to the west. I shiver in fear every time he comes near, knowing he is the one who ordered the cold-blooded murder of the injured Itanyai soldiers. So when he comes over to me, I cower and stare at the ground. He squats in front of me and waits for me to raise my head. His mud-colored eyes are brimming with hatred and promise when I do.

"Icin buna apacekye," he says in a low voice, then draws his finger across his throat. Bajram and the others laugh, but the commander jumps to his feet and draws his revolver. He points it at Bajram's head. The blood drains from Bajram's cheeks as the older man speaks. I get the sense that Kudret is reminding him that he fell asleep on the job. Bajram does not smile after that. He glances nervously at the brilliant sun, perhaps willing it to move slowly and give his comrades more time to recapture the escaped Itanyai.

The sun is directly overhead when the shout comes from the edge of the canyon. Several raiders jog over and immediately let out a cheer. My stomach turns as Melik and Baris stalk into camp, blood smeared on their brown trousers. I search the crowd around them for prisoners and see not a single Itanyai face, and for a moment I feel an irrational surge of hope.

Then Melik breaks loose from the pack and approaches Kudret. He hands his commander a cloth sack stained with more red brown blood. Commander Kudret does not look happy, but he listens to whatever story Melik has to tell, and then he nods. He asks Baris a few questions, and Melik's companion makes quick gestures with his meaty hands as he responds. The commander smiles and shakes Baris by the shoulder, then hands Melik the bloody sack and points to me.

Melik hesitates, but the commander shoves him toward me.

Melik strides over to me, his expression blank, his eyes cold. His shoulders are tense as he tosses the sack at my feet. "We found them," he says in a dead-quiet voice. "Open it."

My heart is hammering against my ribs, and my mouth has gone dry. "No."

Melik gives the commander a sidelong glance, then picks up the bag. "Your father's scalpel was quite useful," he says, staring at me with an intensity that makes me tremble. "We had to travel quickly, so we couldn't bring their bodies. So we brought something else." He upends the sack. Five bloody fingers land at my feet, along with five patches bearing the insignia of the national army. I cover my mouth with my hands and clamp my eyes shut. My skull is home to one long scream that blocks out everything else. It goes on and on, wordless and anguished and raging, until there is no more fuel left inside me to burn.

When I open my eyes, Melik is gone, and so is the grisly gift he forced on me. All that remains is spots of dried blood on hard stone.

That and my newfound hatred of the Red One.

He hunted them. He killed them. He brought back trophies for his master.

That I ever believed he was good is a shame I will never live down.

My hatred is a cold, cold thing. Colder than the air around me. I let it eat me up, grateful that it leaves nothing behind, not sorrow nor grief, neither fear nor regret. I am as still and unfeeling as the rocky peaks above me as Bajram coils the rope around my neck. I am numb as he yanks me to my feet.

Bajram jerks the rope to set me in motion. *"Cuz. Ilerlemaye."*

I stumble over the rocks but manage to stay on my feet. The other Noor are already hiking, bundles of supplies on their backs, a few horses bearing the stolen Itanyai arms. The sun is high over our heads, providing the slightest whisper of warmth as we trudge upward. My breath comes out harsh, feeble wisps of fog in the chilly afternoon. I can't seem to get enough air no matter how hard my lungs work. My head spins. My feet and hands become hunks of unfeeling flesh. But still I walk. If the rope is chafing my skin, I do not notice.

The only thing of which I am aware is a growing certainty. I will not tell these Noor rebels what is coming for them. I think they deserve to be slaughtered. Yes, I believe in mercy. But these men are merciless, so why should they be saved?

It is not a happy realization. It does not bring me any pleasure, not even the savage, animal kind. I thought my own people were the villains, but now I see the truth: all of us are villains. The Noor are just as bad, just as bloodthirsty, just as willing to cause suffering and death. If they had war machines, they would use them. When they have the ability to hurt, they do.

As the sun begins to descend over the west, we reach the peak of our journey, and I get my first glimpse of Yilat. Brown plains crisscrossed with fencing and roads, like careless stitching across ugly fabric. In the distance there is a growth of gray and black, a city. Probably Kegu.

I will never leave this place. This is where I will die. The thought slips in without feeling, without fight. It is just there, a simple truth.

The men settle at the trailside to make camp for the night. They pull rations from their packs and chatter at one another while they eat. Bajram ties my leash to the base of a thick shrub—one too far from the fire to allow me to feel its warmth—and goes to sit with some of his friends. I sink to the ground and pull my knees to my chest. The slosh of water jerks my head up. Melik kneels next to me, holding a canteen. He presses it to my lips, and when I flinch away, he curls his hand around the back of my head and holds me still. Cool water trickles into my mouth, and then I gulp greedily, my body instinctively clinging to life. After a few swigs he pulls it away and offers me a hard biscuit. My hands shake as I take it.

"Tomorrow afternoon we will arrive in the plains. There will be steam-powered carriages waiting to take us to Kegu," he says as I close my teeth over the biscuit. It has little taste, but I gobble it like it is the juiciest meat bun. "We will be at the capital just after sundown."

"Why are you telling me this?" I rasp, wincing at the renewed pain in my throat.

Melik's gaze slips down my face and settles on my neck, where the rope coils around it like a viper on a branch. "Because that is how long you have to decide what to do."

"What do you mean?"

He nudges my chin and makes sure I am looking at him. "You traveled west alone. You were headed for Kegu. And yet I know very well you have no family there, and that you have never been to Yilat. I am wondering why you made this journey."

I stare into his face, the one I dreamed of so many times, the one that now fills me with loathing. "So am I."

His brow furrows. "You should never have come."

"It was my foolish mistake."

"As was freeing those soldiers while you stayed behind to bear the consequences."

"No. That I do not regret."

Like a block of ice beneath the sun, Melik's frown softens a bit. "You have not changed."

You have. I do not say it, but I think he can read the thought in my expression.

He leans close. "Tell me why you came here. Perhaps I can help sway the commander. Perhaps he will have mercy."

"I am not asking for mercy." I cannot believe it will be granted.

Melik lets out a frustrated growl. "You are in no position to be this stubborn."

"I am in the cage you have built for me." It's an old saying, one my mother used to snap during rare fights with my father when she felt he was giving her no choice but to dig in her heels.

Melik takes my face in his hands. As he bows his head over mine, his rust-colored hair falls over his forehead, and his tunic gapes at the neck, revealing the top of his scar, complete with the tiny silver dots from my stiches. "You stepped into it all by yourself, Wen, and you alone are tossing away the key." The tremors of his muscles vibrate into my bones, blurring my thoughts. "I have done everything I can for you," he says from between gritted teeth.

His anguish does not match the blank, cold way he presented me with those trophies of death. "What have you done for me, apart from slaughtering boys I tried to save?" I hiss.

He looks at me in disbelief. "Why is it so easy for you to believe the worst of me? If I were Itanyai, would you feel the same?"

"I spent the last year believing nothing but the best of you!" I cry out, my voice cracking with strain. "I spent every night dreaming I would see you again and every day searching the papers for word of how you were faring. And every moment I was lost in that fantasy of you, strong, noble, and good. So no, Melik, it was not easy, until the last two days, when the living truth stripped those foolish beliefs away."

His eyebrows rise as he hears my bitter confession. "Did you come to find me? Is this because of me? Or has something happened?" He holds me tight as I try to pull away, and he searches my face as if it will tell him what he needs to know. "Please tell me."

As his thumb strokes across my cheek, I push down the desperate, confusing words that are tumbling and crowding inside me. *Hold me. Protect me. Save me.* These are the hands that have touched me in the most tender, secret ways . . . the same hands that sliced fingers from the dead bodies of Itanyai soldiers. He will not save me, nor do I want him to. He is part of this war, and it is bigger than both of us. It has changed him. Torn his mask away. Stolen his goodness. Or perhaps he handed it over willingly. And despite all that, looking into his eyes makes me want to tell him everything. "Leave me alone, Melik," I whisper.

He bares his teeth as his fingers slide along the side of my head, weaving into my hair. *"Zhayapaman,"* he says, low and rough.

He lets me go and walks away. I spend the evening shivering in darkness.

But when I wake, I am near the fire, my head on a folded cap, my body curled warm beneath his coat.

As we descend the steep paths that lead to the plains, my body gives out. After days of barely eating, barely drinking, barely breathing, my toe catches on a loose stone and I fall. My arms aren't strong enough to keep my head from hitting the ground. The hemp rope around my neck pulls tight. Bajram yanks, and I slide along the trail, my vision going black. My ears fill with the roaring of waves in the Southern Sea. It's nice. I'll watch the sun set and see if the steam rises as the water devours the ball of fire. Then my mother will give me a sandwich and tuck me into bed with a song.

When I come back to myself, I am not in my mother's arms. My head is against Melik's shoulder, and his coat is wrapped around me, and I am rocked by his strides. My trembling fingers reach for my throat.

"I know it hurts," he says quietly. "I had to cut the rope from your neck."

"You should have let me die," I rasp.

"Zhayapaman," he says again. His voice is heavy, possibly with regret.

"Put me down."

"Zhayapacaj," he murmurs.

Too weak to fight him, I blink as the world comes into focus. We are no longer in the high passes of the hills, but on a dirt road, entering a small village. The Noor fighters are marching in rows ahead of us.

Mud huts with thatched roofs huddle on either side of the rutted street. Old women wearing colorful, threadbare tunics have gathered, offering the rebels wrapped, grease-spotted packages and live chickens. Old men waddle at the roadside, squarish woven caps on their grizzled heads, waving bottles brimming with some sort of cloudy liquid. Younger women, their hair cascading down their backs in clusters of thin braids, their heads covered with patterned scarves, hover in the doorways, eyeing the rebels with keen interest. The rebels accept the admiring stares along with the gifts, then place their hands over their hearts and turn their palms to the people, receiving wide, gap-toothed smiles in return.

Two rebels—a young man and a young woman—break from the group, running toward a middle-aged couple and throwing their arms around them, laughter and sobs indistinguishable. Another rebel strides quickly to a pretty woman in a long tunic and a red head scarf. He scoops her up and kisses her right on the mouth while his hands fist in the fabric over her back. She melts into him, her fingers tangled in his hair and tears streaming down her face. To these Noor, the raiders are heroes and saviors, not a merciless scourge. They are sons and daughters, brothers and sisters, husbands and wives. They are living, breathing hope.

Outside one hut two small children play in the dirt, their smocks streaked with filth, their brown hair matted around their little faces. They stare at me with their light brown eyes, and I stare back. They are the first Noor children I have ever seen. The younger of them, a little boy of perhaps two years of age, smiles shyly at me. His cheeks are not as chubby as they should be, and his eyes are huge and round in his pinched face. I feel the faint urge to smooth his tangled hair and wrap my arms around him. The layer of hatred protecting me from pain and thought and mercy and conscience begins to melt.

A woman, her dark hair covered with a red and purple head scarf, comes out of the hut and sees the rebels. She waves, but her hand freezes in midair when she sees me being carried along in Melik's arms. Lines furrow her forehead and she calls out something in Noor.

Melik nods and says, *"Zhapacaj,"* which seems to satisfy her. She kneels to kiss the little boy on the forehead, then returns to her hut. Melik looks down at me. "She reminded me that even though you are Itanyai, you are a woman." He lets out a humorless huff of laughter, and for the briefest moment his gaze focuses on my mouth. "As if I had forgotten."

"Why would she say that?"

"She meant that you should be treated with proper respect. It means something different to us than it does to you."

"If you say so." My eyes drift back to the little boy's. He stares intently at me, clutching a carved wooden horse in his tiny hands. He holds it up for me to see as we pass him by. "Where are we?"

"Czizhgie," he says. "The Line. This village, along with many others, is strung along the road that skirts the Western Hills and connects south to north on the eastern side of Yilat. From here it turns west toward Kegu. My village is also on the Line, but far to the south."

"At the mouth of the canyon," I whisper.

What will happen to that tiny boy with the wooden horse when a war machine comes thundering up this road? No matter what Melik has done or become, no matter how cruel these Noor raiders have been, does that little boy deserve to die? How many of these villages lie between the canyon and Kegu, and how many little boys with wooden horses? How many worried mothers with gaunt faces?

"Melik," I say, my voice cracking. "Where are the men?" I have not seen one young man in this village, save for the few rebels who kissed their loved ones and rejoined their comrades on the march, and now we are at its outskirts, approaching five large carriages, their beds lined with benches on either side.

"The men have joined the revolutionary force," he says, as if it should be obvious. "The general has recruited many, ready to meet the national army as they march into Yilat. We will give them a fight."

As they march into Yilat. This general must believe the threat will come from the northern grasslands, then, instead of over the Western Hills. "Is there no one defending these villages?"

Melik frowns. "They should be safe enough if we can repel the army, or at least make them think twice about invasion." His gaze is distant for a moment, and I realize that is the best they can hope for—to put up a fight, to make the invaders think twice. They cannot hope to win. I watch Melik, wondering if he is seeing his own death playing out before his eyes.

He sighs before continuing. "We received word that the army would try to infiltrate Kegu in advance of an invasion from the north, which is why our unit was sent to sabotage the rails, and others are gathering along the northern border. We will join them once we report to the general."

His jaw clenches and he gives me a sidelong glance. Maybe now he is seeing my death play out before his eyes. Perhaps this is why he is so free with this information. He understands that I will never have a chance to share it. He will hand me over to be executed by his general, and then he will leave for the north.

Suddenly Melik hefts me a little higher, holds me a little tighter. As if it has a mind of its own, my arm coils around his neck. I catch myself a moment later, but before I pull away, I realize this may be the last peaceful, gentle touch I receive. I close my eyes and allow myself to pretend that this is the Melik from my dreams, and that I am the bold Wen who lives inside my head, the one who more than once has unbuttoned his shirt and run her hands over his body. My fingers brush the back of his neck, beneath soft locks of his rust-colored hair. I lean my forehead against the side of his face, and my fingertips slide along the bumps of his spine.

Melik shivers, a violent, hard sort of tremor, and leans away. "I wish I'd never met you," he whispers fiercely, more to himself than to me. He scowls at the horizon.

I exhale the moment and all the childish pretend. I could let his hateful expression seal my decision and his fate. If I want him to die for his crimes, all I have to do is keep silent. But instead of making things murkier, his harsh words make everything very clear, because they have rendered a year's worth of passionate dreams irrelevant.

I raise my head and look over his shoulder, past the faces of the Noor rebels, and find the small figure of the boy, playing in the dirt like all children do. I never came to save only Melik. I didn't come to save these rebels, either. And I didn't come to save the Noor simply because they are Noor. This is not about choosing a side. It's about choosing a principle and being willing to see it through to the end.

I came to prevent suffering and death. I came to save that little boy, and his sister, and that woman, and these helpless people who wear their naked hope and love like armor.

I have failed to save a single soul so far, and I am on my way to die. Does all that failure absolve me of the burden of trying again? If my father were in my place, what would he say, and what would he do?

"Melik," I whisper. "I will tell you why I came here."

Chapter Nine

THE RIDE INTO Kegu is bump after bump and mile after mile of dismal sights. I knew Yilat was poor, but I had little idea what this kind of poverty really looked like. In the Ring it is sagging skin and bent backs and a bowl outstretched for a coin. It is grasping and groping and hustling and stealing, a bun swiped and stuffed into a starving mouth before the vendor notices, a penny pinched from a pocket followed by a sprint into an alley. In Yilat poverty looks different. There is no movement to it at all. It is wary gazes and complete stillness. Gaunt and hollow.

Many of the people I see are Noor, but there are Itanyai, too, and in some villages I see the most remarkable thing: faces that are neither and both, eyes and hair and skin that are a melding of the two. I stare and stare, wondering where their loyalties fall. What do they call themselves? Who claims them, and whom do they claim? Where do they belong? Are they wanted and cherished? Do they ever wish they were one or the other instead of being both at once?

I glance up at Melik and find him looking down at me, like he's trying to read my reactions to all I am seeing. I tear my gaze from his and continue to watch as we enter the city. Painted slogans have been scrawled on walls and splattered on roads, accusing the government of abandoning the people of this province. It is only after I've seen a few that I realize I can read many of them—not all are in Noor. We pass a few blocks of smoldering and blackened ruins, and other blocks where the destruction is evident but not complete. The streets appear largely deserted, but a few times I see dark figures running from building to building. Melik points at a woman sprinting across the road behind us. "There are pro-government snipers. It is not safe to be on the streets."

The carriages pull into the municipal compound, which is surrounded by a high wall, part of which is crumbled and destroyed. Guards, mostly Noor, patrol with their rifles at the ready. As Melik lifts me from the truck, a few of the guards call to him, and I recognize them as more men from his village. The commander barks a few orders and then says something to Melik, who turns to me.

"The commander says we must give your report to the general."

"Does he believe me?" Because Commander Kudret is staring at me with raw mistrust.

"I believe you," Melik says. "And the general is a good leader. He will hear us out."

"I am glad." I am fighting fatigue so heavy that I want to ask Melik to carry me again. "What will happen afterward?" *Please say I can sleep.*

Melik takes my arm and leads me into the main building, all chipped paint and tile, water-stained ceilings and blank walls. "We might be able to stop the machines before they exit the canyon," he says. He is close enough for me to feel his urgency, his need to move, to take action. I wonder if he is thinking about his little brother, Sinan, and about his mother, and about all the little boys with wooden horses who play in the dirt next to the road. "We must get a force to Dagchocuk quickly."

"Dagchocuk," I murmur, trying it out. "That's your village?"

He gives me the tiniest of smiles, like he has told me a wonderful secret about himself. "It means 'mountain's child.'" He hesitantly tucks a lock of my hair behind my ear. "And you may have saved it."

I cannot translate the mad thump of my heart when he touches me like that, when he looks at me the way he used to. I cannot reconcile it with the cold man I now know him to be. I stare straight ahead because looking into his eyes is too confusing. His hand falls away from my face. He does not try to touch me again.

We are led into a large meeting room that smells of cigarettes and sweat and strong mint tea. Maps have been laid over the tables, and several men, both Itanyai and Noor, huddle over one, arguing with rumbling, harsh voices. They go quiet when they see us, though. One of them, a tall, lean Noor man with thinning light brown hair combed away from his face, steps forward. He wears the same brown trousers, leather-wrapped boots, and plain tunic as the rest of the men, but when he comes toward us, Melik and Commander Kudret salute with their hands on their hearts.

"General Ahmet," Melik says in Itanyai, even as Commander Kudret opens his mouth to speak. "This girl comes with news from the east that may change your strategy."

General Ahmet arches his eyebrow, and Commander Kudret glares at Melik. The commander begins to speak to the general in Noor. While he does, the general's gaze keeps darting to me. His appraising glances remind me that I must look frightful. My overcoat is torn and dusty, my hair is tangled, my face is dirty, and . . . my fingers travel to my throat, which is crusted with scabs and hot with swollen lines where the rope rubbed me raw. I wince as feeling returns all of a sudden, as my numbness slides away before I'm ready.

"I think the girl needs to sit down," says the general in perfect Itanyai. He barks out an order in Noor, and a chair is shoved against the backs of my legs. I am so weak that I fall onto it with a hard thump. "There we go. Now, it's Wen, isn't it?"

I nod as he moves closer. Unlike the commander and so many of the rebels, the general is clean shaven. His eyes are deep set, his skin stretched tight over his skull. "My name is Ahmet, dear. Tell me why you came here."

"I work in the Gochan Two factory in the Ring, over the Western Hills. It makes war machines." My voice sounds tiny in this big room with these big men.

"I'm well familiar with the Ring and its war machines," says the general. "One of those machines killed my entire family." His hands are clasped behind his back, and his posture is straight and proud. This will be what Melik looks like in thirty years, I think, if he lives that long. "I had a son once," says the general. He tilts his head as he gazes at Melik. "He'd be about your age if he'd lived."

"Then you know about the machines," I say, "and how dangerous they are."

He nods. "But you did not come here to tell me war machines are dangerous."

"No, sir." My cheeks grow warm with embarrassment. "Three days ago, on the eve of First Holiday, the boss of Gochan Two received a large order of war machines from the head of the national army."

Several of the men in the room stiffen, and I know these are the ones who speak Itanyai. But the general does not seem distressed or surprised. "How did you come into possession of this information, Wen?" he asks, his voice gentle. "Are you the boss's secretary?"

"No, sir," I reply. "I work for the surgeon. But I overheard." Well, I heard only a little, but Bo heard all the details. It doesn't feel right to implicate him, though, not here, not when he would hate me for handing over this information. "And that night the factory was supposed to close for the holiday, but it never did. It stayed open all night. Gochan Two never runs at night. They brought all of the workers to live on the compound, then closed the gates. I left just before the lockdown."

The general leans forward, his hands still clasped behind his back. "Anything else?"

I blink at him, then look up at Melik. "That's all I know," I mumble.

The general claps his hands onto his cheeks and looks at me with wide dark blue eyes. "But isn't that enough? The war machines are coming again!"

I nod. "I'm quite certain they are."

"Taslar," he whispers. "And you think I should pull my forces from the north and have them march to the south, to stop the machines in the canyon?"

His cadence and tone remind me of Bajram's mocking, singsong voice as he came down the center of the dining car, stalking survivors, and I feel nearly as hunted as I did then. "I would not presume to advise you on strategy, General Ahmet."

"General," says Melik. "This has happened before. Given how effective it was last time, why wouldn't the national army adopt the same strategy?"

Any friendly amusement on the general's face disappears in a flash of rage. He snaps at Melik, Noor words so fast and sharp that I feel the stab. Melik bows his head and stares at the floor.

The general returns his attention to me. "Wen, Commander Kudret tells me you were found aboard a train full of Itanyai infantrymen. You were traveling with them."

"I wasn't traveling with them. We were on the same train. That is all."

General Ahmet's thin lips twitch upward at the corners. "What a coincidence." He brushes invisible dust off his sleeves. "I am also given to understand that you aided in the escape of several prisoners of war who could have given us vital intelligence."

My stomach drops, but I manage to say, "Yes, sir."

He lets out a snort of laughter. "Thank you for your honesty. Please continue, because I'd like your frank opinion. You see, I am in possession of credible intelligence that tells me the army is putting all its resources into an invasion from the north. Along with that information came the news that a small force would infiltrate Kegu to assassinate me and my commanders in advance of that invasion." He chuckles. "Chop off the head before destroying the body, yes?"

I hope he doesn't expect me to smile or laugh along, because all I can do is tense against the hard chills that run down my spine. Next to me Melik has gone completely still, those vibrations of urgency and action frozen under the general's scrutiny.

"I acted on that information," the general continues. "I sent Commander Kudret and his men to investigate, and lo and behold, they came upon a train packed with Itanyai soldiers headed for Kegu, confirming the intelligence was good. Kudret and his forces dispatched these men, who had been sent to destroy our command center." He smiles. "But then Kudret brings me you."

"General Ahmet, please—" Melik begins, but shuts his mouth when Ahmet raises his hand.

"No," says the general. "Let me finish. If you were in my place, Wen, what would you make of you? An Itanyai girl from the east, who travels with enemy soldiers, who protects them, who aids them in a brazen escape attempt." He begins to pace in front of me, drifting closer with each pass. "If you were me, would you move your forces south to wait in Dagchocuk when you have viable intelligence that the enemy will roll in from the north? Would you risk a single moment or a single life based on what a pretty little Itanyai puppet had to say?"

He grabs either side of my chair and shoves his face in front of mine. "Or would you believe, as I do, that she was nothing more than an attempt at misdirection?"

"Sir, please let me speak," says Melik, loud enough to turn every head in the room.

The general lets go of my chair and stands up. His fingers tap his thighs like he is playing a piano. "Go ahead."

"I know this girl," Melik says. "She is not just any girl."

The general's brows rise, and he looks down at me. "Continue."

"A year ago many of the men from Dagchocuk went to work at a factory in the Ring. We were mistreated and exploited. But this girl . . ." His voice trembles and his fists clench. "This girl, she bought medicine when we were sick, and she cared for us as though we were her own people. She sold her possessions to pay our debts, and did so with no expectation of favors or repayment."

He pulls his tunic to the side and reveals the silver line of the scar that traverses his collarbone and ends in a pinkish starburst below the curve of his shoulder. "She treated my wounds." He points to his neck, where the faint speckled scarring from the noose tells his story. "With her own hands she cut me from the gallows. If not for her, I would be dead."

"And you believe this story she's telling now?" asks the general.

Melik looks at me like he used to, in the unguarded, open, warm, and wondering way that I have been dreaming of for months. It makes my heart beat and my lungs fill. It curls low and tingling in my belly. It is impossible to hate him fully when he looks at me like that. "I believe that everything she is saying is true," he says softly, "because I have never known her to lie, and because I have always known her to put others before herself."

"A brave girl," murmurs the general. "And a caring one."

"Yes," says Melik, his voice worn thin with emotion. The sound of it makes my own throat tight.

The general purses his lips. "She would give her all for those she cares about."

Melik nods.

"So freeing the Itanyai soldiers . . . that would fit your understanding of her perfectly."

The general sets traps as deadly as Bo's. As my mouth goes dry and my ears start to ring, Melik gives me a sidelong glance full of uncertainty.

The general reads it easily. "Don't feel bad, son. She works in a factory that builds war machines, in a Noor-hating city if there ever was one. She has been drenched in their propaganda. How could she withstand such pressure?" He puts his hands on Melik's broad shoulders. "And why wouldn't the government want to make the most of such an asset? Especially when she has a history of consorting with the Noor? She is the perfect spy, the perfect carrier of false information."

Melik's brows draw together, creating a line of worry between his eyes. "But, sir, Dagchocuk is—"

The general shakes his head. "It's a ruse, Melik. An Itanyai ruse meant to destroy us. But we won't let it."

"My village is completely defenseless, sir. All of the fighters who could protect it are here, with you, and—"

"As you should be. Was I not right about the attack that would come by rail?"

"You were, but—"

He claps Melik's arms and shakes him a little. "And I'm right about this, too. We must go to the north and face the enemy there."

Melik draws himself up. He is a few inches taller than the general, but he looks young and unsure. "And the southern villages? Will you act on this information in any way, sir?"

The general steps back, and a ghostly, blank sort of smile slips onto his face. "Oh, yes. I think I must." He barks something in Noor, and two guards step forward.

Melik stares at him, the blood draining from his face. "Sir?"

The general folds his arms over his chest. "You heard me," he says as the guards seize my arms and yank me from the chair. "When the forces assemble tomorrow to leave for the north, we will give them a display to fire their blood for battle, and a story that can be sent over the wires to the east, so that all will know about it." He gives me a hard, cruel smile. "We will execute this spy in the square."

"Melik?" I say as the guards begin to drag me backward,

but his name comes out as little more than a squeak. "Please." *Save me. I don't want to die.*

Melik's arms rise from his sides like he wants to reach for me but is being held back by invisible ropes. The general steps between us, his back to me. "Do you have an objection, soldier?"

Melik's eyes meet mine. I can read the emotion there. I heard his words. I mean something to him. He remembers the things I have done. He knows what I have risked. And he might be young, but he is powerful. He knows how to use his words to sway people.

He squares his shoulders, and I silently cheer. He opens his mouth, and my blood sings with gratitude and admiration.

"No, sir," he says quietly. "I have no objection."

Chapter Ten

MY MEAGER LAST meal of soup and biscuits lies uneaten next to the bars that look out on the corridor. Down the hall a man is crying. Perhaps the provincial governor, perhaps one of his ministers. They are all down here, in the municipal jail, watched over by rebel guards, awaiting some unknown fate. I am not like them. I know my fate. The general made sure of it. He speaks such good Itanyai.

At first I was in shock as they dragged me away from Melik, as he lifted not one finger and spoke not one word to save me. He simply watched as I struggled, as I fought for my life. And I remembered when our positions were reversed, how hard I kicked and slapped and screamed to get to him as the mob descended, how loud I shouted that he had been framed. But tonight he stood completely still. I stared into his jade-green eyes until a door slammed between us. He did not come after me.

At first I could not believe it.

But now it has been hours, and I believe it.

The certainty of death brings with it a kind of peace. My throat hurts, my ribs hurt, my mouth is dry, my eyeballs ache. And yet that pain won't last much longer. My heart is broken, but it doesn't matter. No one has to know.

"Mother," I whisper. "I will see you soon." That is a comforting thought. I've missed her so much. The way she brushed my hair, the way she fussed over my stitches, the way she would sing to me as I fell asleep, the way she navigated the world with her head held high. I wish I had more of her fierceness, her sharpness. Until she got sick, she seemed unstoppable, and in her shadow I felt safe. Now it's gone, and she's gone, and when the morning comes, I will face the glaring, blazing sun alone. "I will keep my chin up as I go, Mother. I want you to be proud."

My fingers trail over the cold concrete floor of my cell, over the rough brick walls. When Bo was barely alive, when he was broken and in agony, my father brought him into the bowels of the factory, to a place with stone floors and stone walls like these. From that he built a kingdom. He transformed his prison into his paradise.

Now that my death is only hours away, perhaps I can do the same. I close my eyes and dream, because wishes are out of my reach. They require hope. Dreams do not; they are fueled by the unreal, the forbidden, the things that will not ever exist in this world. So I imagine a bed stuffed fat with feathers that welcomes the weight of my exhausted body. A pillow that cradles my tired head. Sheets of the softest silk that caress my skin.

A hand strokes my hair. "Why didn't you believe in me?" Bo whispers.

I open my eyes, and he is there, whole and beautiful. He does not wear a mask because his face is perfect, as if the accident never happened. "How can you be here?"

"You're dreaming, of course," he says with a smile. "Now answer my question."

"You are far away." I touch his left cheek, smooth and unscarred. "And you probably hate me."

"That's what I mean. You don't believe in me."

"How can you say that?"

His gaze caresses my face, the adoration so easy to read. But then his brow furrows and he frowns. "You refuse to wish."

The crash of metal on metal jolts me awake. Shivering, I rub my eyes and sit up as a door at the end of the hall slams. My body aches from lying on the hard floor, and my mind is still swimming in the fog of dreaming. Bo was right. I should run to his altar. I need to offer him . . . something. A coin. A shell. And then I will make a wish and hope he grants it.

"What shall I wish for?" I whisper. "How shall I let you know?"

I look down at my coat and its round black buttons. Quick and thoughtless, I yank one loose. Deep inside my head I am aware that I have lost my mooring, that I'm drifting away from reality, but it doesn't hurt and it doesn't scare me, so I don't try to hang on. "Here's my offering, Ghost," I say quietly. "Now I will tell you what I want."

But then I pause. What do I want? Not Melik, not the boy who took everything, who stayed just close enough to my heart that he was able to tear it from my hands and toss it into the fire along with the rest of me. No, I will not wish for him. I will not dream of him either. His dominion inside my mind is over.

No, I will wish for something else. "Please comfort Father," I say, tears forming instantly as I think of my father, his careworn face, his eyes dark and deep with grief and love. If my mother was fierce, my father is constant and steady. His love is less like a protective shadow and more like a path, level and clear, showing me the way to go, the things in this life that matter. Even though I left him behind, I've tried to keep walking it, and as I go to the gallows, I will imagine that path beneath my feet. "But please, if I die in an ugly way, never let him know. Let him believe it was quick and painless, and let him think I did not have time to cry."

A tear slips down my cheek and hits the floor, but I dry it with my sleeve. "And you," I say to the Ghost. "I don't want you to be angry. I want you to forgive me for leaving. I want you to know that even though I did, I loved you, too." I don't think he knew it. It grew slow and delicate, like frost crystals spreading across a windowpane. It wasn't all he wanted, but it was real. It is real. Now I will never watch him work again. I will never again see the intent in his eyes, the pleased smile on his lips, the glow of pride on his face as he created something the world had never before seen. He wasn't a machine in those moments. He was the boy he should have been, brilliant and sweet, vulnerable but strong. And I will never get to tell him how beautiful he was to me, how I needed him as badly as he needed me. The knowledge crushes my heart.

I sniffle and draw my fingers across my face, smearing tears across my cheeks. "One last thing, Bo. The most important thing. Please hold on to the parts of you that I loved. Please do not kill them. You'll want to. You'll want to cut them away and burn them. But if you do, I'll be gone forever. It is in those parts of you that I'll live. And if you keep them safe, I'll always be with you. I'll never leave again. As long as you hold on to them. Please."

I cover my face with my hands. I have babbled on for long enough. "That is all the wishes I had left. I hope my offering is enough."

The lights in the corridor flicker. I peek through my fingers. "Bo?" I whisper.

The hallway goes dark. Heavy footsteps clomp by my cell, probably one of the guards. He calls out in Noor a moment later, a question that goes unanswered. Somewhere outside, a man shouts, but the sound is cut off. Trembling, I crawl toward the bars, groping in the inky murk until my fingers close over metal. "Hello?"

"Turn the lights on!" one of my fellow prisoners yells.

"What's happening?" shouts another.

Down the corridor a door opens and slams shut. Keys jangle. Somewhere two Noor are yelling, their harsh voices muffled by walls.

An explosion rips through the quiet, shaking the floor and raining dust and debris on my head. Shouts and cries grow loud and piercing, and I cover my head as another explosion deafens me. Able to neither hear nor see, I scrabble back against the far wall of my cell and curl into a ball, wondering if the Itanyai army has arrived, wondering if it is about to blow this complex into the sky. The smell of smoke creeps along the corridor. Something is on fire. I huddle ever tighter, my arms clamped over my head and my knees tucked beneath my chin.

Large hands close around my arms and pull me from the ground. I open my eyes but am blinded by darkness. I feel a huff of air against my face and smell sweet, strong mint tea. Someone is shouting in my face, though I hear nothing but a roar. The person yanks me toward him—for it is surely a him, with a firm, flat chest and a hard grip and steely arms that wrap around me and drag me across the floor. Flailing and coughing as the acrid smoke floods my lungs, I struggle feebly while my captor lugs me away. We must be out of the cell, because we have covered too much distance to be inside it still. I blink, but all I see is dense blackness. My ears are ringing, but a few sounds begin to reach me. Screaming and shouting, hard pounding, fearsome hissing of broken water pipes.

"Let me go!" I shriek as my feet lose the ground and begin to kick in midair. The man lifts me high and throws me over his shoulder, then begins to run up a flight of steps. I bump against his body, fighting to draw breath, until he bursts through a door and sprints into the open air. My fists bunched in his shirt, his arm wrapped over the backs of my knees, I lift my head to see the municipal jail, flames shooting from the roof on its far side, and a swarm of men clustered around it. Chaos.

My captor is running away from all that. I let go of his

back and put my hands on his arms. His two human arms. This is not Bo. He is too tall to be Bo anyway. "Melik?"

He clutches me tighter and takes a sharp turn and then another, running past a pile of rubble and along a stone wall until he stops abruptly and lowers me to the ground. Melik's rust-colored hair glints with gold. He is huffing with exertion as he puts his hands on either side of my face. "Are you all right?"

I gape at him. "What are you doing?"

His eyebrows rise. "What does it look like I'm doing?"

"I thought—"

His mouth curves, a bitter twist of his lips. "I don't want to know." He looks over the top of my head and nods at someone behind me, then reaches out to accept the reins of a horse. I look over my shoulder to see Baris heave himself up into the saddle of a second horse. Both animals are wild eyed and restless, stamping the ground and snorting. I cower as Melik draws his horse near and strokes its nose. And then, before I can protest, he lifts me up and sets me in the saddle, then swings himself up behind me. He coils his arm around my waist and looks at Baris. *"Simte bazkozie, eh?"*

Baris gives us a grim smile. *"Sokhizlie."*

Melik kicks at the horse's flanks, spurring it into action. I yelp and grab the smooth leather edges of the saddle, glancing around to see that Melik is sitting behind the saddle, using his legs and balance to hold himself on the creature as it breaks into a gallop and leaps through the hole in the compound wall, its hooves landing with a clatter on the stone-paved street. Melik leans forward, pressing me to the horse's neck as he urges the animal on. The air is filled with thick smoke that rolls from the burning building.

"Where are we going?" I huff, staring down at the horse's hooves pounding the street. The wind created by the animal's speed blows my hair around my face. My fingers are clenched over the saddle and clinging to the horse's mane, and Melik is nearly suffocating me with his grip on my waist. His weight is pressed firmly against my back, and his breath is in my ear.

"More of my friends are waiting near the sports complex. We didn't want to call attention to ourselves."

"But you blew up the jail," I yelp as the horse veers down a narrow road.

"I asked Baris to create a distraction," he says, reining the horse to a halt. "Apparently, he took that very seriously."

He leaps off its back, then pulls me down and steadies me as my feet touch the earth. Then we are running again, toward dozens of Noor voices, quiet and urgent. I hear Dagchocuk mentioned several times in the flurry of their conversation. A bouncing, guttering lantern rounds a corner, carried by a tall, gaunt Noor who leaps into a carriage to our left. By the lantern's erratic light I see two more steam-powered carriages near the sports complex's pockmarked walls, heavy and low, like farm machines. Onto these, Noor rebels are loading wooden boxes and other supplies. The men, with faces I recognize from their time at Gochan One, leap aboard, squatting and holding on to the low wooden walls around the edges of the carts, their rifles at the ready. Melik leads me to one of the carriages and helps me onto it, and the men move to make room. As I squat near the front, one of his friends asks him a question, and by the sharp stab of Melik's words as he settles himself beside me I can tell he is alarmed. He gestures fiercely at the men and shouts something, and our carriage jerks into motion.

He folds his arms over my chest and pulls me against him, his legs on either side of mine. The carriage turns onto a wide thoroughfare, followed by the other two, their yellow lights illuminating our path along the road that leads east, out of Kegu and toward the Line. In the far distance the Western Hills loom, inky black with purple sky above them. Dawn is approaching.

From behind us several shots ring out, and Melik flattens me against the wooden panels of the floor. "Is it snipers?" I ask as Melik bows his head over mine.

He shakes his head. The other men in the carriage have ducked low, but their hands are curled over the wooden slats surrounding the back. They shout among themselves, and Melik goes still. "They said something is chasing us."

"Something?" The army? The rebels? Another carriage? A pack of wolves?

"It's . . . fast." He calls out something in Noor as the carriage accelerates. I crane my neck and see the driver, a man with his cap pulled low and his shoulders hiked to his ears, as if expecting to be shot out of the seat at any moment. Buildings race by in a blur as gunfire punctures every second. I close my eyes and feel Melik's panting, desperate breaths against my back. He is holding me so tightly that my own breaths are shallow and inadequate. I push back against him and he sits back, keeping his arms around me. We streak by a few shacks on the outskirts of Kegu, and then we are rolling down the rutted dirt road that leads to the Line.

The rifles fall silent. The Noor at the back of our carriage crane their necks, peering at the empty road behind the third carriage. "Whatever was chasing us seems to have given up," I say.

Melik shrugs. "Perhaps there never was anything? We are all a bit jumpy."

One of the men shoves a thick, coarse blanket into Melik's arms. All around us the men are lying feet to shoulder, pulling coverings over themselves, tarps and blankets and jackets.

"We have a few hours' ride to Dagchocuk, and we take rest whenever it is offered," Melik says, scooting me against the front edge of the cart, where I sit with my back against a hard, unforgiving side panel. It's better than being dead, though, and the boy next to me is the reason why I still breathe.

"You defied the general."

Melik glances around at his men, his brothers, his friends. "We all did."

"You could have left without me."

He looks down at me. "But I never would have."

We stare at each other. It is a moment so filled with puzzlement and wonder that none of my thoughts make sense. About Melik, about myself, about what I feel for him, about what I know. My blood rushes through my veins, fizzing and sparking, and I let out a shaky breath. I can't . . . I can't sort out any of this, so I look away, back to the city, at the orange glow above the municipal complex.

Melik chuckles and says something to Baris. The stout Noor rocks back and shakes his head, his eyes wide with shock. After a few more exchanges Melik is silent for a moment before touching my arm. "I asked Baris what he used to cause the explosions and set the fire."

"And?"

His face is lit by the distant holocaust. His eyes are crinkled with concern, a deep kind of worry. "He said his distraction was to flood the barracks on the other side of the main building. He had nothing to do with the explosions at all."

Chapter Eleven

THE CARRIAGE GROWLS and jitters along the road as the sky lightens, though dawn is at least an hour away. The other Noor are sleeping, snoring beneath their blankets. Melik spreads ours over our legs. He is wedged close to me in this crowded carriage bed, and my other side is squished against the rumbling front wall right behind the driver. Melik lowers himself onto his elbow and arches his eyebrow. "You'll be more comfortable if you lie down."

I sink back because I do not have the energy to hold myself up, but I face the wall, creating distance between Melik and me. I can't think when he is close. He fogs all my thoughts.

He pulls the blanket over us, cocooning us in a dark, tiny world of our own. I close my eyes and lay my forehead against the wall of the carriage.

"Too many things between us are unsaid," he says to my back. "I want them to be said."

It is a very Noor thing to want. "What needs to be said?" I murmur, my heart thrumming with fear, but also with something startlingly close to hope.

"I will begin with this: I have thought about you every day. No matter where I was, no matter what I saw or did in all these months, I did not forget you. And you did not forget me. That is not nothing."

"But it isn't everything, either." My palms press flat to the wood. Not everything, but still, so much.

"Wen, I never expected to find you like that. I always pictured something different."

I laugh. I can't help it. "So did I, Melik. It never involved that many guns."

"My fantasies never involved any guns at all," he says, low and rough.

"You said you wished you'd never met me." And I remember the look on his face, the anger.

"Because I realized how much it was going to hurt when we were parted again." His hand closes over my shoulder. "Wen, why won't you look at me? Do I repulse you so much?" His voice is hushed. Vulnerable.

"No." I shift onto my back. "But parts of you terrify me," I say, more honest than I should be.

He is propped on his elbow. The dark shadow of his face hovers close. "And the other parts?"

"They make it impossible to let go."

He smooths my hair off my forehead. "I know exactly what you mean."

I pull his hand away from me. "I don't know how to think about what you did. I am trying to hate you."

"Is it working?"

"I might have to try harder."

He is so close that the ends of his hair tickle my cheeks. "We've been through this before."

When I believed he'd gone to a whore, he means. "This is far more serious."

He groans. "It is. So let's go over what happened, yes? Think back to that first night, when the soldiers escaped." His fingers capture mine and intertwine, locking our hands together. "When I gave Bajram the heavy drink from my canteen, did you not consider that I did that on purpose?"

I blink up at the outline of his features, lit only by speckles of early daylight filtering in through tiny holes in the blanket. I cannot read his expression, but I can hear the frustration in his voice, the release of secrets held close for too long.

"And when I slipped my own rations into the bag of food I gave the prisoners," he continues, "you did not notice. You did not wonder."

My heart skips a beat. "I did not look closely. I was too busy working against you. Or so I thought."

"When I spoke loudly and told all my stories, you did not think that perhaps I was keeping their attention to give you time to free the soldiers? Which I knew you would do." His voice is tight and bitter. "And when I gave you my coat and hat to keep you warm on your journey east . . ."

"Melik," I whisper, my fingers bunching in his tunic.

"I did everything I could, Wen. Everything. And still you believed the worst of me."

My fear is melting. My resistance is melting. But . . . "You hunted those boys down."

He lets out a hard bark of laughter. "Absolutely I did. With every bit of cunning and skill and speed that I have. Commander Kudret threatened to drag you behind a horse if the prisoners were not retrieved. He wanted to make you suffer." His breath fans over my face, and I am suddenly very aware of his body against mine. "But ask me what really happened. Now I can tell you."

I touch his face, the long whiskers of his beard coiling coarse over my fingertips. Why did I not consider anything apart from my greatest fears? He did not bring back a single body. And he did not bring back heads. Or hands. Or feet. He brought back pinkie fingers. "You did not kill them."

He shakes his head. "But I did demand a price in exchange for this mercy. One they were all willing to pay if it meant the girl who saved them might live even one more day."

"Baris supported your story to the commander."

"Baris loves me like a brother. And he knows what I feel for you."

"But you couldn't tell me that you had left them alive?"

"If you'd known, you might have given it away. Your true despair was enough to convince the commander that I had completed my mission." He places a scratchy kiss on my forehead. "I hoped that once you knew that your anguish had made you and them safer, you might decide it had been worth it."

I duck my head against his shoulder. "It was. Of course it was. Will you forgive me for not having faith in you?" Again. Again. "You must think I am so stupid and ungrateful."

"I think nothing of the kind. Despite your belief that I was a cold-blooded killer, you delivered the news about the war machines," he says, merely a trickle of sound in my ear. "You were willing to help me save my village and my people, not because of your feelings for me, but because . . . well, I don't know why you did it."

"You don't doubt? Your general made a very good case. It makes more sense for me to be a spy than to think I traveled all this way by myself, through the territory of the enemy, to deliver information that would make me a traitor to my people, that guarantees I have no future at all." My voice breaks as those thoughts spill from my mouth.

He cups my cheek with his palm and tilts my face to his. "I have faith in you." His chest trembles with silent laughter. "Even though you are still the most confusing girl I have ever met." I count the beats of his heart, feeling the silent acceleration before he speaks again. "And I do not blame you, really, for not feeling the same," he whispers. "I have done bad things. I want you, of all people, to believe that I am good, but I am . . . not. These past few months—"

My fingertips slide over his mouth. "Not one of us is good all the time." I think of Bo, and how I care for him despite knowing that he has killed over and over again. I understand that he has taken lives, and that he is not always sorry. I am always aware of his nature. But, still, I do not hate him. There are pieces of him I would protect with my life. And Melik . . . he deserves at least as much from me.

He deserves for me to see him as a man, not as the perfect hero who has inhabited my dreams. "Melik, why were you willing to risk so much? Why free prisoners you wanted to kill?" I saw it, that look in his eyes. That was not an act. "Those soldiers may be in the Ring right now, telling their commanders about the rebel force."

Melik's arm tightens over my back, pressing me against his warm, hard lines. "This war has a big appetite. It devours everything. But I will not let it eat my soul." He tilts my face to his and touches the tip of his nose to mine. "It had sunk its teeth into my heart, but when you appeared, you reminded me that there are parts of me I am not willing to surrender."

I smile, my eyes stinging. "So I saved you from a monster?"

"Not for the first time." He lays his forehead on mine.

"And now you have returned the favor," I say, breathless, unable to stop my fingers from slipping down the warm skin of his throat, from burrowing under the collar of his tunic. My thumb traces the silver scar beneath his collarbone, and he shivers.

His lips flutter against mine as he speaks, filling me with the most powerful kind of craving. "No, I haven't," he whispers. "The things I owe you can never be repaid."

His lips press to mine, soft and searching, and I close my eyes and welcome him. My heart is beating so fast that I can barely breathe, and all of me is tingling. His tongue traces a delicate path along my bottom lip, and I wrap my hand around the back of his neck and pull him closer. He may have been a perfect hero in my dreams, but that perfect hero did not taste like this. He was not warm and trembling like this. He had no weight, no force. But this Melik, the one made of flesh and faults, has all of that, and my body recognizes the difference. It revels in that difference.

He deepens our kiss, his whiskers scratching at my face, one hand sliding down my back to my waist, the other cradling my head above the hard rumbles of the carriage. Parts of me are soft and hot, but others are taut and frantic. I am a jumble of mismatched pieces, but somehow all of them have the same goal. Bring him closer.

I remove my hand from the neck of his tunic to slide it over the bumps of his ribs and curves of his muscles. Such liberties, so bold, but I can think of nothing more necessary than this. Melik moans, a low, desperate sound, and turns so his body is half on top of mine. He crushes me to the floor and I feel the vibrations of the wheels and the hum of the engine against my spine. Suddenly I understand why people slide into this kind of temptation, how the power of a moment conquers years of caution. My hand slips under the hem of his tunic. My palm meets the smooth skin of his waist. And when it does, he breaks our kiss to taste more of me, the soft skin under my chin, and oh, just above the neckline of my dress. His hand is fisted in the folds of my skirt, pressed against my hip. I want to arch into him and see if he'll pull, if he'll touch my legs, if he'll—

The carriage bounces as it hits a divot in the road, and

the engine roars. Melik is tossed away from me, against the back of the man next to him, but he catches the edges of the blanket and holds it close around us. His breath is heavy and hot in my ear as he says, "I'm sorry."

He settles next to me, preserving even the tiny distance between us, the one I want to erase. I frown. "Why?"

He strokes my cheek. "Because this should not happen in the back of a crowded carriage under a blanket that smells like horse."

I lay my head on his shoulder. "Where should it happen, then?" I whisper, my cheeks heating as I realize how brazen I sound.

He holds my head against his body and wraps his arm around my back again. My hand rests over his heart. "Should it happen at all?" he murmurs. "Is that what you want?"

I bite my lip as my thoughts whirl. What am I asking for? I have only the haziest idea, one that involves a good deal more than the ways our bodies could entwine. It seems so foolish, given that we are caught in the middle of a war, that Melik is marked for death—possibly by both sides in this conflict—and that I am without home or family or means or future. And I don't know what he is thinking at all. Perhaps his thoughts are purely about kissing, about touching, about tasting. Because he is Noor, he might tell me if I asked him, but because I am Itanyai, it seems shamefully prying to do so.

He does not demand an answer. Apparently, there are some things he allows to go unsaid. He merely kisses the top of my head, and we lie quiet together, locked in our own minds. Lulled by the rock of the carriage on the road, soothed by the warmth of Melik's hands and body, dragged down by the terror of the night and the weight of my exhaustion, I drift back into sleep. It is black and mercifully free of dreams.

I surface from the murk as Melik shifts beneath me. "We are close to Dagchocuk."

"How do you know?"

He chuckles. "I can smell it." He inches over and peers out through a crack in the wooden boards. "Yes. We're here," he says as the carriage shudders and coughs, then stops.

The men around us are already leaping from the carriage as I sit up and pull the blanket off. We are still on the Line, pulled over to the side of the wide dirt road. A few yards from us is a stone arch, and beyond it lies a sea of stone cottages with thatched roofs. The air is filled with the scent of woodsmoke, the tang of manure, and something slightly sweet and musky—sage on the fire. To our left, towering high above us like a tidal wave of stone is the jutting western face of the hills, and directly behind the village it looks as if a giant has ripped the rock down the middle. The canyon's mouth gapes wide; a walk from one side to the other would probably take several minutes. To the right are endless plowed fields of dirt that stretch, sunbaked and fallow, for miles.

Cries and shouts pierce the morning as the inhabitants of Dagchocuk realize their men have come home. The men run to their families, some disappearing into cottages from which come shrieks of happiness a moment later. All around us people embrace and cry and laugh and kiss, so openly, as if everything they feel inside is much too big to stay there. As I watch, women and old men come rushing out of their cottages carrying strips of embroidered cloth, each one unique, and they wrap them over the shoulders of some of the men, the older ones, mostly.

Melik vaults from the carriage just in time for a tall young man to slam into him. They wrap their arms around each other, muscles shaking with the need to hold tight, talking fast in voices clogged with tears. As they pull away from each other, the young man looks at me, and I gasp. It's Sinan, wearing smudged beige trousers and a brown tunic with a torn collar. He is even taller than he was the last time I saw him, and his shoulders are a bit broader, but his cheeks are hollowed as if all this growing has come at a price, probably because there has not been enough to eat. His rust-colored hair, like Melik's, has grown long, but he has pulled it back with a bit of colored yarn high on the back of his head. His dark blue eyes widen with surprise when he sees me.

"I have a story to tell you," Melik says to him in Itanyai.

"Must be very entertaining," says Sinan, still staring at me. "Hello, Wen. You look really terrible."

Melik squeezes his eyes shut and then rubs his hand over his face. *"Bazan sissilie iyud,"* he groans.

"Why would I be silent?" Sinan retorts. "You wanted me to practice my Itanyai."

I smile at the impudent boy, for that is surely what he is, but I don't mind. It is nice to see his bright, fierce grin. "Hello, Sinan. I'm sure you'll get plenty of practice, because my Noor is no better than it was," I say as Melik grasps my waist and lifts me from the carriage.

I hold on to his arms as my legs buckle beneath me.

Melik gives me a worried look. "You are not well."

"I'm just very, very tired. . . ." My voice trails off as I notice the crowd gathering. Their arms are still around the waists and shoulders of their young men, but their eyes are fixed on me with suspicion and alarm. One of the women points at me, and her harsh tone is unmistakable. I hear it, *"kuchuksivengi,"* and I know the words on either side of it are not friendly.

There is a murmur from the back of the crowd, and it parts to reveal a tall, thin woman with rust-colored hair streaked with gray. Her face and coloring are so striking that I know immediately who she must be—Melik and Sinan's mother. When Melik sees her, he strides forward, his arms spread wide. She is silent as he sweeps her into his embrace and bows his head against her shoulder. Her eyes close and her brow furrows with a bittersweet kind of happiness. Her hands move to his hair, holding him there, but when her eyes open, her gaze drifts past him to focus on me for a moment. She releases him and steps back, looking up at his face. She lifts a strip of embroidered cloth, this one red with delicate green leaves and a border of black diamonds, and lays it around Melik's neck. I think it means he is the man of his household. He accepts it and moves back into her embrace, kissing the side of her head and murmuring into her ear.

A hand shoves me to the side, and I stumble into Sinan. *"Kabilie, kuchuksivengi?"* an old woman snaps at me, her cracked lips peeling back in a sneer.

"I'm sorry. I don't speak Noor," I mumble.

Sinan steadies me and puts his other hand out to keep the old woman from pushing me again, but he looks helpless and unsure of himself. "Melik?" he calls.

Melik spins around and holds his hands out as several others shout *"Kabilie?"* while glaring at me. My heart beats wildly as I wonder if I've escaped one date with execution to be right on time for another. I slip into Melik's arms as he reaches me, relieved to be sheltered by his body.

"Are they threatening to kill me?" I cry.

"No, but I should have thought of this," says Melik, holding my head to his chest as the shouting goes on. "Wen, will you have faith in me?"

"What?"

He looks down at me, his eyes filled with uncertainty. "Do you trust me?"

After our conversation in the carriage there is only one possible answer. "Yes."

Melik raises his head and shouts something that immediately silences every voice in the crowd. His face is utterly somber and his eyes still glint with anxiety as he removes the embroidered cloth from his neck and encircles my shoulders with it. My hands automatically rise to catch the soft fabric when it threatens to slide down my arms, and I pull it around me like a shawl, willing to accept any kind of protection he can offer me.

Astonished whispers roll through the crowd. All around me these Noor stare like it's what they were made to do. Their jaws are slack and their eyes are wide. Melik stands very still and waits. His mother steps forward. She is taller than most Itanyai men, and I fight the urge to take a step back. Her gaze is riveted to her son's. *"Buna zhakabul,*" she says quietly, and then she looks at me. "I accept this."

Melik grins, and Sinan whoops. Many of the men in the crowd cheer, and the children, seeing the excitement, join in. Some of the women whoop and clap as well, but many, especially the ones my age or a few years older, stare at me in stony silence. They are outnumbered, though, and Melik is drawn forward into the crowd as people hug him and slap his back. Sinan tousles my hair and says, "Congratulations, Wen."

"Why?" I ask, my heart hammering against my ribs.

Melik's mother puts her hands on my shoulders. "Because my elder son has just claimed you as his bride."

Chapter Twelve

MELIK GIVES ME another quick, uncertain look before joining the rest of the men in unloading the supplies they brought from Kegu. I am nearly numb with fatigue and shock as Melik's mother leads me to her cottage, her firm, warm hand wrapped around my cold fingers. She tells me her name is Irem but that I should call her Anni, which Sinan told me means "Mama" in Noor. My new mama chatters in Noor with some of the older women, who crowd around me, running their gnarled fingers through my black hair, spanning my waist with their hands, pulling up my skirt and coat and pointing at my feet. I feel like a cow being led to the auction block.

I decided to put my faith in Melik, and I will not avert from that path. But I will admit, I have my doubts here.

"What will happen now?" I ask, leaning close to speak in Anni's ear.

She puts her arm over my shoulder. "We will do this tonight." I blink at her, and she gives me a sympathetic smile. "You will become part of our family, and once you are wed, you will have all the rights and protection we can offer. That is why Melik did what he did."

Does it have anything to do with how he feels about me, or is it simply the only way to extend his protection? I wish I knew which I preferred. "What would have happened if he hadn't?"

"Other families could have chosen to offer you a place in their home." She gives me a sidelong glance. "But I don't think they would have."

"Because I'm Itanyai."

She nods, tugging me free of the grasping hands and pushing me through the low doorway of her stone cottage. A fire burns in the hearth. The floor is smooth dirt, and a straw broom is propped in a corner. There appear to be two rooms, the main living area and the sleeping area. Anni leads me to that second room, smaller than the front room. There are two wool pallets on the floor, and she points to one. "You can take my bed. You look like you are about to fall down." Before I can protest, she unbuttons my coat, her fingers sliding over the threads that held the button I left for Bo as an offering.

"I don't think I can sleep." My head is spinning with all that has happened and all that will.

She smooths her hand over my hair. Her nose is long like Melik's, and her lips are full. There are wrinkles around her mouth and her eyes, and her cheeks are covered in freckles, as if she has spent countless afternoons under a harsh sun. "Rest while you can. Tonight will be long. But pleasant, I hope." When she sees my wide eyes, she laughs. "I am speaking of the feast, *cuz*."

"*Cuz?*" Bajram called me that.

"It means 'girl.' But it also means 'daughter.'"

The tears sneak up on me, and I fight to keep them inside. "My mother," I whisper. "She . . ."

"I cannot replace her," says Anni. "But I will be another *anni* for you."

"Why are you being so kind?"

She lays her palms on my cheeks, and her hands smell of sage. "When my sons returned from the east, they brought stories of the girl who saved them with her kindness and bravery. Sinan ridiculed Melik for losing his heart." She leans close. "And Melik did not deny it. He did not argue, though he rarely turns away from a debate. He merely accepted the teasing of his younger brother and stared into the fire, a small smile on his face. My son has never offered his heart easily or without thought. He is a smart and strong young man, and he has his own mind." She presses her lips together for a moment. "He is very much like his father."

She lowers me to the pallet and covers me with my coat. "You are my daughter now." Her smile is bright. "I've always wanted one."

I sigh. "I imagine you did not expect her to be Itanyai, though." I wonder if the glares from the young women by the carriage were because they wanted Melik. I cannot blame them for that.

"*Cuz*, my elder son would be dead if not for you. Do

you really think that the shape of your eyes or the color of your skin matters to me?"

"Thank you." I sigh as she strokes my hair again. These Noor with their touching . . . sometimes it is nice. Comforting.

Her eyes crinkle deeply at the corners. "When you wake, we will begin our preparations."

It is the last thing I am conscious of until she is gently shaking me awake. I open my eyes and peer at the thatched roof, inhaling the scent of mint. I sit up, and Anni presses a stone cup into my hands. It is heavy and full of steaming tea. "That will bring your blood to the surface and make your heart beat," she says with a smile. "Finish that. I have a bath ready for you."

I drink from the cup, the tea strong and stinging with mint. It's been days since I bathed, and I am absolutely filthy. "A bath would be so nice."

She grins. "Sinan will be glad to hear that. He's been working all afternoon to bring enough water from the spring to fill the tub." She holds her hands up when my eyes go wide with fear. "But he will not be in the cottage while you bathe!" She walks from the room, clucking her tongue.

I finish my tea, letting it sear my throat and wake me up, and then I rise from my bed. When I enter the main room of the cottage, I see that she has hung a cloth over the doorway. In front of the fire is a wooden tub. Anni gestures at me to remove my dress. "I can bathe by myself," I say, praying she will not take offense.

"Of course you can, but you are a bride, and I am your mother, and today is my day to care for you." She arches her rust-colored eyebrow. "Unless Itanyai have body parts the Noor do not, please believe I am aware of what is under your dress. No need to be shy."

My cheeks are blazing. "But I . . ."

She reaches down and lifts my skirt, pulling my filthy, torn work dress over my head. I gape at her as she lifts my legs one at a time and yanks my boots off. I can smell myself suddenly, and my face feels as if it is on fire. I cross my arms over my chest and bite my lip as she pulls my undergarments off. She is so matter-of-fact that I feel stupid protesting. She guides me into the tub, and some of my embarrassment washes away as I sink into the hot water.

"Melik has checked in on you no less than three times since you fell asleep," she says quietly as she picks up a thick bar of tan soap and rubs it over my shoulders while I pull my knees to my chest.

I lay my cheek on my knees and close my eyes as she soaps my back. My tired muscles thrill at the firm but gentle touch. "He has more serious things to worry about than me."

"And he is worrying about them as we speak. He has sent riders to all the villages on the Line, asking for their strongest to come. He's set up a warning system along the main road to Kegu, in case General Ahmet decides to punish Melik and the Dagchocuk men for their disobedience."

My stomach tightens. "Do you think he will?"

She is quiet as she washes my arms, but then she says, "I do not know. He is a good man, but he has been hurt in so many ways. Melik's defiance will not sit well with him."

I stare at the fire. "Do you know General Ahmet?"

"He is from a village at the southern end of the Line. He was a friend of Melik's father's and a village elder, but chose not to go to Kegu with the other elders because he did not trust the Itanyai. It saved him, but when the war machines came through, it did not save his family."

"He has very good reasons to mistrust the Itanyai government."

"We all do," she says, her hands running down my legs. My toes curl at the intimacy of it, but she is not treating my body as if it is any different from a dish she must clean. "But we cannot let those reasons blind us from seeing things and people as they are."

"You believe what I have said about the war machines?" I ask.

Her deep blue eyes glint with the fire in the hearth. "I do not want to. I want to believe that I will never witness such horror again." Her words are strained with memory. "But I trust my son, and he trusts you."

"How can we be planning a . . . wedding . . . if everyone must prepare for an invasion?" It reminds me of what Dr. Yixa told me, about how Noor don't plan for the future and live in the moment.

She lifts one of my feet from the water and begins to scrub it. "That is a very Itanyai thing to say, *cuz.*"

"Why?"

"Because it assumes that there will be a better time to celebrate than right now. When hardship is a constant companion, joy is a welcome guest. We do not assume that things will get easier. We assume now is the easiest and best and happiest time we will ever have." She presses her thumbs into the soles of my feet, and I lean back and sigh, forgetting to be shy. "Are you frightened?"

"Of the war machines? Of course." I've been closely acquainted with their small siblings—Bo's spiders—and the damage of which they are capable.

"No, *cuz.* Are you frightened about tonight?"

"Oh." I smooth my palms over my face, hiding my blush. I do not know what to say to her. Melik did not ask me if I wanted to marry him. He did not seek my consent. And my impression is that he claimed me as his bride because his village was about to trample me beneath their leather-wrapped feet. Will he expect me to behave like a wife? Will he expect to have all the rights of a husband?

Suddenly my heart is beating very hard and fast. "I . . . would prefer not to talk about it."

Her lips curl into a knowing smile. "As you wish." With brisk movements she finishes scrubbing me, then washes my hair and massages my scalp with some sort of fragrant oil. She rubs my skin with a thick cream made from mare's milk. I let her move me this way and that, offering no objection because I am too busy thinking of what will happen tonight.

Anni helps me from the tub and makes me stand on a rug of coarse wool. Then she opens a wooden trunk and pulls out a dark red garment, which she holds up in front of me. "I wore this the day I married Melik's father," she says.

I stare at the dress, buttoned at the throat, with a wide, cream-colored sash for the waist. Itanyai wedding dresses are made of plain fabric in plain colors. Deep red is the worst of luck—the color of blood. "It is . . . lovely," I say quietly. And it is. But if my mother saw it, she would shriek with outrage.

"It will swallow you," she says with a laugh, looking at my skinny limbs. "You are the size of a child."

I press my lips together.

"You do not look like a child," she amends. "But we will have to tie this sash very tightly and fold the excess fabric in the back." She helps me pull it over my head. I feel like a little girl trying on her mother's clothes when I look down at myself, the gown hanging from my narrow shoulders and puffing over my chest, which is substantially smaller than Anni's. The sleeves extend to my fingertips and the skirt pools on the ground at my feet, several inches too long. "Hmmm. Perhaps we will need more than the sash." She walks to her door and peeks out, hollering something in Noor.

An old Noor woman, her sagging bosom resting on her belly, and her mouth pursed with lack of teeth, bustles into the cottage a few minutes later. She laughs when she sees me standing in front of the fire, drowning in Anni's dress, and begins to chatter in Noor with my new mother. Together they pull the dress tight and arrange the sash, wrapping it twice around my waist before tying it at the back. While Anni fusses with the fit of the bodice and rolls up my sleeves, the old lady pulls out a needle made of bone and some red thread. She hems the gown, her stitches tiny and quick and sure. She works almost as fast as my mother used to.

A male voice calls from the outside, and the women shout back. Anni turns to me. "The wedding tent has been erected in the village center," she says. "Melik is waiting for you there."

My heart is choking me. "What am I supposed to do?"

She begins to brush my hair and braid it, her skilled fingers making quick work of my straight black locks. "Speak to him. Tell him what is in your heart."

The same heart that is doing its best to escape my chest right now? "I will try."

Because none of their shoes will fit me, they slide my legs into wool stockings before allowing me to put on my traveling boots. My hair is in seven braids down my back. The toothless old lady places a square, embroidered red cap on the top of my head. She chuckles and mutters something under her breath, and Anni slaps her arm in a good-natured way.

"Is she making fun of me?"

Anni shakes her head. "She was merely commenting on how briefly you will be wearing these garments after all this time we've spent preparing you."

I am sorry I asked. I want to sink through the floor.

Anni takes my hand. "Are you ready?"

Not remotely. "I suppose."

She smiles and leads me from the cottage. Night has fallen, and torches and a few oil lanterns light the way. We are greeted by nearly the whole village, and they clap and cheer and stomp their feet as we walk down the lane toward a large tent made of bleached cloth that has been erected in a large, open area in the middle of the village. Tables have been brought outside and laden with round, flat loaves of bread and several platters of meat. I wonder how much these Noor are sacrificing so we can celebrate tonight. Judging by their sunken cheeks and lean frames, it's clear they do not normally feast like this. To show my gratitude, I smile and accept the white mountain flowers from the children who come running up. They press the blossoms into my hands and hug my legs before fleeing back to their *annis*. I am stunned by the happy faces around me, the villagers' willingness to accept me into their midst after the looks I received when I first arrived.

All because Melik chose me.

It gives me courage as I round the tent and reach the entrance. Sinan steps out, wearing a dark brown tunic with a cream-colored belt around his narrow waist. "We were starting to wonder if you had tried to escape," he says, and his mother gives him a look of warning. He raises his eyebrows. "I think Melik is nervous."

Anni puts her hands on my shoulders. "He has nothing to be nervous about."

I can barely breathe. But I can smile, and so I do. Sinan lifts the tent flap and gestures inside while the crowd whoops. I duck beneath the thick fabric and it falls shut behind me.

The space is lit by a single lantern hanging from the central tent pole. Melik is sitting on a large pallet of fur and wool, but he leaps to his feet when I enter, nearly hitting his head on the angled frame that holds up the roof of the tent. He has shaved his beard and bathed. His rust-colored hair is neatly tied back from his face. His tunic is a bleached wool, and his belt is red like my gown. There is a decorative knife tucked into it. He is stunningly handsome, but his jade eyes glitter with apprehension. "How are you?" he asks.

"Your mother has treated me like her daughter," I reply.

He gives me a flickering smile. "I'm glad, but that's not what I meant."

"What did you mean, then?"

He approaches slowly, and he lightly touches my cap. "All afternoon my head has been filled with your fears."

I swallow hard as he takes my hand. "How do you know my fears?"

He tips my chin up. "You are afraid I will take things from you that you are not ready to give."

I look at his strong, not-quite-perfect face. "I do not think you would do that."

He bows his head over mine. "You are afraid I will keep you here. That I will not let you leave if you want to."

"I hadn't thought of that."

"I wouldn't." He slides a finger down one of my braids. "If you like, once it is safe, I will escort you back to the east, into the arms of your father."

"You know we cannot do that. I am a traitor—"

"Not to those Itanyai soldiers. To them you are a savior."

"But you are also a traitor. They think you are the Red One."

He touches his forehead to mine. "I would wear a disguise."

I chuckle. "You could try. But you, Melik, are a person people notice."

"I would figure out a way, Wen. I do not want you to think you are a prisoner here."

I put my hand on his chest, warm through the fabric of his tunic. "I have a question."

"Now is the time to ask." He looks toward the tent flap.

"If we leave this tent together, we are married."

Outside the villagers have begun to sing. Through the tent walls I see the glow of a large fire. "There is no ceremony?"

"This is our ceremony," he says quietly. "We say what needs to be said, and we walk out together or separately. So ask me your question and I will give you all my honesty."

"Was there another way? Could your mother have claimed me as her daughter? Could you have claimed me as a sister instead of a bride?"

The anxiety returns to his eyes. He looks down at himself, his red belt and his clean trousers. "No other way," he says.

"So you only did it to protect me?"

"I did do it to protect you." He raises his head. "But I also did it because I wanted to."

"Marriage among the Itanyai is for life. It means the woman belongs to the man." I watch his expression carefully, and I see it harden.

"But that is not what it means to us," Melik replies. "In a Noor marriage the man offers himself to the woman. He takes her into his family, not to own her, but to nurture her. Body and heart, health and happiness. A Noor man respects his woman's freedom to choose him, and because she has a choice, he knows it is a gift when she accepts his offer."

"You did not give me a choice."

"You have more than you realize."

"This feels big," I say suddenly, barely sure of what I mean. It is just the way it is, uncontainable, stretching at the boundaries of everything I know.

His fingertips caress my face. "It feels that way to me, too," he murmurs. "This is more than an arrangement of convenience to me."

I'm glad. I don't want to be alone in this. I've felt alone for a very long time. "Melik, we don't know each other well. And this is the most perilous of times. We have no idea what the future holds for us."

He nods. "Would you like to hear my vow to you, then?"

I blink at him, startled. "I suppose?"

He sinks to his knees on the pallet and takes my hands. "I promise, Wen, that I will give you shelter and food and all that you need. I will protect you with my body and give my life for yours if necessary. I will give you all that is due a wife. And in return I will ask you to consider choosing me."

"But isn't that what I'm doing now?"

"No. You are accepting my protection now because you must. I want you to choose me when you don't have to. And until you do, this marriage will be the armor that covers you and the food in your belly. Nothing more."

"What about . . ." My gaze darts to his mouth.

His smile is a slow, seductive thing that I feel low in my belly. "Are you asking if I want to take you to my bed?"

I press my lips together and nod.

His thumb strokes over the back of my hand. "Wanting and doing are different creatures," he says. "So I will tell you about the one that matters. I will not touch you until you ask me to. It is as simple as that."

I see nothing but his eyes as I whisper, "And if I ask?"

He arches his eyebrow. "I think you will find me eager to fulfill your request."

Again, the way he speaks the intimate secrets of his heart and body leaves me breathless. He is on his knees before me, and I can see the pulse beating in a vein in his scarred throat. "What if you decide you don't want me, though?" I say, the pressure in my chest making my voice thin.

His hand tightens over mine. "However it goes between us, you can trust me to be honorable."

I should be reassured by that, but it makes me ache. On the one hand, I want everything, and on the other, I'm afraid of giving in, of giving up this piece of myself to become something Melik and I can only be together. It seems too fast, too huge, too fragile. I could offer my heart, but what if I end up wanting to take it back? What if he ends up not wanting it? Wouldn't that hurt us both?

But in one thing I do trust. Melik will not forsake me. He could have, several times. If he had, I would be dead, but he would be safer. He is frightening to me, and foreign, and he fills me with confusion and desire. But he is a brave man. A strong one. A leader who draws people to him, a treasured son and brother.

He is worth having, worth fighting for, worth risking for.

"Here is my vow to you, Melik," I say, my voice trembling as I twine my fingers with his. I kneel in front of him on the pallet, so we are both on our knees. "You have my trust and faith. You have my hands and my mind. I want to be your helper. I want to do good for the people you love. And I want us to grow together." I bring our hands up, so we are palm to palm and face to face. He folds his fingers over mine, and mine fold over his, and our hands lock together, a bond made weak by flesh but strong by loyalty and respect. "When we get through this war, we will make a decision together. But right now I will be proud to walk out of this tent by your side."

His eyes shine with emotions I can't read. "But will you be happy?"

I release one of his hands and touch his face. "I will be scared. But I will also be happy."

"I will be scared too," he admits.

"But that only means something important is at stake."

He smiles as I repeat his own words back to him. "So important," he says, stroking my cheek.

The songs and laughter outside are interrupted by the clatter of gunfire. I startle, but Melik chuckles. "They are celebrating. And probably getting impatient."

"Should we go?" I start to rise, but his arm coils around my waist.

"In a moment." He kisses me, intoxicating me with the heat of his mouth and the musky scent of his skin. I slide my arms around his neck and surrender to the moment and to him. Pressed together from knees to chest as we are, I feel every inch of him against me, powerful and vibrating with want and need and hope. His mouth is possessive and fierce over mine, not playful like his kisses from last year. As more gunfire erupts outside, Melik strokes the sash at my waist as if he wishes he could pull it off, and soon I begin to wish he would. But that is when he pulls away and wipes his thumb over my lip.

He takes my face in his hands. "To have more, you must ask. And you must be very clear. I know that is

foreign for an Itanyai, but that is what I need from you."
I open my mouth, and he shakes his head. "But not now.
Now we must—"

Screams and shouts drown out whatever he says next.
More gunfire clatters just outside the tent. Sinan rips the
tent flap open, his eyes wide. *"Icin baze murabirse!"* he yells,
his voice cracking.

Melik fires back a question, but Sinan disappears, the
fabric fluttering shut once more.

Melik's brows shoot up and he jumps to his feet, pulling
me to mine. "He said something has come for us."

"The army?"

"I don't know. Stay here."

I squeeze his hand. "No. We leave together."

His fingertips are tender on my throat as he leans
down and kisses my lips, like he thinks it might be the last
time. Then he peers out of the tent and tugs me behind
him. People are pointing down the lane, back toward the
Line. The men have clustered at the edge of the open
area, their rifles aimed. They are calling back and forth
to one another as Melik leads me into the crowd toward
Anni, who is standing next to Sinan right behind the
line of men, peering into the darkness. Melik pushes me
behind him. "They said that something is circling the
village."

"A war machine?"

He looks over his shoulder at me. "Some people think
that's what it is, but it hasn't fired on us. And some of
them say it is too small to be a war machine."

My breath catches as a shadow passes through the
torchlight. The men freeze, their guns aimed into the

night. There is a distant metal creak, and they fire at the noise.

Something lands with a thundering crunch, right in front of the crowd. The ground vibrates beneath our feet. The men stumble back, but before they get their rifles raised again, I scream, "Stop!"

Metal scrapes against metal, accompanied by the hum of circuitry. The thing is covered in a cloak of rich velvet with silver clasps, a garment for a fine gentleman, but it is dusty and the hem is frayed. Nevertheless, the cloth conceals a machine. But it's not a war machine. It's shaped like a man, and as it rises from its crouch and throws its hood back, my heart squeezes tight. His full-metal face glints with fire, and his glass eyes are glowing with piercing light.

I step forward, pushing my way through the men, who are too stunned to hold me back. "Bo?"

The metal monster's eyes wink out, becoming dead and black. His steel hands, one thicker, covering his flesh, reach up and slide half of his faceplate aside, revealing the man beneath. His brown eye focuses on me. "Hello, Wen. I've come to take you home."

Chapter Thirteen

THE MEN GIVE Melik anxious sidelong glances as they aim their rifles at Bo. At this range I don't see how bullets wouldn't penetrate his armor. Sinan is staring at Bo with his mouth hanging open. Melik turns to me, betrayal etched into his furrowed brow. "You didn't tell me he survived."

"He is a secret I am used to keeping," I murmur.

Something flares in his eyes. "I need to give the men an explanation, or they will shoot him out of sheer terror."

"Tell them he will not hurt them." I look at Bo's face as I say this.

Bo's lip curls. "Unless they come closer." His shoulders are covered in a row of metal bumps, and each of those bumps has eight eyes—dormant, fanged spiders, ready to attack. He is wearing the frames he's been working on for the past year, and they cover both legs, his remaining arm, and his torso. They envelop him, making him wider than and nearly as tall as most of the Noor. There is sheet metal contoured over his limbs, covering the inner workings of his artificial body. His fingers are spindly, too long for his hands, with too many joints. His head is covered in a helmet, with that one side that swings open to reveal his actual face. I have no idea how many terrors he's tucked into the arms and legs and belly of this suit, but I think he could kill half this village if he wanted to.

And he looks like he wants to.

"You have traveled a long way," I say.

He lets out a hard laugh. "So have you. Guiren is distraught, Wen. He thinks you're dead."

I cover my mouth with my hand, my eyes stinging. "In the train?" I force out.

He nods. "But I was not willing to let it end there."

Melik's eyes narrow. "You were in Kegu, weren't you?"

Bo tilts his head, his suit letting out an eerie hum. "I was told that's where she would be." He looks back to me. "Your bag was found in a demolished dining car along with over a dozen dead Itanyai soldiers. Guiren was scared to hope." He focuses his gaze on the ground. "But I was scared not to." His joints whir as he stands straighter. "I came through the canyon."

"And you met five Itanyai soldiers who had escaped the vicious Noor rebels, but with only nine fingers each," says Melik as he gently nudges aside the barrel of a rifle aimed at Bo's face, then puts his hand on the back of the young man wielding it and gives him a reassuring nod.

"Correct, Red," says Bo. "They described the girl who cared for their wounds and cut them free. They also told me of the Red One, who sliced off their fingers to save her life. They said the girl was being taken to Kegu."

"But we were at Kegu only three days after I left the Ring," I say. "It takes at least a week to hike the canyon."

Bo rolls his eye. "Wen, I have warned you about underestimating me."

"So you ran through the canyon, all the way to Kegu, in less than four days." Melik glances at Baris, whose forehead is crinkled as he listens to a conversation in a language he doesn't understand. "And then you blew up the municipal complex. How many did you kill?"

Bo shrugs, the metal spiders on his shoulders shifting under the moonlight. "I have no idea, and I truly don't care. I needed everyone completely occupied so I could get out with Wen." He bares his teeth at Melik. "But she was gone."

"Are you sorry I rescued her?" Melik asks in a hard voice. "She was going to be executed at dawn."

"She didn't need you," Bo snarls. "She had me."

"She doesn't need you," says Sinan. "She has my brother."

I put my hand on Sinan's arm. Once again he is too open, too frank, too willing to say exactly what he's thinking. "Sinan . . ."

"Wen, your father needs to see you," says Bo, stepping forward. The Noor men raise their rifles again, and they keep glancing back at Melik, waiting for any signal. But Bo does not seem the slightest bit concerned with them. "It is time for you to come with me."

"I'm not going to—" I begin, but Bo raises his arms, glaring at me.

"You are," he says. "We're wasting time. The first war machines were already assembling at the eastern mouth of the canyon when I left. You cannot be here when they arrive!"

Melik's eyes meet mine. "You were right," he whispers.

"Did you not believe me after all?"

His gaze is both fond and full of regret. "I did, but I hoped you would be wrong at the same time."

I can certainly understand that. I was hoping I was wrong too, but now Bo has confirmed that the nightmare is reality. "How quickly can they move through the canyon?"

Bo looks down at his body. "If it took me four days, it would take them no more than two. We must go," he says to me. "Truly, if they are not here by now, it is only a matter of time."

"*Taslar,*" Melik mutters under his breath. He grabs the shoulders of two of the young men with rifles and speaks very quickly, pointing to the gaping maw of the canyon that leads east. While he talks, several other young men cluster around him. They ask him a few questions and then jog away, along with their women, heading for their respective cottages. "They will set up a scout line all the way to the Quebian Falls. They will leave as soon as their supplies are packed. We'll have signal fires to warn of the war machines' approach."

"It won't save you," says Bo. "Nothing will." He holds out his spindly metal hand to me, but even if I wanted to go with him, I would be scared to grasp it. "Come on, Wen!"

Melik moves so that his body is half in front of mine. "You want to leave with her now so that you can meet the machines in the canyon?"

"We could go high enough into the hills to avoid them," Bo snaps.

"Even if you don't freeze, you are likely to get lost. The high passes are a maze," Melik retorts. "Is that likely to mend her father's heart? When her body is found frozen in a crevasse?"

"If the alternative is being crushed along with a bunch of Noor, then perhaps."

"A bunch of Noor?" Melik laughs. "Is it somehow better if she dies at your side?" My stomach tightens as I hear the bright, overfriendly tone in his voice, as I see the cold look in his eyes. His hand travels to the hilt of his knife.

I put my free hand up, trying to calm the rising storm. "Please. I can speak for myself. I—"

But Sinan steps forward, standing shoulder to shoulder with his older brother. "Wen married Melik. She is part of our family now. Her place is here with him."

I inhale a sharp breath as Bo's face loses all of its tension. He looks as if Melik has slipped that knife between the plates of his armor. His gaze slowly traces my body, my bloodred gown, my embroidered cap, as if he is only just noticing them. "Is that true?" he asks me, his voice trembling.

"Bo, please, you and I should talk," I sputter. "Someplace . . ." *Without all these eyes on us.* "I want you to understand."

Melik's features flicker with raw hurt as he hears my

words, but it's gone in an instant. "Yes, perhaps the two of you should talk," he says in an even voice. He raises his arms and speaks in Noor, gesturing at Bo and at his own body, as if he is explaining that beneath the armor there is a man. Then he turns back to me. "Take all the time you need."

"Melik—"

"No," he says softly. "I need to meet with the village council anyway. We must find a way to prepare for what's coming." He stalks past our wedding tent, and the people follow him, leaving me and Bo alone. Sinan jogs after the crowd but nearly stumbles over his large feet because he keeps turning back to stare at Bo.

I ache as Melik walks away from me. It feels like whatever step we took in those minutes within the tent has been erased, leaving us stumbling back in the wake of Bo's arrival. But my new husband, if that is indeed what he is, has disappeared from my view. I turn back to Bo.

"Can you imagine . . . ," he begins, then clears his throat. "Did you think for one moment about how it might feel to me as I waited for you on First Holiday morning?"

I watch his spindly fingers twitch. "It was very hard to leave, Bo."

"I thought . . . I thought you had chosen me. But the whole time, the entire time, you were planning to leave, weren't you? It wasn't a beginning. It was a good-bye."

"I couldn't tell you," I say, my voice breaking as I raise my gaze to his.

"You are the cruelest girl." His expression is tight with pain. "Why did you let me believe you cared?"

Because I will never stop caring about him. But it is a soft feeling tangled around all the jagged edges of the metal boy who stands before me. "You must be very angry at me."

He stares at my face. "You have no idea how deep it goes. How could you do this?"

"The same way you could come after me instead of leaving me to my well-deserved fate, Bo." It is difficult to return his gaze because he is horrifying like this. He does not look like my Bo right now. He looks like a war machine. "Your heart is not that cold."

"I wish it were," he says, his voice rough. "You can't stay here, Wen. These people are going to die, and you will die with them. The outrage over the train attack energized everyone in the Ring, along with the rest of the country. If any of them were sympathetic to the rebels in the west, this atrocity has changed their minds. They will cheer as the war machines destroy these villages."

"I cannot walk away from this!" I take a step toward him, wanting to dismantle his metal armor, wanting to touch him, not his machine self. "These people just want to live and rule themselves. They are just like us."

"They are not," he shouts. "Shooting unarmed girls and injured soldiers! Burning a train car full of innocent civilians! They are animals!"

"Then we are too!" I shriek. "Do you not hear what you are saying? Machines made only for killing could march through that canyon and into this village at any moment! There are children here, Bo! Pregnant women and little boys and grannies and toothless old men. Mothers and fathers. And our machines will shoot at them and crush them and burn their lives to nothing. Not for the first time, either. How are we not the same?"

Bo's mouth opens and closes, and then he yells, "Because we are Itanyai!"

I rock back, astounded by how horrid that sounds to me now. "For such a smart man, you have an incredibly small mind," I say, my voice shaking.

His metal fists clench. "I can make you come with me."

"You would only have my body. The rest of me would be here. And the part you had wouldn't be worth much."

"It's worth everything to me!" he roars, advancing on me.

I hold my ground. "If I am worth so much, then help me."

"I'm trying." He throws up his arms, which clank and click with the movement. "You're right—I am shamefully shortsighted. Here I thought you were a prisoner. The soldiers said you were being treated poorly." His eye flames with hatred. "And one of the rebels who hurt you is now your husband?" he shouts.

"Melik protected me however he could. You heard what the soldiers told you."

"It's been only four days since I last saw you, but you look as if you've been starved and strangled." He clenches his teeth and points at my throat. "If he is your protector, you need a new one."

"We are in a war, Bo. Melik defied his own general to save me."

His eye narrows. "Save you? If he cared about you at all, this is the last place he would have brought you. I know he is a Noor, but I thought he was smarter than that, so I am assuming he is more selfish than stupid. But I am also assuming he is a great deal of both."

"Stop talking about him like that. My opinion of you decreases with every word." I feel as cold as a peak in the Western Hills. Every muscle in my body is tight. "If you think so little of him—and of me—you can leave."

"I won't leave without you!"

"Then stay and help," I say quietly. "They need us, Bo. If anyone can help, it's you. I can stitch wounds, but you can prevent them."

He takes a step back. "What are you talking about?"

"If we were somehow able to stop the machines in the canyon, or at least cripple some of them, wouldn't that make our government reconsider?"

"I have no idea, Wen, but stopping them is more than these Noor can do."

"You don't know what they can do. But you understand those machines better than anyone."

"I will not betray my country."

I point to the huddled crowd near the large celebration fire. Melik is speaking to them, his long-armed shadow thrown against the thatched roof of the nearest cottage. "They are your countrymen, Bo. They were born here. This is their land. They claim no other nation as their own, and no other nation would shelter them because they belong in Itanya. Please. Help them."

"I will never do anything for anyone but you and Guiren," he says. "You are the only two people in the world I care about."

I lay my palm on his cheek, warm in the cool air of the night. "Then do it for me, if that makes it possible." I close my eyes and breathe deep. As my next words take shape in my mind, they cut to the bone. Am I betraying

Melik, or am I saving him? Am I cursed to do both at once? "And if you help, I will leave with you once the threat is over."

He stares down at me for a long time, distant Noor words washing over us. I lose count of how many times I hear the word *"kuchuksivengi"* before he speaks again. "Promise me," he murmurs. "Promise me you will leave here and return with me."

"I swear to you," I say, my voice strained as it tumbles over the lump in my throat. Leaving Melik will not be easy at all, if the pang of longing in my heart is any clue. But not doing everything I can to ensure his survival would be worse. "I will leave here. But only if you help."

He bows his head. "All right. I will do what I can. We need to talk to them. I need to know what they have to fight with."

"Thank you." My arms rise to hug him, but I don't know where to touch him. All of him seems like a weapon. "Would you . . . like to take your armor off?"

He shakes his head. "I don't feel safe without it," he says quietly.

I will not push him now, because I remember how the people of Dagchocuk responded when I arrived. Melik was my armor, and Bo must supply his own. "Come, then. Melik can translate whatever you need. So can Sinan and their mother."

"How old is that boy?" Bo asks.

"Sinan? He's fourteen now."

Bo grunts. "He was at the factory last year."

"Yes. He is a very unusual boy, I think."

Bo makes another noise in his throat, and we begin to

walk. His footsteps are heavy on the dirt as he makes his strides.

"Is it tiring, having to carry all that metal around?" I ask.

"No. It carries itself. And me." The weariness in his voice tells me he is making it sound easier than it is. "The movement sequences are set, and all I must do is spur them into motion before they do the rest. Like my spiders, the mainsprings are self-winding. It is not perfect, but—"

"It is incredible, Bo. You are incredible." And terrifying. I had no idea he had traveled so far in his journey to become a machine.

As we approach the crowd of Noor, Melik sees us coming and slowly lowers his arms. He watches Bo, his face expressionless.

"Are you arguing about how many rocks you will throw at the war machines?" Bo asks, the edge unmistakable.

"No," says Melik, even and deceptively calm. "We are discussing how much blasting powder will be required to bring down an avalanche of rock on them."

Bo's eyebrow arches. "You have black powder?"

Melik folds his arms over his chest and lifts his chin. "Three crates."

Surprise glitters in Bo's eye. "That is encouraging."

"To whom, exactly?" Melik asks.

"I think I'm going to help you, Red."

Melik scowls. "We do not need your help."

"Really?" Bo chuckles. "What is a war machine's weakest point?"

Melik's mouth is tight as he says, "Its leg joints, I would imagine." Sinan leans over quickly and whispers something in Melik's ear. "Or maybe the hatch that leads to the engine."

Bo smirks. "Your little brother understands them much better than you do."

I don't miss the way Sinan stands a little straighter. Melik doesn't either, and he nudges his brother and gives him a small smile.

"But you are both wrong," Bo says, erasing the brothers' pride in an instant. "The machines are built for uneven terrain and dusty conditions. Raining rocks on them with blasting powder is possible, if imprecise and risky, and three crates will not bring down enough to do more than temporarily slow them. Their leg joints are actually the most protected and well-constructed parts of them. And though their hatches are more vulnerable, they are still armored. A better strategy is to attack from the ground and stop their beating hearts. I know exactly how to get to them too. Now tell me again that you do not need me."

Melik's nostrils flare. "We might. But we also do not trust you." The men and women around him may not understand my language, but that wariness and dislike is etched into their features. Not only does Bo look like a war machine—he is clearly Itanyai, and clearly unfriendly. They would not hesitate to shoot him if Melik gave the word.

Bo's smile does not warm the cold look in his eyes. "Under most circumstances, Red, you shouldn't trust me." His suit hums as he looks down at me. "But in this case I have every reason to help you."

Melik's gaze crosses the distance between Bo and me,

and from his frown, I suspect he believes that space is smaller than it is. "You have tried to kill me twice before— for the same reason."

"And I also saved your miserable life."

"Which makes balance between us. Now you are free to try again."

"I'd love to do more than try," Bo says. "But I won't."

"Because of Wen." Three words, and their weight on me is crushing.

Bo nods. "Because of Wen."

Melik stares at me for a long moment. One during which I wish he would say exactly what he is thinking, but he doesn't. "Very well," he says softly. "We will accept your help."

Chapter Fourteen

MELIK AND A few of the others trace the outline of the canyon in the dirt, carving bends and ridges from memory. Melik uses his paces to measure miles, talking nonstop to the men and women gathered around him. But as Bo moves forward to look, shoulders and hips and elbows and backs create a wall of flesh, edging him out. Instead of pushing his way through, which he could do easily, Bo drifts to the back of the group, giving me a look that says, *See? They will not let me help.*

Then Sinan pokes Bo's metal arm. He jerks his hand back when the spiders on Bo's shoulders raise their fangs, but he seems more fascinated than afraid. "Teach me about the machines," Sinan says, as much a challenge as a request.

Bo stares at the boy's face, at his defiant stance and the

eager glimmer in his eyes. "Why don't you go argue about crates of dirt and blasting powder with your brother? Not all of his ideas are stupid."

Sinan folds his arms over his chest. "None of his ideas are stupid. But I think understanding the war machines themselves will make us more able to defeat them."

Bo tilts his head. "Very well. We'll see if you are capable of understanding them. They are far more complicated than a horse-drawn plow."

Sinan's mouth twitches, like he wants to grin but is trying to look like a man. I sit on a low stone fence and watch as Bo takes a sharp stick, one used as a spit for meat devoured earlier in the evening, and makes drawings of his own in the dusty earth.

The war machine's body and legs take shape quickly. "Eight legs with three segments each. This configuration allows the legs to take on a bow-shaped structure that is both powerful and flexible," says Bo, his metal fingers wrapped around the stick as he slides it along the ground. "The movements of the legs are very efficient." He holds his hand, palm down, parallel to the ground. "The thorax and abdomen of the machine are stable, with no vertical oscillation, as the legs propel it over the ground."

Sinan wears a grimace of concentration as he listens. I am sure he does not understand Itanyai words like "oscillation," but he seems to pick them up from the context. "Are they able to jump?" he asks.

Bo shakes his head. "But they can accelerate quickly and maneuver over uneven ground easily. They are capable of climbing inclines as steep as sixty degrees, though that burns a lot of fuel. The front and rear legs are synchronized on each side, with the middle legs synchronized to the opposite side." He gazes fondly at his drawing. "It really is marvelous."

Sinan frowns. "But if the legs are synchronized, what does the pilot do?"

"He creates modifications in the patterns with the levers in the cockpit. He is heavily protected. There is a metal hatch at the top of the thorax, but no windows. Only the small eyes at the front. Some of them are connected to openings on the sides and rear of the abdomen with a mirror system." Bo's eye briefly meets mine as I realize how much he has learned from these animals of war.

Next Bo draws two long guns where a spider's fangs should be. "The front gunner sits in a compartment below the pilot, but there is also a way for the pilot to control the guns from the cockpit if necessary. The machine is most dangerous head-on, but there is also a top gunner here." He taps the top of the spider's round abdomen. "He is protected from ground attack but would be easy to take out from above. His chair is positioned over the fireman's compartment. That crew member manages the engine, adding coal to the firebox and monitoring the boiler's water levels. His hatch is on the rear of the machine, also armored. It can be penetrated, but it is not easy. There is something else, though. A panel, here." He pokes a spot where the thorax and abdomen are joined. "Beneath that panel is a kill switch of sorts, meant to be used if the boiler catches fire or the pilot is incapacitated."

When Bo sees Sinan smile, he starts to laugh. "It is much harder to reach than you would think," he says.

Sinan stares at the sketch for a moment longer before asking, "What is the range of this machine? Is there a way to starve it? Cut off its fuel?"

Bo considers the rust-haired boy. "You have a very good mind," he says matter-of-factly, and Sinan beams. "Water is the most significant limitation of these machines." He leans forward. "I overheard the factory boss talking to a general. They are anticipating a quick, easy campaign with no detours or major battles because they have sent false intelligence that the entire army will attack from the north."

Sinan calls out something in Noor to Melik before returning his attention to Bo. "You must tell my brother everything that you heard."

"Or I could tell you, and you could tell him," says Bo in a flat voice.

Sinan rubs the back of his head and glances at me. "If you insist," he mutters. "So, they are planning to march up from the south and approach our forces from behind?"

Bo shifts his weight from one steel boot to the other, and I know him well enough to recognize the pain he is trying to hide. "That is the strategy. Infantry troops will follow the war machines through the canyon, but it is only an occupying force. They will be laden with supplies."

"And days behind the machines," says Sinan, absently gouging the ground with his stick. "The drought will make it harder for the spiders. How much water must they carry?"

Bo grins. "You ask the right questions, boy. Their tanks carry five thousand gallons. The upper rear level of the abdomen holds the coal—approximately eight tons. With that load their range is a hundred miles. There will be a carrier spider behind them, loaded with coal. It looks different from the others." Bo sketches a massive body and short legs. "It is even more heavily armored."

Sinan glares at it as if he has a personal grudge. "But if we could destroy it?"

"Then the machines could be stranded."

Sinan's eyebrow arches. "Or used against the oncoming infantry forces?"

Bo smiles as if he admires the boy's thirst for destruction. "We should focus on stopping the machines first."

As they continue to banter, I look up to see Melik staring at the three of us. I am suddenly very aware of my red dress and cap, of how I am dressed like a Noor woman but still don't bear the slightest resemblance to the ones who are crowded around him, looking as fierce and strong as he does as they all make their plans for battle. Instead, I probably look like a little girl in a costume, playing pretend. Melik's rust-colored hair glints with gold in the light of the bonfire. Again I want to know what he is thinking, what he sees as he gazes at me, dressed for the wedding that never was. I wonder if he knows how much I am willing to hurt both of us to make sure he and those he loves continue to breathe.

I rise to my feet, working up the courage to tell him, but he looks away quickly and returns to his plans. The night suddenly feels very cold. I sink to the ground and lean my head against the stone, listening to men I care about planning to fight a war with terrible odds and painfully high stakes. Hearing Bo talk about all the ways a war machine can be destroyed gives me hope, though, and I drift into nothing on the raft of reassurance it provides. When I shiver myself awake, most of the villagers have disappeared into their cottages for the night. Melik is gone, and so is Sinan. Bo is hunched over his drawing, muttering to himself.

"You must be so tired," I say, slowly pulling myself to my feet.

He sighs. "I should probably get some rest." His spider-laden shoulders sag. "I need to do maintenance on this suit if I want it to remain functional."

"You need to do maintenance on your body if you want it to remain functional," I remind him, laying my palm over his cold metal forearm.

He looks down at my fingers, which look weak and skinny on his steel body. "I will see you once the sun comes up, then."

"Where will you sleep?"

His gaze rises to the low ridges of the canyon. "In a place safe from greedy, sabotaging hands and wide, staring eyes."

"Why would they hurt you? You're helping them."

He steps away from me, shedding my grasp easily. "Tomorrow, Wen." And then he strides away as if he cannot put enough distance between us.

Too exhausted and twisted up to chase, I trudge back to the wedding tent, hoping Melik is still awake, hoping he will talk to me, hoping he will take me in his arms and let me fall asleep listening to his heart beat. But when I lift the flap, the tent is empty. The pallet has been arranged for sleep, with a soft wool-stuffed pillow and a warm blanket, and someone, probably Anni, has left a woolen nightgown and a plain tunic and trousers. They are small and probably belong to one of the village boys, but they are practical and I am grateful to have them. My muscles heavy with dread, I remove the embroidered cap and bloodred dress, folding them carefully. I sit on the ground and pull the ties from my braids one by one, then put on the nightgown and slide under the blanket.

This is my wedding night, and it is worse than I feared for none of the reasons I expected. I curl onto my side, alone in my white tent. I wonder where Melik is, and if he's sleeping, and whether this is part of his promise to be honorable. If so, there are few dishonors that would hurt more.

It takes me a long time to fall asleep.

I wake to the sound of roosters crowing and pull my trousers and tunic under my blanket, dressing in the warm cocoon instead of the chilly air in the tent. I use one of the ties to corral my hair in a low ponytail and slide on my boots, knowing I look more like a young boy than a woman. But maybe that is good, because I can hardly scramble across rocks and ridges in a wedding dress.

Melik did not come to me. He found somewhere else to sleep. But even so, I will not mope or feel sorry for myself. I will not think about the loneliness and foreboding gnawing at my heart. No, today I will make myself useful in the only way I know how. My feet make no sound on the dirt as I march to Anni's cottage. Yes, part of me secretly hopes to catch Melik at his breakfast. Yes, that part of me wilts when I see that he is not in front of the hearth. But I smile anyway as Anni beckons me inside. If she is aware that Melik and I were apart last night, she does not let on.

"Good morning," she says. "I am making flatbread for the fighters who will occupy the high ridges. Will you join me?"

"I would, but I have something else I must do," I say. "Is there a doctor in this village?"

Her eyebrows rise. "A doctor?" She chuckles. "The nearest doctor is in Kegu, *cuz*. But we have a healer."

I accept a chunk of warm flatbread with a bow of thanks. "May I speak with that healer?"

She frowns. "Are you ill?"

"No. I want to offer him my assistance."

"Her."

"Her, then," I mumble with a full mouth, covering it with my palm until I swallow. "If we are going to battle with war machines, there will most certainly be injuries. I have assisted my father for over a year and have seen all manner of wounds. I can help."

She gives me a pitying look. "And you have likely had the benefit of equipment and medicine far more sophisticated than we have here. *Cuz*, if our men are shot, we carry them home and give them enough heavy drink to ease their pain as they die."

My stomach knots as I hear the resignation in her tone. "We can do more than that."

She lays her palm on my cheek. "You are welcome to try. Come, I will introduce you to Aysun."

I polish off my bread as she pulls a patterned red head scarf over her rust-colored braid. I follow her through the scattering of cottages closest to the cliff that leads up to the plateaus above the village. Anni claps her hands before entering the cottage, which I can only assume is the equivalent of knocking. A skinny woman with sharp brown eyes peers out, and those eyes narrow as they land on me. She's the one who shoved me yesterday before Melik claimed me as his bride. Anni converses with her in Noor as I take in the woman's appearance—a blue head scarf that covers a thin white braid, sallow skin that suggests a liver ailment, and large, knobby knuckles that tell me she must be racked with joint pain.

Aysun the healer lets out a bark of laughter as Anni puts her hand on my shoulder and gestures at me. She shakes her head and waves her gnarled, veined hands like she's trying to ward me off. Anni gives me an apologetic look. "She says she will not accept your help."

"Then I will work on my own," I say loudly, knowing I am being shamefully bold. There is too much at stake to worry about it. "Anni, I need cloth, a very sharp knife, and a curved needle and thread. I also need to look at what herbs you have. Please."

Anni hesitates. "What are you planning to do?"

"I'm going to travel with the fighters, and I'm going to treat them on the field," I say, tightening my muscles to keep from shaking. "I'm going to save as many lives as I can."

She blinks at me, as if surprised to hear such big statements coming out of my little body. "*Cuz*, Melik will not be happy to have you so close to the danger."

I stand as tall as I can and lift my chin. "Melik knows what I can do."

Her mouth softens into a motherly smile. "Very well. How can I help?"

"Please ask Aysun if she has san qi root." I describe the plant, and after Anni spends several long moments arguing with the healer, the older woman disappears into her cottage and emerges with the homely, bumpy dried root. I hold my hands out and she drops it into my cupped palms with a muttered *"kuchuksivengi."*

With Anni as my translator, I gather a small collection of healing herbs from the snarling medicine woman, then return to Anni's cottage and sit in front of the fire with a mortar and pestle, grinding mixtures that slow bleeding and ease pain. I create cloth packets for each, tied with strings of various colors. Despite her refusal to work with me, Aysun repeatedly pokes her head into the cottage to see what I'm doing. I don't miss her nod of approval as I pack a precious jar of honey to disinfect wounds. Anni brings me a metal needle, and though it is straight instead of curved, it is thin and will suit. She offers me what I suspect is her finest thread and helps me cut a bolt of unbleached cloth into strips to use as tourniquets and bandages. After I sort and fold them, I wander the ditches by the road and the edge of the village, plucking sticks to be used as splints. Throughout the morning I am so focused that I don't have time to feel the sting of Melik's absence or to worry about Bo.

Once my medical kit is assembled, I pack it all into an old satchel Anni provides, along with a loaf of flatbread, a canteen, and a sleeping blanket. I sling it onto my back. It is not too heavy to carry. I am strong enough. I think.

Anni gives me a tight hug and returns to her cottage to finish her baking, and I hike to the village square to find Melik and Bo. Like last night, Melik is surrounded by village elders and young men. He has changed into a plain brown tunic and trousers, but his hair is still tied back. His jaw is shadowed with stubble and there are circles of fatigue beneath his eyes. I want to run to him. I want to ask what is happening between us. I want to know why he is avoiding me. But then I remind myself that he is dealing with something very big, and now that I am safe within his family, I should rightfully be very low on his list of priorities.

He does not look up when I pass, so I approach Bo and Sinan, who are once again off to the side, quibbling over a diagram of a war machine. Both of them are smiling, and I am struck by the identical fire of intense curiosity that I read on their faces. I wonder if Bo used to be a lot like Sinan, bold and unafraid of his elders, unapologetically thirsty to learn, too confident and eager to be aware of how small he is in this world.

Bo looks up and notices me. He waves, but I read the fatigue on his face.

"How are the preparations?" I ask.

Sinan stretches his long limbs, though he doesn't look tired at all. "There are a number of ways to attack these machines. They are more vulnerable than I imagined."

He sounds gleeful, the way only a teenage boy can, and his delight draws a smile to my lips despite my concern for Bo. "That is encouraging."

"Melik has already sent a group ahead to prepare," says Sinan.

"But he is determined to keep the men high on the ridges," sneers Bo. "He'll be hard pressed to stop the machines that way, no matter how much blasting powder or dirt he uses."

"Dirt?" I ask.

Bo's mouth quirks up. "He believes he will damage the gears of the machines if he dumps enough small-grained debris on them."

"Is he correct?"

Bo grumbles "yes" before saying, "But more can be done from the ground."

Sinan frowns and glances at his brother. "He wants to protect the fighters."

"And in doing so, he will condemn everyone else."

"I can hear you, Ghost," Melik says loudly, raising his head from the diagram of the ridge at his feet. "And as I've told you, I welcome your suggestions, but they are not the only ones I will consider."

"They are the ones that will work best," Bo retorts.

Melik says something to his group and then strides over to us. "We have only a hundred men right now, and a handful of women," he says quietly. "Though I have sent riders to nearby villages, no one has come, and that is because most of their fighters are with General Ahmet in the north." His eyes narrow. "Assuming he is still alive after your destruction of the compound in Kegu."

Bo rolls his eye. I know very well the general's life does not matter to him at all.

Melik is stiff with tension. "I have to stretch this tiny

force as far as I can," he explains. "If I put all of them on the ground, as you suggested, we could be wiped out in the first wave. That is why I am trying to protect them."

Bo's mouth snaps shut over whatever acid remark he was preparing. He looks away and nods. "Some should be on the ground, though."

"Perhaps," says Melik. "We can prepare for both types of attack."

Bo kneels next to his dirt sketch and begins to make a few calculations, and Melik turns to me. "Are you planning a hike?" he asks, unsmiling, his gaze sliding from my boots to my trousers to my pack.

"I'm going with you and the fighters," I say.

Bo shoots to his feet so quickly that the spiders on his shoulders move, their legs twitching. "What?"

"You heard me." My fingers close over the strap of the satchel. "I have made a medical kit for use in the field."

For a moment Melik looks at me in the way I love, the way that makes me believe we can close whatever rift has opened between us with Bo's arrival. He bows his head and chuckles. "Wen always has medicine," he whispers.

"That is all you have to say?" Bo snaps. "Weren't you the one telling me I was leading her to certain death if I took her through the canyon?"

Melik straightens. "Yes, but I wouldn't have stopped her if she wanted to go, and I won't try now." He pulls the collar of his tunic aside to reveal his scar. "I am not Itanyai, Ghost. I am Noor, and we value our women for what they can do." He gestures to the group that will journey into the hills, some of whom are female. "We do not shackle them the way you do. They may not fight at the front line, but they are strong, and they do fight."

"Wen is Itanyai," Bo snarls. "And she—"

"Both of you, please be quiet," I say, rubbing my temple to try to quell the headache that is forming there. Melik's words were encouraging, but the way he said them, with no warmth, only logical assessment, as if I am any other female, stings in a way I don't want to think about. "I am able to help, and so I will. Stop arguing and talk about something that matters."

The two of them stare at me like I've kicked them in the shins, but Sinan laughs and says something to Melik in Noor that draws a faint smile to his face. Melik is opening his mouth to reply when a shout turns our heads. A rider plastered over the back of his horse races down the lane from the Line. He shouts something in Noor.

"He said an armed carriage is coming this way," Melik translates, his entire body coiling for action.

All of us look up to see a dust cloud billowing from the road—the rider didn't beat the carriage by much. Melik calls to his fighters, and they pick up their rifles and scramble to the sides of the lane, kneeling and aiming at the road.

"Ghost, conceal yourself. Your presence will only make violence more likely," Melik says as he picks up his own rifle, which tells me violence is a real possibility. He turns and says something to Sinan, who scowls. Melik repeats the command, shouting it and shoving his little brother toward me.

Sinan wraps his arm over my shoulders. "My brother

has suggested we retire to our cottage," he says in a sulky voice as he leads me from the square. "He's been expecting this."

Behind me I hear the clamor of shouted instructions and the clanking footsteps that tell me Bo is doing as Melik asked. After watching Melik run to the opening of the square and stand with a few of the other men, Sinan diverts me into the nearest cottage and winks. "We'll be able to hear much better from here."

He and I peek from the doorway as a large steam-powered carriage rumbles right off the road and into the village. At least twenty rebels armed with rifles are sitting in the back. I recognize several of them from the raid on the train, including Bajram. The carriage slows and then stops at the entrance to the square, where Melik waits, his rifle slung over his shoulder.

Commander Kudret stands up from the passenger seat at the front and begins to speak.

Sinan, mercifully, translates. "'Your flight from Kegu coincided with a vicious attack on the compound orchestrated by government sympathizers. They freed the spy. Many men were killed and several vehicles destroyed. It has taken us nearly two days to settle the citizens and regain control. Now that is done, and the general sent me to deal with you.'"

Melik keeps his empty hands out to his sides as he replies. "He's telling them he was driven by honor and conscience to return to Dagchocuk," Sinan says, "and he's asking the commander to tell General Ahmet that the men of this village will remain here."

Commander Kudret's face is impassive as he listens to

SARAH FINE

Melik, and then he slowly shakes his head. "'We have come to take you back to the north,'" Sinan translates. "'Come peacefully or we will'—*taslar*." He tenses. "They're going to shoot them."

I grab his arm before he can run into the open. "Sinan, don't distract Melik!" I say in a sharp whisper. "He needs to focus."

This reaches the boy, and he sinks into the dark cottage once more. "Melik is telling him about the machines," he says. "He is saying he is certain they are coming very soon. But the commander doesn't believe him."

The rebels on the carriage take up positions around the commander, aiming their weapons at Melik and the men at the front. My fingers curl tightly over Sinan's forearm. "No," he mumbles. "The commander is saying Melik is a traitor to his people."

I barely need to hear the words in Itanyai because I see the tension in the shoulders of the fighters from Dagchocuk, the way their fingers are twitching closer to their triggers. And Melik stands tall right at the front, the only one without a weapon in his hands.

When the rebels open fire, Melik will be the first to fall.

My heart is beating so fast that I am panting with the strain. My mind whirls with what I will do if they start shooting, how I will get to Melik, which supplies I will reach for first, where Sinan and I could drag him to protect him. Nonsense, all of it, because we would be cut down too, but I know that, like Sinan, I could not sit here and watch Melik die.

Melik shouts, angry now, and gestures at the canyon before his tone softens.

"He is begging the commander to listen," Sinan whispers.

But the commander points at Melik, and all the rebels aim at him, the barrels of their weapons gleaming under the sun. Sinan lets out a childlike noise. Both of us brace to run.

The men around Melik try to step in front of him, but he puts his arms out and holds them back. *"Miev zhasivunmokie!"* he roars. He looks around at the determined faces on either side of him, and his fingers spread wide, shaking with tension waiting to be unleashed. *"Bizev bazesivunmokie."*

"'I will defend my home,'" Sinan says in a choked whisper. "'We will defend our home.'"

Commander Kudret's gaze strays along the line of men in front of him. His dark eyes betray his doubt, the conflict inside of him, and his own men are starting to lower their rifles in response to Melik's pleas. So many of them are probably from other villages on the Line. Any order to fire on these Noor would surely sit sour in their stomachs.

A woman in the square cries out, and heads jerk up. Melik raises his gaze, as do most of the rebels. Their eyes go wide.

"The signal fire!" Sinan yelps. He takes my hand and drags me out of the cottage. We crane our necks and look up at the high ridge about a quarter mile into the canyon. Smoke pours from it, fed by the orange glow of a fire.

The village square becomes a flurry of barely organized commotion. Sinan and I run toward Melik, hand in hand, as he yells something at the commander.

And I don't need a translation. I know what he's saying. The machines are on their way.

Chapter Fifteen

COMMANDER KUDRET HOLDS his arms up and his rebels lower their rifles. Melik is past caring what his former commander does, though, as he sprints across the square to grab a supply pack, which he swings onto his back. His eyes keep darting to the ridge, where the smoke puffs are floating high above the ground. "There are four machines," he says to me as I join him.

"How do you know?"

He points at the smoke. "We arranged a system. Knowing they were coming was not enough."

"When will they arrive?"

"If they are not stopped, they will probably arrive in a day, given how far I sent the scouts and where the first one is positioned. There is no way to determine exactly when they will arrive at our battle position, which is a five-hour walk from here." He looks at my feet. "For a person accustomed to that kind of climbing, that is."

I lift my chin and clutch the straps of my satchel. "I will keep up."

Bajram and a few of Kudret's men come over and talk to Melik, and Melik issues a few orders before waving them away. "Kudret is staying to determine whether the threat is real. He will remain in the village with a force, and some of his men will come with us."

"So they are holding the village hostage," I say quietly.

Melik's nostrils flare and he nods. Sinan strides by us and picks up a pack, but Melik's hand clamps over his forearm. "What do you think you're doing?" he says to his little brother.

"Getting ready to leave." Sinan tears his arm from Melik's grip as Bo strides out of a nearby cottage, his head swiveling toward the ridge.

Melik reaches for the pack, but Sinan skips out of his way. Melik's eyes flare with frustration. "You are not coming."

"He knows a lot about the machines," says Bo. He wears no pack, nor is he reaching for one. I wonder if he has supplies wherever he slept last night . . . or if he truly believes he has become a machine.

Melik rounds on Bo. "I don't care if he knows everything about the machines." His voice is a knife, sharp enough to rend bone from muscle. "He is my brother, and he is fourteen years old. He will stay with my mother here in the village."

"I'm not a child!" shouts Sinan. "I have been to the east, and I have worked on a factory floor, and I've hiked the canyon, and—"

"And you are staying here!" Melik roars, advancing on his brother with thunder in every step. "Sinan, I have enough to worry about. I will not add the thought of carrying your body back to our mother."

Sinan's expression is steel. He might be a skinny boy, but right now he looks like a warrior. "As if she would be less sad if I had to carry your body back."

Melik slaps his own chest. *"Zhaliriesie!"*

"Man of our family or not," Sinan says, breathing hard, "you will be better off with me among your fighters."

Melik's face is red with fury as he tears the pack from Sinan so abruptly that it makes the slender boy stumble. "Enough," he says, making an abrupt gesture at the ridge. "We are leaving."

"Wen can go but I cannot?" Sinan's voice drips with disgust.

"Wen can do things no one else can," Melik snaps.

Sinan's mouth drops open, and his eyes shine with unshed tears. "And I cannot?"

"Bazeyatartismakie." Melik hands Sinan's pack to a middle-aged man as he jogs past us, headed for the ridge.

"When will we talk about it, then?" Sinan asks. He sounds as if Melik has punched him in the stomach.

"When I return." Melik waves to Anni as she approaches. "We are leaving," he says to her. "Sinan will remain with you."

Anni looks back and forth between her sons and puts her arm around Sinan's bony shoulders, but he jerks away and runs for their cottage. Not quickly enough for me to miss the tears that streak his face, though. My chest aches for him, but he will be safer here, and I believe that will make Melik safer too.

Melik bows his head and gives his mother an apologetic glance. "I spoke harshly to him."

"He will forgive you," Anni says, crossing her arms over her chest. "Go with a clear head."

Melik nods and takes her in his arms. They whisper to each other in Noor as she strokes his hair. I look over at Bo, whose gaze is riveted to Sinan's back.

"I will go say good-bye to him," says Bo. "And catch up with you."

Melik watches Bo stride after his little brother, but then Anni takes his face in her hands and kisses his cheeks before letting him go. "Fight well," she says, then turns to me. "Heal well."

I accept her fierce, sage-scented hug. "Thank you, Anni." She releases me and clasps my hand, then leads me to Melik. She takes his hand and presses it to mine.

"Take care of each other," she says, her voice strained. She turns abruptly and walks away.

Melik and I stare at our joined hands for a moment. He lets go first. "Are you sure you want to come, Wen?" he asks.

I rub my fingers over the spots he was touching, feeling the warmth fade. "I am sure."

His mouth is a tight line as he nods. I follow him across the square toward the line of fighters with huge packs on their backs. The front of the line is already winding up a steep trail along the inner wall of the canyon. I keep hoping Melik will use this time to speak to me, that he will share what is in his head. Though we Itanyai tend to dwell within our own thoughts and keep most of them private, I have grown used to knowing Melik's mind—and I like it. I bite my lip, trying to think of how to ask, but he quickens his pace and catches up with a few young men and one young woman. They begin to converse in Noor, and I am left to myself.

I do not understand. But again I refuse to sulk. I am here to be the healer, and that requires all my focus. As we hike, I consider the supplies in my pack and develop a plan for triage. Melik wants to keep as many of his people able to fight as possible, so I will have to focus most of my attention on those I can save. Which means I will have to leave the gravely wounded to their fates. The thought does not sit well, so I turn my mind to hoping that Bo's strategy combined with Melik's will be devastatingly successful and yield few casualties.

Higher and higher we climb, like mounting an endless staircase. My breath huffs from my lungs and my thighs scream. I keep my eyes on the feet of the woman in front of me and let her steps set my pace. The sun beats down on us, and though the air is chilly, I sweat within my tunic and trousers.

Something heavy and clanking lands hard at the trailside, shaking the ground. The Noor woman and I fall to the trail, and for a moment I believe we are under attack—but then I see Bo rising to his feet. "I am going ahead," he huffs. "I will see you at the end of the trail."

He crouches, his metal limbs whirring, and then jumps onto the rock wall above us. The Noor woman in front of me whispers *"taslar"* as she watches his progress. He crawls like a spider along the wall before leaping forward again to land next to Melik, who is far ahead. As Bo lands, Melik swings around, his rifle slipping down his arm and into his hand, but then he rolls his eyes when he sees it is Bo. I hear Melik's harsh words from where I stand, telling Bo that he risks getting shot if he insists on sneaking up on people like that.

Bo laughs and walks next to him for a short time before leaping ahead again. I watch the sun glare off his armor until he disappears from sight, wondering how hot it must be in that suit. I hope he is drinking enough water, but I don't even know if he's carrying any.

As the sun descends into the west, we arrive at the spot Melik has chosen for battle. It is a spot in the canyon just to the east of where the ground is wide and flat. The concave rock faces to the west of this position give the appearance of a bowl, but we are in a narrow choke point. I smile as I take in the details of this location: the mostly dry riverbed with a trickle of water down its center, the flat ridges high above the ground. Melik was very clever to select this place. If we could stop enough machines here, it would make it very difficult for others to pass through. The scouts who left earlier have already set up large wooden crates on the ledges and have shoveled them full of dirt. The newly arrived fighters laugh and talk as they clean their rifles and make camp. Melik is standing next to a set of yellow strings. He shoos away a man who attempts to set up a campfire nearby, chuckling and mimicking a massive explosion. The man accepts Melik's teasing with good-natured grace and moves his fire several yards away.

My gaze follows the path of the strings, which diverge

and disappear into cracks in boulders near the eastern part of the bowl, where the canyon opens up. The strings are fuses, and I am guessing the advance scouts have spent the last several hours packing blasting powder into holes and cracks they've chipped into the boulders with the pickaxes leaning against the wall near some of the supply packs.

We are at least fifty to sixty feet off the canyon floor, like being at the top of Gochan One. I lean over a ledge and see why Melik is concerned about putting men down there—it would be so easy to be shot or crushed, by metal feet or falling rock. My gut clenches as I consider that Bo wants to be down there. If he dies, I will feel the weight of his loss in my soul.

I keep my pack on as I walk slowly around the ridge, searching for Bo. Finally I spot his squared footprints in the dirt and follow them around a bend. From there they disappear, and I climb over the rocks when I hear cursing and metal clanking behind a boulder a few yards away.

Bo crouches in a flat, dusty area, sweat dripping from the exposed half of his face. His whole body is shaking. I scramble over the rocks and drop my pack. His head jerks up, and his face is pale with strain. "Leave me alone," he whispers.

"Absolutely not," I say, marching over to him. "You are destroying yourself. Tell me how to get this thing off you."

"No," he breathes.

I kneel in front of him and touch his face. "Look at me," I say gently, stroking my thumb over his clammy cheek. His brown eye meets mine. "You must take care of yourself, or you will not be able to fight."

He lets out an unsteady breath. "I don't feel safe—"

"Bo, please. Do you feel safe with me?"

His chuckle is hoarse. "Never. But I do trust you." He closes his eye. "With some things. Help me undo the arm first?"

He murmurs instructions and I follow them carefully, my fingers slipping over gears to find latches that disconnect the framework over his human arm from the shoulder of the suit. It is tricky, slow business because I am scared that the spiders on his armor will awaken and slice off my fingers. Finally I open the arm like a clam and find his naked, trembling limb inside. His fingers twitch as I carefully pull the metal arm loose and set it on the dirt.

"No," he snaps, then clamps his eye shut and softens his tone. "Please. Do you have a blanket in your pack? If the exposed gears get grit in them, it will wear them down."

I retrieve my sleeping blanket from my pack and lay it over the ground, then set his metal arm on it before returning to him. Next he has me take off his helmet, but he asks me to leave his mask in place. His ebony hair is plastered to his head. I smooth damp strands from his face as he tells me to open the chest plate. He has strapped his tools, a bottle of machine oil, a length of cable, and a sack of spare parts across his ribs, over a dirty, sweat-stained undershirt. There is a small compartment beneath the armor over his abdomen that holds a loaf of flatbread and strips of dried beef.

With his teeth clenched, he stares at the rock wall as he explains how to unhook the armor from his machine limb, the one that's connected to his body at the stump of his amputated left arm. We leave that in place, since he's accustomed to wearing it and I believe he needs it to feel whole. Once his upper body is freed from its metal cage, Bo himself removes the metal frames over his legs. His flesh hand falters over the latches, but his machine hand is smooth and skittering and sure. His worn trousers are cleaner than his shirt, but still damp with his exertion. His ankles are swollen and bruised, and so is his wrist. There are worn, blistered spots at his elbow and along his collarbone. If he removed his pants, which I know he will not, I am sure I would see more blisters and bruises—signs that this metal skin he wears is eating him alive.

"How long have you been wearing this?" I ask, trying not to wrinkle my nose at his smell. He left the Ring almost a week ago for my sake, something he said he would never do. He came after me because he was unwilling to let me go. And as angry as he is at me, he is still my friend, still my Bo, my Ghost.

"I tried to take it off last night," he mumbles, his eyelid drooping with fatigue. "But I couldn't quite manage it. I am sorry. I know I am a filthy mess."

I take a cloth from my pack and pour a bit of water from my canteen over it. "Let's clean you off, then." Moving slowly so that I can sense his needs, I peel the soggy shirt from his skin and run my cloth over his flesh. He shivers as my fingers pass over his bare stomach and lies back on the blanket. As the sun dries the sweat from his hair, I clean his body, my jaw tight with anger as I see what he has done to himself. "Bo, you must spend more time out of these frames than in them."

His fingers skim my arm as I hand him my canteen. He drinks slowly before sinking back to the blanket. "How much advance warning do you expect us to have before the machines arrive, Wen? An hour? More like a few minutes. It takes me several to get the armor on."

"I would help you."

He shakes his head. "Please. Do not force me to argue with you about it."

I stare at his half-face, wanting to rip his mask off. Before I met the Noor, I was never aware of how much we Itanyai leave unsaid, how rarely we seek help when we need it, but now my head is pounding with that knowledge. "You are beautiful and fine without the metal," I say, my voice catching. "I like you better without it too. The parts of you I love the most are made of flesh, not steel."

His eye shines before he blinks the surprise away. "Don't say those things to me. You don't mean them."

I slap my palms onto my thighs. "Are you accusing me of lying?"

He shuts his eye. "Wen, what's the use of saying it? You married Red, and then you say words like that to me and I can't stand it."

I cover my face with my hands. "It was the only way the Noor would allow me into their village. Would you have had me wander alone with no place to stay?"

"Honestly? I'm not sure which is worse."

My hands fall away and I stare at him. "I'm not even sure if we are married," I say quietly. "I'm not sure how it works. They have such strange customs here, and your arrival interrupted whatever was happening."

The corner of his mouth twitches. "I will not lie and say I'm sorry."

I'm sorry. I bow my head, wiping grime from the backs of my hands. "Well, at least you will speak to me," I say, clearing my throat to conceal the tremor in my voice.

Bo's fingers close over my wrist. "Is he mistreating you?"

Melik is treating me no way at all. Those words almost come out of my mouth, but it would be shameless and cruel to complain about this to Bo. I pat his hand. "This is not for you to worry about."

His machine arm twists and his metal palm plants itself in the dirt. It pushes him up to a sit. "Do not speak to me like I am a child," he says, low and rough. "Is . . . he . . . mistreating . . . you?"

"No," I whisper.

"But you will come with me when this is over. You will return to the east, where you belong."

"Yes." At this point I'm not sure Melik would notice.

"Good. It will be as if this ridiculous marriage never happened."

My stomach drops at his harsh words, and my heart follows it down when he snaps, "How long have you been eavesdropping?"

I turn to see Melik standing next to my pack. "I just wanted to see how you were doing after the hike," he says to me in a flat voice. "I did not mean to interrupt your . . . conversation."

"Melik—"

He puts up his hands. "It's all right," he says quietly, then turns and heads down the rocks toward the trail.

Behind me, Bo is cursing and clanking as he pulls the metal frames over his legs. I move toward him, meaning to still the frenetic movements of his hands, but he bares his teeth at me. "Leave me alone," he barks, his voice harsh with humiliation. "Get away from me."

I shrink back at the vicious rumble of his tone, grab my pack, and scramble down the rocks away from him. Not wanting to appear in front of the fighters looking like I'm about to sob, I head farther down the trail, away from the camp, until I find a little nook between two boulders. I scoot inside and pull my knees to my chest, then lower my head onto them and try to slow my breathing. I hurt someone I care about no matter what I do.

Footsteps crunch up the trail, and I raise my head to see Melik standing in front of me. He peers at me for several long seconds, then sighs and tucks himself into the nook beside me. Together we stare across the canyon. "What was last year like for you?" he asks.

My eyes slip along the desolate peaks above us and the sky beyond them. "I was half here and half there."

He pulls at a loose thread along the seam of his worn, dusty trousers. "And when you were there, you were with him."

I lower my head to my knees again. "Obviously, he survived the building collapse."

"Obviously. Many other things are obvious as well."

I imagine what Melik must have witnessed just now, me with my hands on Bo's half-naked body, us talking about my maybe-marriage, and I cringe.

"You have shared many hours with him," Melik says quietly. "Far more than you have with me. And you know each other. You understand each other."

"Do we not understand each other?" I murmur, even though I know the answer.

"There are things I will never understand, Wen. Like there are things you cannot possibly understand, even if I explained them."

"Even with time?"

"Even if we had time, I think not."

I lift my head, dread squeezing in my chest. "That does not sound very hopeful."

He leans back, bracing himself with his palm on the rock next to my hip. His fingers skim a lock of loose hair from my cheek. "I don't need to understand everything to be certain of some things. Of one thing in particular."

I look into his face, at the freckles across his nose and cheeks, the rough golden red stubble on his jaw, the shadow of fatigue beneath his eyes, and I know he is right. I don't need to understand everything about Melik, where he comes from and how he thinks, to know that he is worthy and fine and good. But I might need to understand more than I do now to make him happy. "What if it is not enough?"

His jaw tightens. "I am not sure it is worth wondering about 'what if.'" He brushes grit off his hands and looks out at the canyon again. "It seems your decision to return to the east is already made, despite what you said to me in the wedding tent."

I swallow back the hurt that is clamped like fingers on my throat. "I promised in exchange for Bo's help."

He is quiet for a few moments. "Did you do it for us, then? Or because you wanted to?"

That is a complicated question. My cheeks burn as I consider it.

"Bo did not look good," Melik says suddenly. "This journey has been very hard on him." He leaves the rest hanging in the air between us: *But he did it for you.*

"I don't think he would want me to talk to you about it." I wish I could tell him all my worries. But Bo sounded so angry and embarrassed just now, and I can only imagine what he would think if he knew I was talking with Melik about the frailty of Bo's body.

"Fair enough," Melik murmurs. "At least he has you."

I touch his arm. "You are very gracious for understanding and accepting that."

His eyes flare as he looks down at my hand. "I accept it because I must." Every word is a slice. "Do not mistake my silence for peace."

I pull my hand away. "What should I mistake it for?"

Like he often does when he is angry with me, Melik takes my face in his hands and weaves his fingers into my hair so that I cannot escape the heat of his gaze. "*Yorh zhasev*, Wen," he whispers harshly.

"What does that mean?" I ask in a choked voice.

His expression softens, lines of pain crinkling around his eyes. "Telling you now would hurt too much."

"I'm not trying to hurt you." I don't know how to bridge this canyon that has formed between us. I don't even know how to start.

"I know." He kisses my forehead. "You have only ever looked after my well-being. Sometimes I think it would be easier if you hadn't."

He sounds so regretful that I want to cry. "But you

have done the same for me," I say, my voice cracking.

He touches my forehead with his. "That will not change, no matter the decision you have made." His eyes bore into mine. "And no matter how much it tears at my heart."

I blink at him. Though he is speaking Itanyai, he might as well be speaking Noor for how well I understand it. What words can I choose to throw a rope from ledge to ledge? Which ones will help me crawl over the chasm and reach the other side? I cannot promise him I won't leave. I cannot ask him if he is my husband—that seems like something I should know, and I am afraid of revealing my ignorance. I put my palm over the center of his chest and say the only other thing that comes to me. "Your heart is very important to me. I don't want it to tear."

He lets out a huff of laughter. "Do you have medicine for that?" I kiss his cheek, and he sighs as my lips touch his skin. The corner of his mouth curls with mischievous amusement that almost covers the sadness. "That is a good start."

"You need a higher dose?" I kiss his lips and taste the salt from the hike, the tea he drank in front of the fire, the taste of Melik, one I want to savor. I cannot help my smile as I ask, "How about that?"

"I'm afraid the ailment is very severe." His nose nudges mine as he leans to kiss me again. Beneath my palms the ridge vibrates, and a few small stones roll over my fingers. Melik raises his head, his smile gone. "Did you feel that?"

We sit in silence for only a fraction of a second before it happens again, a deep tremor in the ground. We stare at each other, and when we feel it a third time, I know. "They're here."

Chapter Sixteen

"STAY NEAR THE canyon wall and get behind the boulders," Melik says to me just before he lets me go and sprints up the trail. I follow him, unable to keep up with his long strides. The thumps are numerous now, the footfalls of enormous machines. Ahead of me the ridge is a swarm of activity. Men and women cluster behind any cover they can find, lying on their bellies and aiming rifles at the eastern opening of the bowl. Given the armor on those machines, I can only imagine they are planning to aim for the top gunners, the least protected members of the crew.

Somehow Melik has also acquired a few heavy weapons, tripod-mounted machine guns positioned at the eastern end of the ridge. Next to them crews gather on an outcropping with the crates of dirt and the pry bars meant to overturn them. I veer away from the gathering fighters to find Bo. He'll need me to help him get his frames on, and possibly to talk him out of going below. In all the bustle of making camp, there was no further discussion of sending anyone to go with him. I scramble up the rocks and slide in the dirt as I round the boulder. My blanket still bears the dark, wet mark from where his sweaty body lay, but Bo and all his metal body parts are gone.

The thunderous footsteps of the war machines are close enough to hear now, even over the constant shouts from the Noor fighters. I can hear the fear and strain, but also the determination. I emerge from behind the boulder to see Melik, a rifle slung over his shoulder, running from the heavy guns to the dirt crew. He slaps each of them on the back. His voice, as always, is authoritative and full of confidence, even though I can see the worry in his eyes. Suddenly adoration for him bursts the bounds of my heart and spills into all my empty spaces. He knows this might be the last few minutes of his life, of all their lives, and he is using his time to give others hope, to make them believe victory is possible. He will never stop fighting and will never bow down.

And I am in love with him. Simple and certain, complete and devastating. I don't understand everything, but this . . . this is something I know in my bones.

"I love you, Melik," I whisper, needing to hear it out loud, knowing I may never get to say it to him. But like him, I will hope. And like him, I will fight for that moment.

I edge myself into the shelter of a cluster of boulders just above the trail, clutching my medical pack. I plan my paths, the different ways I can safely get to the injured, the places I can try to drag them to get them out of danger. My palms flatten on the rock as I hear a growing cry, over and over again, spreading in a ripple from person to person down the ridge: *"Muraonlan! Muraonlan!"*

They are pointing at the eastern opening of the bowl. I squint at the place where the canyon walls narrow and catch a dark shadow flicker on the rock walls. My breath catches as I see what's casting it. The forelegs come into view first, deep gray with soot and dust, stomping steadily. Nearly three stories high, they arch above the fat body of the machine, where the crew nestles inside. The thing hisses as it moves along, spewing steam from the rear of its abdomen. Atop its back sits the top gunner, surrounded by a low wall of metal armor. He wears a helmet that resembles Bo's.

The Noor heavy machine guns swing toward the first spider, but Melik shouts for them to stop, to hold fire, probably until it is closer. But that means they have to let it get closer, and that is a nightmare of a thought. And so is knowing that Bo is probably on the ground, watching them approach. I dart from my shelter and peer over the ledge. Something beige moves behind an outcropping of rock down there, and that must be him. I want to scream at him to climb up, to get out of the way.

Explosions deafen me as a wave of heat rolls across the back of my neck. I flatten myself to the ground as Melik's blasting powder shatters the rocks at the eastern opening of the bowl, causing a small avalanche of stone. Rocks pour down the steep slope, followed by the clanging and crashing of earth on metal. Faltering engine noises make the Noor cheer, but then the war machines begin to climb over the debris, the one in front reaching the summit of rubble in a few steps. Its gears grind over rock and dust, but this is not enough to stop it.

Gunfire drowns out the noise as the first war machine steps into the bowl section of the canyon. It moves to the right, away from our ridge, to make room for the one behind it, which is already climbing over the rock spill. Melik was correct—there appear to be four machines, all twice as large as I imagined, with thick jointed legs and wide-barreled guns. The Noor on the ridge fire on the metal creatures as all of them enter the bowl, and at first the machines are slow to respond. Bullets pock the legs and backs of the spiders but do not penetrate. But then the machine closest to our position speeds up suddenly, and as it passes, its top gunner swings his weapon up and fires.

Rock explodes along the ridge, followed by wretched screams. I throw myself behind my boulder shelter as the machine walks by, showering the canyon wall with bullets as big as my hands. I peer out to see the dirt crates overturn on top of the spider even as its gunner sends another volley at the ledge. The air fills with a smoky, dusty haze, but the shrieks of wounded Noor penetrate it easily. I slide to the eastern side of my shelter and hover behind the rocks as I try to see through the fog to the owners of the voices.

As I wonder if one of them is Melik.

The Noor heavy guns boom and echo, one of them

focused on the machine right below the ridge, the one I can hear grinding and chugging. The dirt trap appears to have given it some trouble, slowing it down, and now the Noor rain bullets on it. A deep pop followed by billowing white smoke tells me the engine is likely gone, and the cheers that follow probably mean one of the machines is down for good. But as soon as the jubilation starts, it is over. Bullets slam into the ridge all around me, creating stone shrapnel that pelts my back and head. Another machine is attacking. I pull my pack up to pad the back of my head and press myself against the rock as the Noor heavy guns go silent.

When I focus on the spot, I see bodies, bleeding and twitching.

I do not hesitate. Even as rifles fire and shrapnel flies, I race down the trail, sliding my pack down my arm as I do. I keep jogging, ducking behind boulders whenever I can, pulling strips of bandage from the satchel. Pausing at a spot less than twenty feet from the wounded gunners, I take a deep breath. If I die, I hope it will be quick.

I lunge into the open, blinking as bullets hit the rock next to me and send a cloud of stone dust down on me. My stumbling steps carry me nearly all the way, and then I dive to my hands and knees and crawl. The first fighter I reach has taken a bullet to the leg. *"Yorh zhaosteyardie,"* I huff, wrenching my bandage around his thigh and tying it tight. I grab a pinch of my coagulating blend and push it into his mouth, then press my canteen to his lips, wishing I knew how to tell him to drink. His brown eyes, streaming tears, meet mine. "You'll be fine," I coo to him, stroking his hair.

Dimly I am aware of the world exploding around me, but I pay it little mind. My fear fades and so does the noise. My ears roar with my own heartbeat as I squat behind him and hook my shoulders beneath his arms. I drag him backward as he pushes with his other leg, understanding that I am trying to get him out of danger. Together we manage to get him behind a row of large rocks. I press his hands to his wound and hold them there when he tries to pull back, wearing a grimace of agony. "Pressure," I say, and even though I'm sure he doesn't understand the word, he nods.

I kneel by the rock and locate my next patient, a woman with her long brown hair in a dozen braids spread across her shoulders. It's the woman whose steps set my pace on the hike to this war zone. She is bleeding from wounds in her left arm and her throat but is still trying to crawl toward me. I dart into the open and coil my arm around her. We half run, half crawl back to the rocks, where I bandage her arm and pack her neck wound with cloth. My first patient holds her hand as she lets out wet screams. I leave them to hold each other, but when I peer from behind the rocks, I gasp. The Noor heavy guns are firing again—because Melik is pulling the trigger.

Two of the machines are stomping around the far edge of the bowl, but another seems to be stuck close to the ledge, and Melik is merciless, his jaw ridged and his eyes fierce, bullet casings bouncing and spinning in the air around his legs, his shoulders tense as he holds the tripod-mounted weapon steady. The besieged war machine chugs and falters as Melik focuses fire on its abdomen, which holds the steam engine—and the flesh-and-blood crew member—inside. The gun lies silent on its back, the gunner sprawled across its long barrel.

There's a sharp crack and then a dull thunk—the machine's abdomen bulges outward and then explodes, and I duck behind the rock as black smoke rises and metal shrapnel zings close by my head. When next I peek from my shelter, Melik is gone. I lean out to see him racing down the trail, shouting. They've taken out two machines, but two more are about to escape the bowl and head for Dagchocuk with nothing to stop them. I scurry onto the trail and run after him. His shouts are agonized and desperate as he sprints for the ledge and disappears over it.

Noor bodies clutter the path between where I am and where he's gone, and they remind me of my role here. As much as I want to throw myself over the edge just to see that Melik's all right, I drop to my knees next to a man with gray streaked at his temples and a penetrating wound to his shoulder. I pack it, fold his shaking hand over the bandage, and fill his mouth with my coagulant brew, anything to slow the bleeding. Then I move to the next and the next, doing whatever I can to ensure they'll live a little longer, before diving for the next patient. Some are far past saving, like the man with scars on his cheeks who takes his last breaths while looking into my eyes, or the woman who has been shot twice in the belly. I grit my teeth and step over her because I know there is nothing I can do, because I must get to the ones I can help. My legs ache as I drag them to safety. My lungs burn with every breath. But my eyes are dry. My heartbeat is steady. My body is in constant motion—stopping would allow room for panic.

I wish my father were here. He would know what was best. But he is not, so I must do the best I know. A volley of shouting draws my attention as I crouch over my latest patient, a young man who will surely lose his foot. I tourniquet his lower leg to keep him from losing his life, then lie on the edge of the trail and look toward the floor of the canyon.

What I see shoots bolts of fear along my limbs. The machines are nearly to the exit of the bowl. The remaining Noor fighters on the ridge are firing at the top gunners, and one of them falls backward and rolls off the abdomen of the beast. He is stomped by its rear legs a moment later. But he is not the only man at the mercy of those clanking metal legs.

Bo is hanging from the side of one of the creatures, steadily climbing a steel cable that is attached to his metal chest and secured by a grappling hook wound around the top of one of the creature's side legs where it connects to the thorax. He is not wearing his full faceplate, so I can see the half smile he wears as he gazes up at the machine's underbelly.

A hoarse shout from a spot directly below me has me leaning over farther. Melik is huddled beneath the ridge, his rifle aimed at the remaining top gunner, but he is hesitating. His shoulders tremble, and his voice cracks as he yells and waves to the other rifle-bearing fighters. And I see why—there is another young man climbing a rope between two churning legs of the other war machine. He has a tool in his hand, possibly a wrench, and he drags himself up the rope toward the spider's back with steady, quick yanks.

It's Sinan.

Below me Melik is a picture of agony, caught between action and fear as he watches his younger brother scale the rope and huddle just beneath the swell of the machine's abdomen. From where Sinan hangs, the gunner cannot get him, and doesn't even seem aware of his presence. Bo is in the same position beneath his machine as he reaches up with his mechanical hand and begins to fiddle with a panel in the dip where the thorax and abdomen connect.

Sinan works on the same area with his wrench, but the look on his face—pure concentration and determination, along with a hard, jagged kind of joy—is so similar to Bo's that they could be twins. Brothers.

Both war machines are still stalking steadily toward the western edge of the canyon. They are mere steps away, carrying Bo and Sinan with them.

Bo's metal hand pops the hatch on the side of the machine, and he plunges his fingers into the spider's guts.

After one more step the steel monster stops dead, then falls forward with a rending metal crunch. Bo disappears beneath a tangle of spider body and legs, each piece capable of crushing him. But my attention is drawn from the wreckage when Melik shouts Sinan's name and aims his rifle. The top gunner on Sinan's machine has emerged from his armored position and is leaning over, trying to get a clear shot at Sinan. The boy looks up just as the gunner points his revolver.

A sharp crack echoes from the ridge below me and the gunner's head splits like a melon. Sinan clings to the rope as the dead man slides off the war machine's abdomen, but then the boy goes back to work. The machine is seconds away from leaving the bowl when he gets the hatch open and reaches inside. The Noor scream and cheer when Sinan manages to scramble upward as the machine teeters. He perches on its back as it crumples to the ground.

For a moment there is silence, broken only by the hiss of the steam engines flooding.

"Bo," I whisper, staring at the heap of metal that swallowed him.

As if he hears me, Bo pops his metal head up from between two of the legs of the machine he took down. Sinan sees him and pumps his arms in the air, and the two of them grin at each other. Even from this distance I can feel Bo's fierce happiness.

The Noor fighters are ecstatic, shouting and hugging one another. So many casualties, so much work to be done, but there are four machines down and a minefield for the next machines that try to come through. From where I lie, I see Melik's smile, warm like a sunbeam, full of pride and love.

But then his lips drop open in a howl of warning.

Sinan looks up at the ridge as he hears his brother's voice. Melik jerks his rifle up again.

The hatch over the cockpit of the downed machine is open, and the pilot has his revolver trained on Sinan. Bo crouches, bracing to leap for the man. The crackle of gunshots makes me flinch. The pilot slumps over the steel thorax of his beast just as Bo lands next to him, metal hands outstretched to kill. When he sees the pilot is dead, he whoops and spins toward Sinan.

His joyful expression freezes.

Sinan looks puzzled as he touches his fingertips to the blood blossoming across his tunic. He glances at Bo as if his friend might know how to fix him, then sinks to his knees as Melik screams his name.

Chapter Seventeen

IT IS AS if my brain cannot accept the horror unfolding before my eyes. I cling to the ridge, frozen, as Melik slides and leaps down the steep trail to the canyon floor. Bo catches Sinan in his steely arms and gently lays him on the spider's back, but he steps away from him quickly, blinking down at the blood on his metal hands. As Melik reaches the ground, Bo leaps across to the machine he downed, rips the top hatch off, and pulls out its dazed pilot. He strips him of his weapon and tosses him aside, then jumps onto the machine's abdomen and tears away the rear hatch. A moment later he drags the limp body of its fireman out and pitches him onto the ground. His movements are violent and merciless. He does not look at Sinan, who is writhing now, curled into himself as the pain winds through him.

Melik sprints to the machine where his brother lies sprawled. As he throws himself onto its back, he shouts my name. The desperation in that one syllable gets me moving, reminds me of my purpose. I hike the satchel onto my back and clumsily crawl down the steep trail, following Melik's path, the sliding prints of his boots in the loose rock and dirt. I focus very hard on each step and try not to listen to Sinan's anguished cries.

I huff as I race across the narrow space between the canyon wall and the wrecked machine. As I reach up, Melik grabs my arm and pulls me onto the thorax, which is hot under the sun and with the fire that burned within.

"Wen," Melik says in a raspy whisper. "Please." His face is twisted with pain as he turns back to Sinan.

I scoot across the spider's back and kneel on the other side of Sinan. He is clutching at Melik's shoulders, crying in pain. When I touch his body, he screams and tries to turn away. "Melik, you have to hold him," I say.

Melik lets out a trembling breath and pins Sinan's shoulders to the machine. He begins whispering to him, kissing his forehead between each sentence. My gut clenches as I tear Sinan's tunic up the center and see the wound. He has been shot in the stomach, just below his ribs. I run my palm along his back, and his skin is smooth and unbroken—the bullet is still inside him. I glance at his face and see the blood on his teeth. It is creeping up his esophagus. Even if I had opium and bright lights and a scalpel and clampers and antibiotics and my father, I am not sure I could fix what has broken. Suddenly I feel the bitter helplessness I saw in Anni this morning as I proudly and stupidly announced I could save the wounded. Suddenly I understand her resignation.

Melik wipes his brother's lips with his sleeve. His pale, bloodshot eyes meet mine. But I cannot say what I am thinking. I cannot bear to tell Melik that his little brother is going to die.

Melik grimaces, like he is holding in a scream of pure pain. "Please, Wen," he whispers. "Please?"

I clamp my lips shut and open my satchel. But I do not use my san qi, because I must save it for those who have a chance, and it might only prolong Sinan's agony. Instead I reach for my jie cao. I pour a bit of water into a small bowl and mix it with the powder I made this morning, until I have a paste. "Sinan," I say gently, edging toward his face. "This will taste awful, but it will help."

Melik holds his head as I push bits of the paste between Sinan's graying lips. "Will this stop his bleeding?" he asks in a hushed voice. "Will it heal his insides?"

The hope in his voice is like a knife traced along the tender seams of my heart, slicing the stitches that hold me together. I do not look at Melik as I say, "It will ease his pain."

Melik lets out a strangled sob and holds Sinan tighter. I focus on getting as much of the jie cao into Sinan as I can while Melik strokes his hair. The boy is wretched with searing agony. "Help me, Wen," he gasps, his blue eyes filled with tears. "Don't let me die."

"Shhh; it's going to be all right," I say, forcing each word from my throat. I smile at the dying boy while his older brother shakes with tears he is trying not to shed. I touch Sinan's face. "You did so well. You are a hero."

His lips twitch in an attempt at a smile. "We did it," he

says, even as blood trickles from the corner of his mouth.

"You saved your village," I tell him. "You have done your people proud."

He closes his eyes, his breathing rapid and wet, each exhale a squeaky moan. "But I don't want to die. Please, I don't want to die. Melik, *oluma zhayaben. Oluma zhayaben.*"

Sinan whispers his plea over and over until his voice goes quiet, and then Melik's voice takes over, a broken song, choked words of love and devotion. I creep backward as Sinan's curled fingers relax, as his skinny legs slide along the spider's back, as he fades away. And I am thankful. The bullet must have hit an artery. He has been saved from the agony of a slow death as his guts spilled poison into his abdomen.

I slip my fingertips over his wrist and feel the moment his heart stops. I bow my head. "Melik—"

"No." Melik tenderly lays Sinan's head on the machine and slowly gets to his feet. His chest is splattered with his brother's blood. His face is so pale that each freckle stands out, as does the smear of crimson along his jaw.

"You," says Melik, his voice a brutal, hoarse accusation. His gaze is not on me. It is on Bo, who is standing behind me, looking stricken and helpless and small despite his fearsome armor. "You did this. He was going to stay in the village. He would still be alive if not for you."

Bo stares at Sinan's body. "He knew he could help," he says weakly. "He knew what to do."

"He was a child!" Melik roars, striding forward, his fists clenching. "He was my only brother. You had no right to interfere!"

"He was his own person," Bo says, taking a step

back, putting his arms up. The spiders on his shoulders twitch restlessly, as if they respond to Bo's heartbeat, his internal distress. "I couldn't have stopped him." He glances around us to see the Noor staring at him, shock and anger in their gazes.

I push myself to my feet. "Melik, stop."

Melik raises his hand and catches a rifle tossed by Bajram, who is glaring at Bo as if he is a monster. My rust-haired Noor swings it up smoothly, like it is part of him, like he has become a machine too. "You have taken too much, Ghost," he says, the promise of death in every word. "Your disregard for my life is understandable, even forgivable. Your disregard for Sinan's . . ."

"If not for Sinan and me, these machines would be out of your reach and on their way to your village," Bo says softly. If he is afraid, he is not showing it. "And you and the others ignored me. You did not listen to the knowledge I offered. Only Sinan did. Without us—"

"Shall I thank you by making yours a quick death?" Melik asks, his voice shaking with rage.

When his finger slides to the trigger, I step between him and Bo. "It wouldn't make up for what you have lost." My voice is the steadiest here, though I am trembling in my bones. The barrel of his weapon is pointed at my forehead. "Melik, we have to get the wounded back to Dagchocuk. Many can be saved. There is much to be done."

Pain flashes in his jade eyes as he holds the weapon steady. A tear slips from his cheek and slides along the stock of his rifle. "My brother is dead, Wen," he whispers, his gaze boring into mine.

I step to the side and push the barrel down, and Melik does not resist. "I know, Melik," I say, my throat closing over the horrible sorrow of it. "I know." I reach up to smooth his hair from his face, but he steps back and points at Bo.

"Go. Now. I do not want to see your face ever again. I do not want to think of you and what you have done." His voice is quiet, but it is impossible to mistake this for weakness. The fire in his eyes is bright and hot. "Leave or I will find a way to kill you."

I tense, expecting Bo to fire back, to snarl, to challenge him. But my Ghost is silent. He doesn't even breathe. I watch Melik's face, trying to figure out what he needs, what he wants. Does he wish I would leave too?

He gives no signal either way. He does not reach for me, nor does he look at me. "I have to take Sinan's body to my mother," he says, hollow now. Sagging. He looks down at his rifle and his face crumples with disgust as he tosses it to the ground. He kneels at his brother's side and scoops Sinan into his arms. The boy's head lolls in the crook of Melik's neck, and Melik murmurs words of love as he edges to the side of the machine and slides off its back. The Noor gather around them, some of them wailing, others sobbing, all of their feelings on the outside, filling the air with grief. In the Ring, when Tercan died, they did not show their despair to us, but here they are not afraid to cry. I turn away and see Bo walking along the floor of the canyon, toward the eastern end of the bowl.

I scramble after him, breaking into a run to catch up. "Bo," I call out.

He stops. "Do not try to follow me."

I pivot around his metal body and face him. "Melik is heartbroken. He will for—"

"No, he won't," Bo says, his voice thick with pain. "And he should not . . . should not ever forgive me."

"Did you tell Sinan to follow the group?"

He winces. "We made the plan together because he said he would come either way. He was so bright and so capable. He knew what he was doing. He may have been young, but . . ."

"You saw yourself in him." The boy who lived and lived and lived even when he should have died. If only Sinan had been more like Bo. "You wanted him by your side. It didn't matter that he was Noor. You understood him, and he understood you."

Bo bares his teeth and lets out a sound of total agony, ragged and halting. "Stop."

"You could not help but love him."

Bo's hands swing up to ward me off, and his spiders raise their fangs. "I destroyed him. Like I destroy everything. Like I ruin everything." The spiders rattle and shift as he steps away from me. "Like I ruin you, just by being close to you."

"You have never done that."

"Haven't I? All the hours you and Guiren spent with me—you could have been with real people. Living people. You could have been with each other, even. Both of you should have left me to myself a year ago, but you kept coming back."

"You have a right to live, and to feel, and to love. You are not really a ghost, Bo." I reach for him, but his metal circuits hum as he jumps back.

"I am," he snaps. "And ghosts must let the living be." His expression splits with a harsh smile. "Your father used to read me a story from *Kulchan and His Warriors*, about a princess and a bandit. I thought the story was idiotic when he first read it to me, but after I met you, I gained a new appreciation for it."

I put my hand on my stomach. I vaguely remember the story. The bandit, a carefree and fearless soul, rescues a princess from certain death. She wears an enchanted necklace, and after the bandit claims a kiss as his reward, he loses his free will and is bound to her. "What are you saying?"

He laughs, but it is wracked with regret. "Even after he dies, the bandit cannot leave her. His spirit guards her for the rest of her life. She marries. She has children. And still he haunts her. He is a very stupid ghost. I will not make his mistake."

"Stop this," I say, scared of the hopelessness drenching his words. "Melik will realize what you have done for his village and his people. He cannot do that now because he is hurting so much. But he will. You can follow behind the group. You can—"

"Leave me alone, Wen," he says.

"Bo, please. Stay. Camp on the ridge. I will bring you whatever you need."

"I release you from your promise." He makes an easy leap onto the side of the canyon wall, his long metal fingers slipping into cracks and anchoring him. "Send word to your father when you can."

There is an odd, sad, certain note in his voice that makes my heart speed. He is not returning to the Ring, and he is not coming to Dagchocuk. "Where are you going?"

He shakes his head. "Where I belong."

Now panic is rising in me. My Ghost, the boy who could not relinquish his grip on life, sounds as if he is letting go. "Sinan would not want this. He would have wanted you to stay and help the people he loved. You owe that to him."

"I owe him nothing!" Bo shouts. "He was a silly Noor boy who did not see me for what I am. And you are a stupid girl who thinks I feel more than I do, who thinks I am worth more than I am, and who is the reason I have betrayed my own people." He sweeps his arm across the scene of carnage, the smoking machines, the bodies, the grieving survivors. His eye swivels back to glare at me. "Maybe it is you who have ruined me."

"Blame me if you need to, but don't leave. We still need you," I plead. And he needs us. Somehow I know it is the only thing keeping him human. "There might be more machines coming."

"I am done. With you and everyone else. I am done. Nothing is worth . . . this." He sounds as hollow as Melik did, like something inside him is broken forever. He crawls up the rock wall and heaves himself onto the trail above. For a moment he looks down at me, and I stare at him, silently begging him to come back. He opens his mouth, and my blood sings with hope.

"Tell Guiren I tried," he says. "And tell him I am sorry."

With spindly metal fingers he closes his faceplate, hiding any trace of his soft, human self. His steel muscles hum as he crouches, and his armor clanks as he lunges upward. In a few seconds he has disappeared into the narrow canyon. I listen, clinging to the sound of him, until the only noise that reaches me is the cries of the Noor as they prepare to carry their dead back to Dagchocuk.

Chapter Eighteen

THE CRESCENT MOON hangs over the plains of Yilat like a sickle poised to cut us all down. I hike at the rear of the procession of Noor, tending to my patients as best I can. Some of them can walk, but they are slower than the rest, and whenever we stop, I pour jie cao and san qi tea down their throats and smear honey on wounds to keep them from festering. Some of the wounded are carried in makeshift stretchers made from sleeping blankets, and I apply fresh bandages and check for bleeding, fevers, breathing difficulties, and faltering heartbeats. I grit my teeth in frustration when I cannot do more for them. But we must keep moving.

The dead are at the front. The Itanyai prisoners are in the middle, surrounded by Noor rebels. Everyone is grim. We have twelve dead, but Sinan's death was the one that destroyed the triumph.

We left about half the fighters at the bowl, preparing to fight a second wave. The rest of us are returning to Dagchocuk for supplies, and to bury the dead and allow families to care for the wounded. I sometimes hear Melik's voice at the front of the procession, worn with grief but still sure and quick. I have no idea what he's saying, but whenever we stop for a break, we leave fighters behind, possibly to keep watch for more machines.

I have no doubt Melik will return to the bowl, but not until after he buries Sinan. My stomach churns every time I catch glimpses of him, a tall form far ahead of me. He cradles his brother's shoulders and head against his side while Baris and Bajram walk close behind and support the rest of the boy's body. Like the rest of the dead, Sinan has been wrapped in a blanket, but Melik has not allowed his brother's face to be covered. He walks with his fingers in Sinan's rust-colored hair. He must be thinking that this is the last chance he has to touch his brother, to look at his face. He is hoarding every moment.

Like I always do, I remain busy as a way of holding off despair, though my thoughts wrap tightly around two of the men I love. Bo has torn himself free of whatever web he thinks I cast around him, and I am afraid that what he has really released is himself, his humanity. He will stave off his grief by hardening his heart, by nestling within his machine self and pretending that is all he is. I am not enough to save him, not fast enough, strong enough, smart enough. The same might be true with Melik. But he is surrounded by people who treasure him. Unlike

Bo, Melik is loved by people who understand who he is, where he came from, how he thinks and feels.

And by some who don't.

We descend into Dagchocuk, a tired, sad procession. The wailing begins before my feet touch level ground. The villagers see the blanket-wrapped bodies and light torches in the square. The survivors lay the dead down in a row and make sure their faces are uncovered so their families can find them. Knots of people surround each one, weeping and wailing, while several men trek to the southern side of the village with shovels in hand. I stay with the wounded who are too injured to walk to their families. They are brought to the wedding tent, where I set up a hospital of sorts. I stitch wounds with my straight needle and coarse thread. I make herb poultices with supplies brought by Aysun the healer, who joins me in the tent and sings to her patients while she slathers oily mixtures of her own over their wounds. Some of them smell quite suspicious, but the Noor seem reassured by her presence.

Once I have managed the most dire of their injuries, I squat on the floor and make each patient as comfortable as I can, using strokes of my hands and gentle smiles when no medicine can help. At least one of them, the woman with the throat wound, will probably die. Her color is not good and her breathing is faltering and labored. I catch Aysun's eye and nod down at the woman, and Aysun seems to see the same truth I do. She looks at me and says, *"Anni,"* before slipping from the tent. It takes me a moment to realize she is not getting my *anni*—Melik's mother—she is fetching the young woman's mother.

I hold the dying woman's hand as she drifts in and out of consciousness. All around me I can hear the Noor words of lament. *"Bazegovyasi bazebogmikie"* . . . *"Migovyasi zhabogmikie"* . . . I hear these phrases over and over again. They are so loud, shouted, screamed, torn from throats until their voices are shredded. It is exhausting to listen to, like sandpaper against my skin.

Itanyai are silent in their grief. To be so loud shames the family, the lost loved one, the memories you shared with him or her. To be so uncontrolled is a weakness of character. At my mother's funeral I stared at her grave while we all sweated under the late-summer sun. My heart had been crushed, but I refused to embarrass my father by crying. I refused to add to his grief by forcing him to comfort me.

We cry in private. We cry alone. We do not burden others with our sorrow. To share that kind of thing is rare. But not for the Noor. They cry together, and none of them are ashamed of tears or runny noses or sobs, even the men.

It makes me feel as if I am wrapped in a transparent, impenetrable veil, watching them from the outside. They can see me, and I can see them, but we will never reach each other, not really.

The problem is that I want to try.

More than anything I want to soothe Melik in his grief, but I would not even know where to start. His loss is so massive, so devastating, that I cannot imagine my presence being helpful. And then there is the reason I am now hiding within this tent, pretending my sleeping patients need me: My greatest fear is that I would make his grief worse. The way he looked at me in the last minutes of Sinan's life . . .

"Wen always has medicine." How many times has he said that to me? So fondly, so reverently. I squeeze my eyes shut and clench my fists. I want to go to him, but I fear that is selfish. I will not force him to relive those horrible moments, my helplessness and failure. I am scared to remind him of the fact that Bo was in Dagchocuk because of me. If I stitch those truths together, they amount to one big, horrible indictment—Sinan is dead because of me. I know that is not really true, but what if Melik thinks it is?

The dying young woman's mother comes to the tent with several men, and they carry their daughter-sister-cousin-lover away so that she can die in her home surrounded by those who love her fiercely. Before the tent flap settles over the doorway, Melik pokes his head in. "Wen, can I talk to you?"

I blink at him, hope surging within me. "Of course." I leave my patients with Aysun and join him in the square. He has changed his bloody tunic and washed his face, but he looks as if he has lived a thousand years in the last few hours. "What can I do?"

He will not meet my eyes. "I need you to talk to the Itanyai prisoners."

My hope evaporates. "Oh. What would you like me to say?"

He folds his arms over his chest. "I would like you to do what you did in the hills, with the other prisoners. I would like you to convince them that you are a prisoner too, and gather whatever information you can. I need to know what else is coming for us, but they are well trained. Trickery will work better than torture."

I have not eaten in hours, but this task makes me feel sick. Still, not as sick as I'd feel if these Noor tortured the captured Itanyai. "I will do it."

Melik nods. "They're in a cottage down the lane." He walks by my side, and when we are a few houses away from where the prisoners are being held, he hands me some flatbread and a canteen to offer them. "Thank you." He begins to walk away.

"Melik?" I call, but when he stops and turns to me, I find I have no words. Or rather, I have many, but all seem full of obligation, like an expectation that he would respond in kind. *I hurt for you,* I want to say. *I will do anything for you. I adore you. I love you.* But none of it feels like enough.

"What is it?" he says softly.

"I will do my best," I say, my voice cracking.

He meets my eyes briefly. "I must complete the funeral preparations for my brother, but I will find you later." He strides away.

Like a condemned woman, I carry my burdens down the lane. If this is the one thing I can do for him, then I will do it as well as I can. I nod at the rebel guarding the door and slip inside the cottage. Three Itanyai soldiers are lined up in front of the hearth. Their hands and feet are bound. One of them has black smears along his arms and shirt—he must be a fireman from one of the machines, while the others are probably pilots or front gunners. Their eyes widen when they see me. "Sister," the fireman says. "Where are you from?"

"I came from . . . Vuda," I say, deciding to hold tight to as much truth as I can. "I was in the train wreck and captured by the rebels. I have been here for a few days, no more than a week."

The wiry young man at the end of the row looks awestruck. "You are the one! The girl who saved the prisoners in the hills. They returned to the Ring as we were preparing to leave."

I bow my head. "They were very kind. I am glad to hear they made it back to the Ring."

"Are they treating you well?" the wiry fellow asks. "Is the Red One here? There are so many stories and rumors." He raises his eyebrows. This feels like dangerous ground.

"I am alive," I say. "And they have not abused me. But I was hoping to be rescued."

The fireman looks ashamed, but the other two, younger and angrier, curse under their breath. The one in the middle, with a broad nose and cheeks thick with red spots, shakes his head. "The canyon was supposed to be clear," he snarls. "There is obviously a spy in our ranks—they were prepared for us, and they have war machines of their own. I've never seen anything like it."

Bo is the war machine, and I am the spy, but they do not seem to suspect. "You did not expect an attack at all, even after they ambushed the train?"

They shake their heads. "This attack plan was top secret."

The wiry fellow grimaces. "We were out of radio range when we were attacked. We did not warn the rest."

I force myself to smile. "But there are more machines

coming? That is good!" My heart thunders with fear.

The soldiers' smiles are tempered. "I wouldn't be too hopeful, sister," says the fireman. "When they come, they will tear through this village like a paper dragon on First Holiday. There are twenty of them, and the crews' blood will be fired when they see the wreckage in the canyon."

The spotty soldier nods. "At least they will know what happened. At least they will be ready."

"We can be grateful for that," I say, my toes curling within my boots. "Perhaps we can hide when they come. Find cover."

The wiry soldier looks hopeful. "If you could help us get loose . . . there is an infantry force behind the war machines. They will hunt the survivors in the hills, and when they arrive, we'll know it's safe."

"Hunt the survivors?" I blurt out.

Spotty bares his teeth. "This will not be like the last uprising. This time we will not show mercy."

I tear off a hunk of bread and press it to Spotty's mouth. "Eat. You must be hungry." And I need him to stop talking, because his words make me feel ill. "So," I say to the others as he chews. "How long do we have until the invasion force arrives?"

The wiry fellow watches my trembling hands tearing the bread. "Fear not, sister," he says quietly. "Our orders were to destroy this village and lay the path for the others. They are set to arrive in two days. I know it seems like a long time, but—"

"I will cheer their arrival," I say, "and I will do my best to free you before that time so we can take cover. I believe there are caves within these hills."

Spotty glances at his wiry friend. "The sooner the better."

The fireman looks somber as he allows me to feed him bread. "You are very kind," he mumbles.

I give them each sips of water and leave breathless with information and the hope of saving these prisoners. I know I am betraying their trust, but I will do what I can to preserve their lives. When I emerge from the cottage, I walk for a few steps before running to find Melik. He is in the square with Anni but meets me halfway. I give him all the information I gathered, and he thanks me. "I will inform Commander Kudret," he says. "It's possible we'll be able to get reinforcements from the north in less than two days."

"What will happen to these men?"

He stares at the ground. "These soldiers who killed so many of mine?"

"It will be your choice to show mercy."

His voice is hollow as he says, "I will do what I can for them."

"Thank you." My own heart is overflowing with admiration and love for him, but one look tells me he doesn't feel it at all. In fact, I realize that I've hurt him again by asking for such a huge gift right now. Melik is on the other side of this canyon between us, and every rope I grab to throw across falls apart in my hands.

He glances at my face before turning away. "It is time to bury the dead," he says. He pauses for a moment, a space in which I almost reach for him, almost take his hand, but then Anni raises her arms and beckons to him, and he walks away.

Feeling stupid and toxic, like an infection in a wound, I return to the wedding tent to check on my patients. I soothe myself by doing small and good things—silent acts, seeing as my words always seem to be wrong. I check bandages and help patients find comfortable positions. I hold a cup of cold tea to the lips of a thirsty man and wipe his mouth when he has drunk his fill. I rub the cold hands of another and tuck a blanket around someone else. Most of them are awake, listening to the mourning outside. It seems as though they cannot sleep, that they would rather share the pain with their family and friends than shut it out. One woman, whose ribs Aysun and I had to bind tightly, gives me a weak, pained push toward the tent flap, as if telling me I should go and be a part of the grieving.

I only add to it, I want to tell her. *I only make it worse.* When all my work is done and I'm unable to invent more, I huddle within the canvas walls, fading with exhaustion while the fires outside burn, while the wailing and weeping continues, until I finally leave to use the pit latrines at the outskirts of the village. The air is laced with sage and lavender and other heady scents, and there is a haze of smoke above the village, trapping the torchlight in a foggy dome.

As I return to the square, the funeral procession is heading for the southern side of Dagchocuk. Sticking close to the cottages, concealed within the almost dark, I follow it until we reach a graveyard, plots marked with piles of rocks from the Western Hills.

There are twelve freshly dug graves, each adjacent to a pile of stones. A thick post has been hammered into the ground at the foot of each plot, and tied to them are the family colors, delicate scraps of sorrow fluttering in the breeze. Melik and his mother kneel in front of the post bedecked with the red cloth embroidered with leaves and black diamonds, saying their final good-byes to Sinan. His body has been washed, and he has been dressed in a simple cream-colored tunic and pants. He is pale and handsome and perfect and young, far too young. Melik holds Anni as she kisses Sinan's freckled cheeks and white eyelids, smoothing his hair, her tears falling on his unblemished brow.

His eyes dry and his face blank, Melik climbs into the grave and carefully lays his brother down. For a moment I cannot see him at all, and my chest squeezes tight as I wonder what he must be thinking, walls of earth close around him. Finally he slowly rises, and Anni helps him climb out, because for once he looks too weak to do something for himself. He grits his teeth as he shovels dirt over his brother. Though all those around him are weeping as Sinan disappears into the ground, Melik is silent. He keeps tipping soil into the grave, smooth and empty. It is so unlike him, so unlike what I expected, as if his soul has dimmed completely. By Itanyai standards his calm is admirable, but for Melik it just seems . . . wrong.

Anni covers her face with her hands, her shoulders shaking. Melik outlines the grave with stones, positioning each one with care, and then he pulls his mother into his arms. Whatever he says to her makes her nod and hug him tightly.

When she lets him go, he strides away. Right toward my hiding spot. I press myself against the wall of the nearest cottage as he walks by, looking neither left nor right. He ducks into his mother's home and emerges a few minutes later with a pack, which he slings onto his shoulders as he walks toward the canyon. I stare at his back as he fades into the darkness.

"Why did you not come to the grave site?" Anni asks in a choked voice, making me jump. I have no idea how long she's been standing next to me. "I made sure Aysun remained with the wounded so you could come and stand by Melik's side."

"I . . . I didn't want to intrude on your grief," I say.

"So you abandoned Melik to his sorrow instead? He is so lost in it that he cannot cry. He said he cannot even stay here tonight. He was afraid the grief would swallow him." She covers her mouth with her hand. "I'm afraid it still might."

I turn to her, this strong woman laid low by what she has lost. Her rust-colored hair is in a single gray-streaked braid down her back, but several strands have come loose and hang around her face. She looks twenty years older than she did this morning. "I did not abandon him, Anni. I am here. I have been here. If he asks me for something, I will offer it—"

She tilts her head, her brow creased with puzzlement. "Should he have had to ask you for comfort? Why wouldn't you give that to him freely?"

Tears start in my eyes. "I don't know how!" I throw my arms up. "I don't want to hurt him, but I seem to, no matter what I do. And Melik, he usually says what is in his heart—"

"His heart is shattered, Wen," says Anni. "It is in ruins. There are no words for that."

I swipe tears from my cheeks, embarrassed to be crying in front of this woman who has lost her younger son. "I don't want to burden him."

She takes me by the shoulders. "Do you love him, *cuz?* Be truthful."

I look into her dark blue eyes, Sinan's eyes. "I love him."

"Why do you think your love and comfort would be a burden to him?"

"Because I don't know if he feels the same, Anni. And I don't want to impose—"

She mutters something in Noor under her breath and shakes her head. "The two of you. He tries to be like an Itanyai for you, and if he had only been himself, or if you had understood us better, you would know exactly what he needs."

I think back, over all the times lately he has avoided saying what is in his mind, and I wonder if she is right. Maybe he hasn't wanted to burden me, either. Maybe he hasn't wanted to push. And as a result he has denied himself things I would have happily given him. "Anni, what does *'yorh zhasev'* mean? Melik said it to me in the hills, but he would not translate it for me."

She presses her lips together as her face crumples under the weight of her sadness. Her eyes glitter with tears. "It means you are the only one who can reach him now, *cuz.*"

Hesitantly I reach up and smooth my fingertips over her cheeks, catching her tears. I would never do this to another Itanyai, but with Anni it feels necessary and right. It makes me feel strong. And so does the memory of Melik saying *"yorh zhasev,* Wen" so fiercely, like it was true whether he wanted it to be or not. I think I know what it means now. I think I understand.

"Then I will find him, Anni, and I will bring him back."

Chapter Nineteen

DAWN IS STILL a few hours away as I trek across the canyon and begin to ascend into the hills. Anni was not completely sure where Melik would go, but she had an idea and described the path to me in great detail, the shapes of the rocks, the subtle markings by the trailside that one would never see if one didn't already know they were there. But now I know, and so I drag my fingertips across the boulder with the creased face, continue past the group of jagged rocks that looks like a group of old women gossiping, walk along the stone that could be a wounded warrior lying down to die. I carry the satchel Anni packed, a lantern in my hand, and all the hope and determination my body can hold.

As I hike, my mind treads across memories of Bo and stretches to imagine where he might be right now. I hope that with every step he moves closer to peace of whatever kind he is capable of finding. I do not blame him for allowing Sinan to follow along, for taking joy in having a partner in his plan. For Bo, his deepest satisfaction has always come in his work. His quiet moments have been spent immersed in problems that needed to be solved. His greatest triumphs have been in machines well made, in watching them fulfill the purpose he assigned. It was about the power of his mind, the delight in having such a magnificent tool and weapon hidden within his skull.

In Sinan, Bo had found a kindred spirit, but unlike Sinan, Bo never had a family, not really, and so he did not think about what it would be like for Melik. Or maybe he did not care. I know, though, that his harsh words as he left me behind were poorly fashioned tourniquets— desperate attempts to stop the blood gushing from the soft spot in his heart. My fear is that his next step will be cauterization, burning away those parts of him until he is numb. Or worse, amputation.

I hurt for Bo. I wish for him to be safe. But he and I, we have made our choices, and we are walking in opposite directions.

My legs ache, and I have not slept in a very long time. I haven't eaten, either, but I have food and water in my satchel—packed by Anni for Melik and me. My breath is ragged and my feet hurt as I finally find the narrow chasm that marks the entrance to the cave. I hold the lantern up and examine the space, puzzling at how someone as big as Melik could possibly fit through a space this small. But then I see the slide of rocky dirt at my feet and know he must be here, that he wormed his way through on his belly because the opening is wider near the ground. "Melik?" I call.

I am greeted with silence. No matter. I will search until I find him. I edge through the space by sidestepping, my chest and back scraping against stone as I sink into the darkness. After a few steps there is a black opening in front of me, and I move forward, raising my lantern and following the rocky tunnel until it opens into a cave.

It is already lit from within by another lantern, and I set mine down, my throat tightening with sorrow.

Melik is on his knees, facing a large, relatively smooth breadth of rock covered in markings. He does not look at me when I come in; his attention is focused on the cave wall. "When the machines came all those years ago," he says softly, "Anni brought us here. We were in this cave for over a week." His large hands skim over the stony expanse, and I step behind him to see what he sees. "Sinan had so much energy. He did not want to be trapped in this small space. Anni was terrified that he would sneak out and fall or be seen by the soldiers. I wanted to help."

The markings on the wall are drawings, made with chalky stone in a childlike hand. A dragon, or perhaps it is a lion, marches across the rocky terrain with a small person on his back. "We could hear the sounds of war from the village, and it echoed through the canyon," he says, his eyes on the tiny hero astride the fearsome animal. "I didn't want him to be scared, so I made up a story." His fingertips brush over the creature. "I told him there was a boy king, and he had made the world his playground, and while he was having playtime, it was safer for us to have our own playtime in here."

He chuckles, but it is a pained slice of sound. "Sinan did not like this story. He wanted to have a winged lion of his own." Melik's palm smooths over the primitive mural, the hills and trees and lakes and birds . . . and another boy atop an even bigger winged beast with a massive head and huge eyes. "So I made him one, and Anni and I made up stories about his adventures. He liked that. Even when he could barely walk, he was not satisfied with small dreams."

I bite my lip and move close to my red Noor, laying my hands on his shoulders. I bow my head and kiss his hair, thinking of the devotion of an eight-year-old boy for his baby brother, a powerful love for a child to carry. My heart beats a hard rhythm against my breast as I brace for Melik to flinch away from me, but he does not. Strands of his hair tickle my lips as I search for my words. "You will always carry him inside you, Melik. I know it is not enough, but it is not nothing."

"It is nowhere near enough," he says in a choked whisper.

My arms encircle his shoulders. "I know. I know, and I ache for you."

"From the moment he was born, my father told me to watch over him," he says, voice cracking over the words. "And from that moment until this afternoon I did. Not well, but I did." His body trembles and his mouth stretches into a grimace. "As he was dying, he looked at me like I could save him. Like he believed I could." Melik sinks to the floor, and I coil my arms around him as we descend, unwilling to let him go unless he orders me to, and perhaps not even then. He is shaking with grief, his mouth open in a silent scream of agony.

"I'm here," I whisper, stroking his hair and pulling him back against me. "I will not leave you. You can cry an ocean if you need to. I will not let you drown."

Melik turns so that his head is in my lap. His arms coil around my waist and I bow my head over him, providing him shelter. His knees are pulled up like a child's, but his legs are so long that his body is curled around mine, my back resting on his thighs. We are a knot of sorrow. I touch his face and feel the tears, and for the first time in my entire life I am relieved to know someone is crying. I think it is bad for Melik not to cry. The sight of his blank expression as he walked away from the grave was far scarier than his wracked sobs now. His shoulders heave as he weeps for what he has lost, and my eyes sting and tear as I feel his pain in my own body. He squeezes me tight, hanging on like the current is tugging at him. "I have you," I murmur in his ear. "I will not let you go."

I will never let him go.

I am not strong. I cannot shoot a gun or wield a knife. I am no soldier, no fighter. But as it turns out, I can do this. With my voice and my hands and my warmth, with everything that's in me, I hold Melik to the earth, refusing to relinquish him to the rising tide of his grief. He fists his hands in my tunic and buries his face in my side. I feel every tear and every sob, every time a memory hits him, every time the reality sweeps over him, every time his future without his brother sucks him down.

I have no idea how much time passes before Melik falls silent, before his breath becomes steady again, but as I drift in my thoughts, his voice reaches me. "Did my mother ask you to come?"

I lean back and find him looking up at me. "She did."

He swipes his sleeve across his face and sits up. "It was kind of you," he says quietly, turning his face away and wiping it once more.

He is pulling inside of himself again, and my first instinct is to do the same. To believe that he does not want me close. But if Anni is right, that is not what is happening here at all. "I did not come to be kind, Melik. Or out of a sense of obligation. *Yorh zhasev*," I whisper, reaching to touch the side of his face.

He lets out a raspy laugh. "Do you even know what that means?"

I rise to my knees and climb into his lap so that my legs are on either side of his. I take his face in my hands. Never have I been so bold, but I don't care. "I will tell you what it means to me, and you can tell me if I understand it." I kiss the tip of his nose. "It means I ache when you ache, and I am happy when you are happy. It means that I cheer when you have victory, and I stand beside you when you fight. It means my whole self is yours as a haven, a place to rest, a place to grow strong again." My voice shakes as I say, "It means I adore you." I kiss his mouth, and at first he seems too stunned to do anything but let me. "It means you have my heart."

His lips meet mine again, warm and salty. My hands slide into his hair as his spread across my back. I breathe him in as my mouth fills with the taste of him. Melik takes my chin between his fingers and breaks our kiss. "You do not have to do this, Wen—"

"Did you need me to find you tonight?"

He looks up at me. "I needed it more than anything else."

"Do you want me to leave?"

"That is the last thing I want."

"Do you feel the same?"

His eyes close and my heart stops. "For me it is different." His arm loops around my back as I stiffen. "Different, but not less," he says softly, opening his eyes. "To me, *'yorh zhasev'* . . . Wen, you are so mysterious to me. You are the smoothest dark waters, beneath which there is an entire world that I cannot see or understand. Yet I know it is there, and I know it is beautiful." His fingertips trace along my brow. "I could spend a lifetime looking at this surface and wondering." The corner of his mouth twitches. "And perhaps exploring."

He watches his hand slide up my sleeve to my shoulder, where he plays with the collar of my tunic. "I want to memorize every flash of your eyes and every smile. You have so many different smiles, and all of them mean something different." He skims a finger over my bottom lip, making my stomach flutter. "The slope of your neck, the furrow in your brow, the way you watch and watch and watch but rarely share what is inside you. I want to know all of it." His eyes meet mine. "And I admit: I want to be the only one who knows all these secrets about you. Unless . . ." He sighs.

"Unless what?"

"Unless someone else already does," he murmurs, his eyes straying to the wall of drawings behind me.

"You are speaking about Bo." When I say his name,

Melik tenses beneath me. "I will not lie to you and say that Bo is not important to me, and I will not pretend that I do not think of him, even now." I think of how he has decided to kill his soft, human side, how he will die a machine, and it fills me with sorrow so deep that it is its own kind of grave, one from which I must walk away. I lean my forehead on Melik's. "But I spent the last year dreaming of you, Melik." I poke him gently in the nose. "And saying your name in my sleep."

His gaze returns to mine. "I would like to hear about those dreams. I wonder how closely they match my own."

"You think we found each other there?"

"All I know is that I searched for you every night until I found you, and when I did, you always welcomed me."

"Is that what *'yorh zhasev'* means?" I whisper.

"Yorh zhasev ve bana sevye," he murmurs, clasping the back of my head and kissing my neck. "It means all those things."

I bow my head against his shoulder. We hold tight, and I feel the moment another wave of grief hits Melik. But I have him, and I wrap myself around him, and I offer him the comfort of my body. "What do you believe happens to us after we die?" Melik whispers.

"Many Itanyai believe you go to a nice place, a beautiful place, where you join your ancestors and watch over your family and your descendants."

"Do you believe that?"

I rest my forehead against his throat. "I don't know. I want to. I like the idea that my mother has not left me completely, even though I cannot feel or see her. What do you believe?"

"We believe you return to the birthplace of all souls, a beautiful glittering sea that is the source of all life, from the beginning of time until the end." He presses his face to my hair. "You rejoin all the souls who have ever been, and perhaps you will be born again once more. Like you, I want to believe, but right now it seems as real as the story of the boy king and his winged lion."

I thread my fingers into his hair. "I did not know Sinan as well as you did, but if anyone could swim his way through a mystical sea to be born again, it would be your little brother."

Melik lets out a raspy chuckle, and his arms pull tight around me. "I believe you are right. He was so alive." His voice breaks again and he takes a deep, shuddering breath. "Maybe he will find a way to return someday. I hope that is possible."

We go quiet with that thought, that hope. It seems we have few words left now, and few tears. Sinan's loss is just as big, and the fight to come is just as frightening. But Anni told me that the Noor never assume that there is a better time to be joyful and thankful than the present, and I believe that now. I will take the solace of being here with Melik, and I will not spend this time worrying. I will bear what we've lost, and I will be thankful for what we still have.

I kiss the side of Melik's neck. In the lantern light goose bumps ripple down the column of his throat. I pull back the collar of his tunic to follow their progress. Melik's head falls back, and my fingertips drift down his skin. When they settle over the exposed stretch of the scar on his chest, he presses his palm over mine. His heart bumps heavy against my hand. "Wen . . ."

"I am being very clear," I say, caressing his face with the back of my other hand. "And you can make of it what you will. But I am here tonight, and I am your bride."

"If this is because you think you must—"

"It is because I love you, Melik, and it is that simple."

He opens his eyes and stares at the ceiling of the cave, our shadows flickering in the lantern light. Slowly he takes my hand and lays it on his rough, stubbly cheek. He searches my face, and I smile, waiting for him, my heart skipping, until he seems to accept what I have said. He kisses my palm, then reaches into my satchel and pulls out the sleeping blanket. I scoot off his lap and he spreads the thick wool over the floor of the cave, then I kneel on it, already reaching for him. He pulls me into his arms, and together we are warm and whole, tentative but certain all the same. My hands tremble as I lift his tunic, as I touch the places I have healed and the places that I am claiming for my own.

I know how these things go in theory. I understand how people come together, how they overlap. Until this moment, though, I did not understand what it could mean. Melik stares into my eyes as his fingers slip beneath the hem of my tunic, as I lift my arms and allow him to remove it. I have never willingly bared my skin for another person, and my cheeks blaze as his gaze slides over me. It is not a bad feeling, though. I am made of anticipation, so full of want that it overwhelms everything else.

Melik knows how to touch me in ways that make my fingers dig into his skin. He is bold and curious, and I give myself over to him, craving every stroke. As much pleasure as it gives me, I sense he needs it as well, to numb the pain, to feel connected and loved, to be held to the earth. But when his mouth closes over my bare shoulder, when his hand slides along my waist and guides me down, when we are skin to skin, it is not a taking. It is a mutual offering, a gentle and complete surrender on both sides. It is frightening, and yet still I feel safe, because I trust him and we are in it together.

Somehow, tonight, we have forever even though we do not know what tomorrow brings. We weave our future with our interlocked fingers and mingled breaths. We do not need the promise of another sunset. We are alive now, together now, fragile perhaps, but we will not break. I promise him with every kiss, as our foreheads touch, as our eyes close—I will fight for this until the end, and I know he will too.

When we are spent, sapped of words and sighs and strength, Melik wraps us in the blanket and walks his fingers along the bumps of my spine while I close my eyes and listen to his heartbeat. I am sore and exhausted, but I am also warm and happy. It is not hard to drift into dreams, and when they come, I am on a high cliff above an endless ocean that shimmers and teems with life. Melik's hand slips into mine. "Don't let go," he says, and then we jump.

I wake with a start, blinking and sniffing at the air, my heart hammering. "Melik?"

"Hmmm?" he asks sleepily, winding his arms around my body.

"Do you smell smoke?"

He sits up quickly, his nostrils flaring, every muscle tensing. I wait for him to tell me it is just the scent of Dagchocuk in the morning, but after one or two breaths he curses and rises to his feet, yanking his pants from the floor. "It's the signal fires."

"The soldiers said the machines would not arrive for two days."

He looks down at me, raw horror in his gaze. "I think they lied."

Chapter Twenty

MELIK WRENCHES ON his tunic and ties his hair back, every movement a snap of frantic energy. "I'll wait for you outside," he says as he disappears through the passage to the ridge, leaving me to dress myself with shaking hands.

When I make my way outside, the sun is high above us, and Melik is perched on an outcropping, looking toward the east, where wisps of black smoke stretch high into the sky from three distant points within the canyon, and from one just to the east.

"I'm ready," I say, because he does not seem aware of anything but the view.

He tears his eyes from the horizon. "Would you consider staying here?" he asks quietly.

"What?" I clutch the strap of my pack. "Why?"

He jumps from the outcropping and lands on the trail next to me, scooping his pack from a boulder. "When this is over, you can find the soldiers. Tell them you were held prisoner. Tell them who you are. They will get you back to the Ring."

"Melik?" My throat is so tight that it comes out as a squeak.

He grasps my shoulders. His eyes are red rimmed and bloodshot, shining with fear. "Wen, the machines will be here in a few hours at most."

I crane my neck to peer at the smoke. "How can you tell?"

"The distance between the smoke puffs, and their number. There are nineteen headed this way, and they are past the point of the battle yesterday." He swallows hard. "Which means my men destroyed one of the twenty— and are probably dead. And we have no reinforcements. I sent word with Commander Kudret yesterday, but even if the general decided to send anyone, they would not arrive until tomorrow."

I cover his hands with mine. They are cold and sweating. "What are you going to do?"

He looks toward the east. "I will fight until I am dead, Wen, but we cannot stop them all. And even if I survived this attack, the soldiers would execute me on sight." He bows his head and closes his eyes as my hands slide into his hair. "But I have to do what I can. Maybe if I could—"

"And you would leave me behind?" I ask, choking on the idea of losing him now. He talks like it is a certainty.

"I want you to live through this!" he shouts, his voice breaking.

My fingers pull tight in his rust-colored locks. "But you can't make me stay here while you go," I whisper, standing on my tiptoes and drawing his face to mine. "Not now. I can help. You know I can."

Our kiss is desperate with grief and terror. "I cannot watch you die," he breathes against my mouth.

"And I cannot sit here and do nothing. You would never accept such a thing. How can you ask me to?" I step back and put my hand over my heart, then turn my palm to him. "You cannot keep me from this fight."

He stares at my hand outstretched, and then he takes it in his own. "Then we will go together."

He tugs me down the trail, and I jog after him. I savor every slide of his palm against mine, every time he steadies me with his hand on my waist, every exhaled breath. I stare at his broad back, his shoulders, his booted feet as he nimbly weaves through the passes and descends toward the village.

When I was young, I sat at my father's desk and played with an hourglass he kept there. I would turn the thing over and listen to the quiet hiss of sand as it tumbled down. As the bottom filled, the sand stopped falling in a steady torrent, and it became possible to spot individual grains. I feel like that now, examining each second separately, trying to memorize and hold it in my mind.

As we reach the lower part of the trail, Melik turns to me. "Find my mother. Tell her what is happening." His thumb strokes over the back of my hand. "See if the two of you can load the wounded onto a cart and head south. Warn the other villages on the Line."

"Focus on what you need to do," I say to him, wishing

my voice weren't shaking, wishing we weren't down to a few grains of sand, a few seconds before we reach our good-bye.

He pulls me to him and flattens his palm between my breasts. *"Mican tisamokye,"* he whispers. "You carry my heart." He kisses the top of my head and lets go of my hand. His face is lit with a ghostly smile. "So no matter what happens to the rest of me, it is up to you to take care of that."

He pivots on his heel and sprints toward the village, leaving me to scramble in his wake. The lanes are filled with scared Noor, pointing up at the smoke that signals the beginning of the end. As I run toward Anni's house, I hear Melik's voice, rallying his men. I place my hand over the spot he touched and pick up my pace. "Anni!" I call.

She comes out of her cottage, her eyes going round as she sees the others pointing at the sky. Her face is puffy and pale after a night of crying, and she opens her arms to me. "You found him," she huffs as I throw my arms around her waist and squeeze.

"I found him, and he is with the other fighters." I pull away from her. "The machines will be here much sooner than we thought. Melik asked us to take the wounded south."

Her eyes stray toward the center of the village, to the makeshift hospital within the wedding tent. "There are many more besides the wounded who must go south. Can you prepare the ones in the tent while I spread the word to the elders and the families with children? I will meet you with the cart."

I leave her to warn the others, and jog to the tent. Old

Aysun is inside with the patients. Her eyes narrow when she sees me. *"Kuchuksivengi,"* she says.

I squat in front of her and turn my palm up. I crab my other fingers like a spider's legs and walk them along my open hand, then point in the direction of the canyon.

Aysun squawks, *"Devi!"*

At that word the patients begin to rouse. Their chalky complexions tell me of their pain, and I take a few moments to distribute my jie cao, because this trip will be bumpy and unpleasant even for those who are not desperately injured. With Aysun's help I change bandages and adjust splints, speaking soothing words despite the terror inside me. My knees are flat on the sparse grass floor of the tent, and when I feel the first vibration in the ground, I go still, hoping it is a trick of my mind. It is too soon, far too soon. We will never get these people to safety in time. Surely I am imagining the tremor. . . .

But another comes a moment later, and another, and Aysun tears open the tent flap and screams Anni's name. I push past her and exit the tent, needing to escape the enclosed space for a moment, hoping to see Anni rushing toward me, because I cannot drag some of these patients all the way to the carriage by myself—some of them weigh twice as much as I do.

It is strangely quiet in the square as the ground trembles beneath my feet. At the south side of the canyon mouth I hear a shout in Noor, and it draws my eyes along the ground to a spot at the base of a low hill. Melik is there, rifle over his shoulder, holding a long, thick coil of rope with a hook at one end.

In his other hand is a wrench.

Several men, including Baris and Bajram, stand around him, equipped in the same manner. They are going to try to take down the machines the way Bo and Sinan did. They are pointing into the canyon, and I swear I see the stark shadow of a spider leg against the cliffs, the metal gleam of a steel body under the glaring sun.

"Wen!"

I spin around to see Anni waving to me from the front of a large horse-drawn farm cart. She steers the two horses down the lane as we hear the first clatter of heavy gunfire echo against the rocks. My ears roar with the knowledge that these might be the last minutes of our lives, and I look over my shoulder to find Melik staring at us.

He puts his hand over his heart and extends his palm to us before loping out of sight. Anni's hand is still held out when I turn back to her. "We must load them quickly," she says to me as I climb onto the side.

"Aysun can help us," I tell her as she guides the animals into the square. My shoulders are hiked to my ears as I jump off the cart. The ground shakes with the horde of approaching killers, and the air splits with the boom of gunfire.

I will fight until I am dead. That is what Melik said. Not until he is wounded or tired or too scared to go on. Until he is dead. And that is what I will do too. Until I am no longer breathing, I will move and I will help. Anni rips the tent flap open and issues a stream of instructions. She disappears inside. I go around the back of the cart and imagine who should go where. The injured more at risk for bleeding should ride at the front, where there will be slightly less jostling, and—

Panicked shouts and crashing metal footsteps steal my breath. Heavy fire shatters the rocks all around the fighters, and they scatter in search of cover. Except for one. As the first machine lumbers into view, Melik runs straight under it, ducking between the columns of its legs. Its front guns are silent and its top gunner slouches limp in his seat, already dead. Even if he weren't, though, Melik is out of the reach of the machine's guns.

But not out of the reach of the guns of the war machine behind it.

Melik throws his rope straight up, and when it catches, he leaps onto it as bullets strafe the ground at his feet. The machine stalks forward quickly with him dangling from the coupling of its thorax and abdomen. It stomps out of the canyon and into the village with the other spider on its tail, the front guns swinging this way and that, trying to get a good shot without damaging its brother. Steam and smoke roll out of the backs of the machines and billow into the air. All I can see is Melik's legs now, the rest of him obscured by the massive body of the monster coming toward us.

Hands close over my shoulders. "We need your help to—" Anni screams when she sees the war machine astride the lane, its massive feet collapsing the cottages on either side as it roars forward, with another right behind it.

I am prying her fingers from my body when Melik is shot.

Blood spatters around his leg and he falls, landing on his back with the legs of the enormous machine caging him. His wrench lands several feet away. His face is a mask of pain. It is one of those grain-of-sand moments, tumbling through the air and allowing me to see every facet. The swell of Melik's chest as he draws a labored breath. His hands reaching for his rifle as blood streams from his leg. The big gun that took him down, dipping to take another shot.

"No." It comes from me quietly, but as it does, I sprint forward, my hands up. "No!" My feet pound the dirt and my ears roar as I barrel toward my death, unable to watch Melik shot to pieces in front of me. The machine above him steps over his body but by some miracle does not crush him with its enormous feet. It strides along the path as I approach from the other side, screaming and waving my arms.

Melik rolls onto his stomach, and his jade eyes meet mine as the hulking spider that shot him approaches from behind. I run straight toward him while the other spider, the one with the rope still hanging from its belly, makes a turn toward me. Melik heaves himself onto his knees and swings his rifle up. He fires past me at the machine he tried to climb, then pivots, aiming for the other.

"Melik!" I dive for him and grab his shoulders as he fires a few futile shots at the metal beast coming toward him. I drag him backward even though I know it is hopeless.

"No, no, no," he says, his fingers clutching at my arm. He's been shot through the right calf, and blood soaks his trouser leg. "Run, Wen. Go!"

But it is too late to run. The machines are on either side of us, and as the battle rages in the canyon, we are here, the sole focus of these two monsters. As the guns swing down toward us, I step around Melik and take his face in my hands. "Don't let go," I say, echoing his words from my dream. I press my lips to his forehead.

"I will never let go," he says, his voice shredded with pain.

The world explodes with gunfire, deafening me. Melik twists over me, crushing me to the ground. My arm coils around his neck and I press my face against his chest. It goes on and on and on, and I know I am screaming, but I can't hear myself. Melik is a fierce and relentless weight, every muscle trembling as he tries to shield me.

Metal crashes against metal, shrieking and whining. I open my eyes to see Melik's face above mine. He blinks and rolls off me, and we turn to see one of the machines, the one that shot him, crumple slowly to the ground, smoke blooming from its back end. There are large-bore bullet holes across its spider face and along its sides. We twist to look at the other machine, the one with the rope hanging from it. Its front legs are planted on either side of the lane, and the front guns are smoking. With a hissing hum the body of the spider moves lower until it is resting on the lane.

Its top hatch opens.

The pilot's helmet reflects the sunlight as he climbs onto the top of the machine. Melik grabs for his rifle, but as he does, the pilot leaps from the war spider and lands in front of us with an unmistakable metal clank and hum.

We stare into his face as he slides half of his metal visor to the side.

Bo looks at Melik's leg and then at me. "Can you fix that? Or at least make it stop bleeding?" he asks me.

My mouth opens and closes a few times before I manage to say. "I think so?"

Bo nods, quick and matter-of-fact. "Perfect. Because I need him."

"What are you doing?" Melik asks, grimacing as he holds himself upright.

Bo tilts his head, looking for all the world like a sentient machine. "I'm delivering you eighteen war machines, Red. Do you want them?"

Melik gapes at him.

Bo's mouth curves into a smirk. "Good. Get on your feet and come with me."

Chapter
Twenty-One

"WHAT HAVE YOU done, Bo?" I ask as Anni races over to us, offering forth my satchel and then hovering over Melik, who speaks to her in rapid-fire Noor.

"I created slow leaks in the water tanks and sabotaged the gauges in all the machines except the one I was piloting," he says, nodding at the small puddle of water forming beneath the downed machine behind us. "They've been slowly draining since we set out this morning, but the firemen have no idea. I calculated the rate of water loss, and . . . ah. Yes. Look." He points his spindly metal finger at the mouth of the canyon, where one of the war machines slowly sinks until its abdomen and thorax hit the dirt. "If you patch the holes and refill the tanks, they will be fine, but only if they are not destroyed." He watches the Noor fighters rush forward with their rifles raised before he swivels his head down and looks at Melik. "Which means you have to call your men off. Get them to capture the crew, but tell them not to hurt the machines."

I open my satchel and pull out several long strips of cloth. Teeth gritted, Melik wrenches up his trouser leg to reveal a long gouge along the back of his leg, as deep and wide as my thumb and twice as long. It is a bad wound, but not a fatal one, and though it needs to be cleaned and carefully stitched, there is no time. "Melik, I can bind this, but—"

"Do it," he says, "as quickly as you can." His narrowed, bloodshot eyes are focused on the opening of the canyon, where the boom of gunfire and the shouts of the Noor tell us that a desperate battle is going on.

A shout from the rear of Bo's machine makes me flinch, and we look up to see the grime-streaked fireman, who must have emerged from his hatch when he realized his pilot had attacked another machine. He's aiming a revolver at us, but before he can pull the trigger, Bo's metal hands move in concert, plucking two spiders from his shoulders and flinging them at the fireman. The man's thick arms pinwheel as the two metal demons land on his chest and belly, and I look away as he begins to scream.

Melik and Anni are silent as the fireman hits the ground and goes still. Anni's eyes are so wide, and her lips tremble as she cuts furtive glances at Bo. Melik's every muscle is tense, but he does not cry out as I wind the cloth around his lower leg and pull it tight. I put my hand over his. "This will bleed if you try to walk."

"I know," he says. "But I am not dead yet. I can still fight."

I wish he would not say it like that. I am having trouble suppressing my wish to drag him to the cart onto which Anni and Aysun have loaded the wounded. He is still alive. He could stay that way. But now he is bracing himself and trying to rise from the ground. Bo offers a metal hand, and Melik takes it, using his good leg to push himself up. He leaves bloody fingerprints on Bo's steel palm.

"Do any of your people know how to manage a boiler?" Bo asks.

Melik looks toward the slaughtered fireman. Bo's spiders have buried themselves in the man's chest and are still at work. "What is required?"

"Adding coal to the firebox and monitoring the gauges to keep the pressure at a level that allows me to pilot the machine. There is a communication system inside. The fireman will be able to hear my voice, and I will tell him before I need more power."

"What more is there to do?" I ask. "You've said the machines will shut down on their own."

Bo nods. "They will. But the carrier machine is coming, and I did not have time to sabotage it. It is a very powerful machine with two heavy cannon at the front. It would have no trouble destroying this village and your survivors." His eyes stray toward Aysun and the cart full of injured Noor.

Melik leans on Anni as he tries to put weight on his injured leg. He keeps his mouth clamped shut to hold his groan inside. "I will manage the boiler if you show me how."

"But your men—" Bo begins.

"Cannot speak Itanyai," says Melik. "I'm the only one who can."

"Wen and I will tell the fighters what they need to know," says Anni. She turns to me. "Many of them will be injured."

I stand up and swing my pack over my shoulder. I can do little but bind and tourniquet and splint, but that is not nothing. I raise my head to find Bo staring at me, a frown on his face. "Wen, the guns on the war machines will still be functional," he says. "It is not safe."

"All the more reason for me to go and help." I move closer to him, drinking in the sight of his face, of his concern for me. He has allowed that part of him, the human part, to live, and it feels like a gift. "I will be careful," I add.

Bo looks back and forth between Melik and me, and I know he is wishing Melik would agree with him and tell me not to go. And Melik looks like he wants to. We stare at each other for the briefest moment, and then he says, very quietly, "Remember, Wen. *Mican tisamokye.*" *You carry my heart with you.*

Anni makes a choked sound in her throat and puts her arm over my shoulders. I put mine around her waist. "I will never forget that," I say to him.

Bo turns away and strides to the back of his hijacked war machine. "Now, Red. The carrier will be here in a few minutes, and we have to make it past the downed machines." He gestures at the perforated war machine several yards away. "Their guns can penetrate our armor."

Melik half limps, half hops to the rear of the machine. "And the carrier?"

"Heavily armored. Our guns are nothing to it. We will have to either access its kill switch or take out its pilot."

Melik frowns. "Both of those involve climbing on top of the machine."

Bo gives him a grim smile. "Obviously." Together, he and Melik peer into the boiler chamber of the war machine. "You're a little big for this space, Red."

"I'll fit," Melik says, his voice strained. He accepts Bo's arm as he climbs into the back. As Bo explains how to work the boiler, I turn to Anni.

"We must go," I say to her. "If the fighters can get the crews out of the machines, they will not be able to shoot at this one."

Anni casts an anxious glance at Melik, who has folded himself into the boiler chamber of the war machine. My stomach clenches. So many horrible things could happen to him in that tiny space full of fire and smoke. Bo slams the hatch and strides over the top of the machine. He looks down at me. "I'll try to keep him safe." He closes the plate over his face, becoming all steel.

I take Anni's hand. "We have to warn the fighters so they don't try to stop Melik and Bo." I squeeze her fingers as the giant metal spider carrying two men I love lets out a hissing groan and rises from the ground. Anni calls out to Aysun, who sets out with the cart, heading south. A string of Noor are already ahead of her on the Line, moving as quickly as they can away from the danger that Anni and I now run toward. We weave our way past the stone cottages and press ourselves to a low rock wall.

Maybe a hundred yards beyond it is the battle, and we can see only a small part of it, where the canyon opens to the west. Gunfire is constant, both from rifles and from the heavy guns of the war machines. The ground shakes as the hijacked machine trundles past its dead brother and makes its way toward the fight.

From our vantage point I can see a few Noor peeking around the low hill and firing at something deeper in the canyon. One war machine lies silent right near the path. A few Noor are peering into its rear hatch as smoke rolls from it. "I think we can go," I say to Anni, and together we scramble over the wall and sprint for the hill. My boots tangle in the scraggly weeds and a cold wind whips at my hair, but I am strong with desperation.

Anni begins calling out in Noor before we reach the hill, and the fighters turn to her and listen, their gazes darting toward the hijacked war machine bearing down on them. Once she explains, their mouths twist into bemused smiles and they shout to their brethren— hopefully, telling them to hold their fire. Anni turns to me as I press myself against a boulder when more gunfire erupts. "They said there are many injuries. They are trying to silence the guns on all the machines now."

By killing the gunners, I am sure. I poke my head out and crane my neck to see deeper into the rocky canyon. It is littered with the corpses of giant spiders, and Noor swarm over them like ants, pulling gunners from their perches and yanking pilots from their cockpits. As I watch, several charge from between the legs of one machine and attack the pilot's hatch with a wrench. I tear my eyes from the sight and search for the fighters who need my help.

I find Baris easily. He lies bleeding near the trail, his thick fingers clutching at a wound in his side. With a quick scan of my surroundings, I dart onto the trail and run to him. "Melik?" he says when he sees me. "Melik?"

I point to the hijacked machine. Bo is skillfully piloting it past the sleeping war spiders, maneuvering its heavy legs as if they were extensions of him, delicate and nimble. He must be so happy. The thought comes and goes quickly, but I smile as I turn back to Baris. I lift his tunic to see that the large bullet has gone right through him, and only time will tell if it destroyed something vital inside him. I squeeze his hand and pack the wound with cloth, trying to stop the bleeding.

The ground beneath my knees trembles in jolts out of time with the pounding of Bo's spider feet. I squint at the place where the canyon bends to the east and my breath catches. The carrier spider is twice the size of the war machines, with thicker legs and a body two stories high. It has two cannon for fangs. When its pilot sees the carnage in front of him, he halts the giant machine.

Bo marches his spider straight toward it. Baris asks me a question that includes the word "Melik," but I don't know how to answer him. And even if I could, I might not. I'm too busy praying that the carrier spider believes Bo is a friend, because if those cannon blaze, Bo and Melik are dead. They have no chance.

I look over my shoulder and see Anni coming up the trail. "Take care of Baris? Move him carefully."

She nods, her mouth tight as she watches the slow,

careful progress of the hijacked spider toward the massive carrier beast. I slide along the rock wall, heading up the trail to where Bajram lies dead, huge holes ripped right through his chest. His death came quick, at least. I close his eyes and keep moving, knowing I am creeping closer to danger but needing to keep the battle in sight.

I kneel next to a woman who is curled onto her side. Her hand has been shot off, leaving her with only a stump. I whisper to her as I tie the tourniquet, and stroke her hair as I push san qi paste into her mouth, but my attention is on Bo and Melik.

The two spiders are only a hundred feet away from each other in the dry riverbed. I am only a hundred feet behind them.

I am close enough to see the moment the cannon swing toward the hijacked spider. Perhaps the pilot sees the rope dangling from its middle. Perhaps they have a radio signal that Bo is not answering. Whatever it is, they know they have an enemy now, and they are going to destroy it.

The first explosion shatters a boulder next to the spider's legs, and Bo jerks his machine into action. It moves like a real animal, changing directions before spinning and charging at the carrier. As the cannon swing heavy and slow toward it, Bo darts across the front of the machine.

When the pilot realizes he is being flanked, the carrier spider charges forward along the riverbed, firing its cannon. It lands a direct hit on the war machine where several Noor are standing, and the air fills with smoke and screams and flying bodies. I dive behind a boulder and reach out to drag the Noor woman with me. She shrieks and whimpers, tears streaming down her face as the big guns boom.

I have trapped myself here, so near the danger that rocks rain down on our heads and heat from the machines fans across my cheeks. I stare at the carrier spider as it stalks past my position, wondering where Bo and Melik are, if they were hit, if their machine lies dead near the bend in the canyon.

I do not have to wonder long.

With thundering footsteps, Bo's war machine barrels up behind the carrier spider. Just before it crashes into the colossal machine's abdomen, Bo's spider rears in the air and pounds its legs onto the carrier's back. Metal tears and squeals as the war machine's front legs tangle with the carrier spider's rear legs. The carrier's rear hatch opens as the massive arachnid drags Bo's machine along the ground. I cry out, imagining coal raining out of the firebox onto Melik, trapped in the tiny chamber at the back of the war machine.

Bo emerges from his cockpit, his metal mask gleaming in the light. He hurls several of his small spiders at the carrier's fireman and then jumps onto the back of the carrier spider, crouching near the open rear hatch and listening to the screams coming from inside. Smoke puffs and billows from the opening, but the carrier continues to move. It is nearly to the downed spiders now. The Noor have scattered, running for the village, but several wounded men are lying amidst the metal carnage.

Bo leaps from the carrier's abdomen to its thorax and hunches over the cockpit hatch. Perhaps alerted by the sounds of Bo's machine hands hard at work, the pilot inside halts the carrier. And then, just as Bo opens the hatch, the massive spider makes a violent right turn, heading straight for the opposite canyon wall, dragging the hijacked war machine behind it.

"Bo," I whisper. "Melik."

Before I can think about it, I have climbed out of my rocky hiding place and am running toward the dry riverbed. I can see what's going to happen, what this carrier machine is doing, and the scream unfurls from my throat, savage and agonized.

Bo dives into the open cockpit hatch as the carrier barrels forward. He yanks the pilot up. A man of flesh is no match for one of metal, and the pilot shrieks as Bo ends him with a wrenching twist. But the machine still moves, running across a short open space before ramming into the rocky canyon wall at top speed. Bo flies into the air, his steel body spiraling across the sky before colliding with stone and dropping to the ground three stories below. The hijacked machine with Melik in its belly slides heavily over the top of the carrier and collides with rock too.

"Anni!" I scream. "Melik is in the back!" Smoke billows from the rear of the hijacked spider, where Melik is trapped inside. Sickness winds up my throat as panicked shouts rise from behind me, as Anni's tortured voice calls out to her elder son.

She has lost her husband and Sinan, and now she is losing Melik.

I scramble up the riverbank to the other side and follow the giant footsteps that lead to the collision. Spurts of flame, coming from the open hatch of the carrier beneath, rise around the body of the hijacked machine. The carrier's boiler has caught fire, and it will cook the smaller machine on its back in a matter of seconds.

I am almost there when the boiler explodes. I am thrown backward as a wave of heat rolls over me. My ears ring as I raise my head. All that remains of the hijacked spider is a burned shell that slides off the back of the carrier into a smoldering heap of rubble.

"Melik!" yowls Anni. She and several Noor rush past me, on my knees and staring, and run to the wreckage. But it is too hot to allow them to reach the dented hatch over the boiler, where my red Noor is entombed.

They keep trying. I watch, helpless and hopeless. Because I know. I already know. Melik is dead. He is gone from this world, to join his brother in the crystal sea of souls. I rise, my feet numb and my head throbbing. When I touch my fingers to my temple, they come away wet and bloody. How interesting. I am injured.

I stumble forward, but I do not stop at the blackened coffin where Melik lies. I do not want to see him burned and ruined. It will kill me. So I make my way around the wreckage, searching for the only other person I need to see.

Bo lies crumpled against the canyon wall, thrown clear of the burned hulk of the carrier. As soon as I find him, I regain my bearings and purpose. I run for him and crouch at his side. His chest plate is caved in, and the frame around his right leg is mangled and twisted. Blood seeps from it, red drops falling from ragged torn metal edges. "Bo?" I squeak, reaching for his faceplate.

I slide it to the side, and his brown eye meets mine. His lips move, and his metal hand scrabbles over his chest. My fingers fumble and shake as I follow by memory the set of steps required to open his metal suit. I loosen his right arm from the shoulder and gently pull it off, freeing his human limb. I open his chest plate.

His chest is dented and swollen. Broken ribs. Internal bleeding. And the severe injury to his leg. "You can't fix me, Wen," he whispers.

I lean over him and pull his helmet off. His sweaty hair is soft beneath my fingers. "I can try."

His trembling human hand covers mine. "No." His gaze slides along my face. "You're bleeding. Are you hurt?"

"I'm fine." A tear falls from my face and lands on his cheek. "You have done a great thing, Bo."

He lets out a shuddering sigh and winces. "I have done many bad things too. So many bad things." His voice is only a shadow of what it was. Every word takes effort.

My fingers entwine with his. "No one is good all the time."

He smiles, but it twists into a grimace. "I wish Sinan could have seen this," he murmurs. "He would have loved to pilot one of those machines."

I ride a wave of sorrow. "Thank you for coming back. I thought I had lost you."

He wheezes. "Remember the end of the story about the bandit and the princess?"

I sniffle and lay my head on his shoulder, ignoring the stabbing pain in my temple. "The bandit dies, and he is still doomed to haunt the princess."

"That is not the end." When I raise my head, he continues. "In the end the princess gives her necklace to her daughter. But the bandit ghost still haunts her. Do you remember why?"

My throat constricts as I think of it. "He loves her. He realizes that it was never the necklace that held him to her, nor any enchantment. It was his heart."

"Very good, Wen," he whispers.

"But I don't want you to haunt me. I want you to stay here."

"That is a wish I cannot grant," he murmurs. A tear slips from his eye as I lift his hand and lay it on my cheek. He swallows painfully. "Will you let me haunt you? I do not want to be alone."

He has had no family but for me and my father. No ancestors to look forward to seeing. He does not think anyone will be waiting for him, wherever he is going.

"Mican tisamokye." I kiss his forehead and place my palm gently over the center of his chest, where his tender heart beats, weak but frantic, clinging fiercely to life but rapidly losing its grip. "You carry my heart with you, Bo. You will never be alone."

Slowly I reach up and remove his mask, revealing his whole face, half beautiful and half ruined. He lets out a small, vulnerable sound as I lay the mask over his chest.

I take his face in my hands, and I kiss his mouth. He sighs a broken thank-you as I lay my cheek on his forehead and listen to his life ebb, his breathing going shallow and erratic. I hold his hand and kiss his fingers while he dies, and I look into his eye as the spark of brilliance fades from it.

Once it is gone, I put his mask back on his face. I know how he would feel about people staring. Numb and hollow, I rise. I touch my temple again, and blood dribbles over my fingers, slick and fresh. With vague interest I look down at my tunic to see my shoulder and sleeve stained crimson. I trudge clumsily around the side of the carrier, my feet like blocks of ice. A group of Noor stands a good distance away from the wreckage, over by the riverbed. Even through my blurred vision I see the rust-colored hair of my Noor mother. "Anni," I breathe, "I think I'm hurt."

My ears fill with the ocean's roar as I sink to my knees. Distant shouts fly past me, and then I am rolled onto my back and faintly familiar faces hover above me. I try to smile as Anni strokes my face. Something soft is pressed to the side of my head. "You'll be fine," she says, her voice strained.

But I will not be fine. I could never be fine again. Melik is gone. Bo is gone. And I would rather be with them.

I close my eyes, let myself sink into the dark and the cold, and invite death to swallow me.

Chapter
Twenty-Two

DEATH IS NOT pleasant. My head pounds and pinches and throbs, my muscles ache, and I cannot get away from the noise. Instead of rising into the sky, I descend into the earth, too heavy to move. Bo and Melik are close—I see them, hazy shapes and colors, shadows just out of my reach. I call for them over and over again. Bo perches on one side, and Melik on the other. Dark and light. Both beckoning, offering to take my hand and lead me to wherever they are. They promise they are real, and that we can be together.

"Come with me," Bo says. "Choose me."

"Mican tisamokye," whispers Melik. "If you leave me, you take my heart."

They are so different from each other, and I don't want to let either one go. But finally both of them fade away and leave me alone.

I curl in on myself. My mother is not here. There is no crystal sea of souls and no ancestors to enfold me. This is the opposite of peaceful. I want to cry, but I have no tears. I want stillness, but all I have is jostling and prodding. I want silence, but my ears fill with clatter and chatter, as well as the endless crashing and hissing of machines.

"Shouldn't she have awakened by now?"

I have lost too much to return.

"Her body needs rest, and so she is resting."

I wish for rest, but all I have is clamor.

"Does she know we're here?"

Hands smooth over my hair and there is a tug at my temple. "I believe she does."

Something in the weary yet gentle tone of that voice pulls the veil of oblivion away from me. Yearning swells in my chest. "Father?" I whisper.

Someone squeezes my hand and lets out a low, strangled noise. "I'm right here, daughter. I am holding your hand."

I slowly open my eyes, and his face is above mine. "Father."

He smiles and quickly swipes a tear from his cheek, then tugs a blanket higher on my chest. There is a thick pillow beneath my head, and my body is warm and tightly bundled. "You lost a great deal of blood."

Someone else takes my other hand, and the flash of rust-colored hair in my periphery is a painful jolt to my heart. "It's been all we could do to get enough dang-gui tea into you," says Anni.

My father touches a bandage on the side of my head. "You were cut with some shrapnel. We are thankful it didn't kill you." He smiles, a gentle, soft curve that I have missed so much. "I stitched you good as new. Your hair will cover the scar."

"How are you here?" I ask, my voice cracking and hoarse. My gaze flits from him to the stone and mud walls around me and the thatched roof above. I am in Anni's cottage. Strange noises come from outside, the roar and hiss of steam engines and shouts in Noor. It is like the battle is still going on, and I shudder. Anni puts her hand over my stomach, weighing me down, holding me where I am.

"I have had an adventure," my father says, his wrinkled face bemused but also full of quiet pride. "I was grieving my beloved daughter when five young soldiers walked out of the Western Hills and into the Ring with an amazing story that was too strange to ignore. Hoping Bo had been right when he refused to accept the news of your death, I packed my things and set off into the canyon ahead of the army. I stuck to high trails and got lost a few times, and I ended up in a village several miles to the north of this one."

Anni lets out a fond chuckle, and I am amazed that someone who has lost so much can make that kind of happy sound. "He spoke enough Noor to get to Dagchocuk. He arrived the night after the great battle, and we were very thankful. Your father is a great doctor, and you were not his only patient." She pats my shoulder and leaves the room as the ground trembles.

Father looks toward the door. "You have been sleeping for two days. The Noor have been repairing the war machines. Sixteen are operational, but it is taking some time to fill the water tanks using their wells and the spring. They are teaching themselves to pilot them." He lets out a snort of quiet laughter. "They have only crashed one. Really, I think they are doing very well."

But I cannot feel that triumph. My losses curdle in my stomach, and I wish I could sink into unconsciousness again. As awful as it was, being here is harder. "Bo did this. He delivered the machines. He . . . he—"

Father sighs. "We buried him yesterday, with the rest of the dead. There were many. Wen . . ."

I squeeze my eyes shut. I don't want to hear him tell me about Melik. I cover my mouth to stifle a sob of grief. This is too much. "Please don't say his name."

Uneven footsteps thump toward us from the front room. "Wen?"

My eyes pop open at the desperate, familiar sound of his voice. "Melik?"

He appears in the doorway, blocking out the light, his broad silhouette unmistakable. His rust-colored hair is wild and his tunic is smeared with soot. My father dodges out of the way as Melik lunges forward and reaches my side in an instant. His hands smell of machine oil but I don't care—I am in his arms and his lips are on my forehead and I am alive, so alive that my heart bursts with it. My fingers curl into Melik's sleeves as he kisses me, scratching my skin with his scraggly stubble.

"I was so afraid you would not come back," he says in a choked voice.

"Are you real?" I whisper stupidly as his hair tickles my cheeks.

Anni peers in from the doorway. "Real enough to

have been pestering your father constantly about your condition."

My father chuckles and rises to his feet. "I did not mind," he says, looking down at me. "When you are ready, we have bread and more tea for you." He and Anni disappear into the front room, where the fire glows warm and throws shadows on the wall.

Melik raises his head and looks down at me. The circles under his eyes are purple, and even his freckles are pale. "You kept saying my name, and Bo's name, and you sounded so lost." His eyes glitter with unshed tears. "But you did not hear me when I answered. Your father finally told me I had to stay away. He thought it was upsetting you."

"I saw you die."

"No, you did not." He kisses the tip of my nose. "When the carrier began firing and charging ahead, we were behind it. Bo ordered me to load the firebox with coal—and then he told me to jump out. It was a hard fall. I was lying in the riverbed, and my leg . . ." He shifts uncomfortably, and I glance down to see the cane that he discarded as he dived to the floor to reach me.

"He was alone in the machine when he attacked the carrier," I murmur.

"He told me I had better not die," Melik says, sadness shadowing his face. "He said I owed my sorry life to you, and I had better repay the debt."

"He was trying to make amends." In his own way. Always in his own way.

"I know," he says quietly, laying his forehead on mine. "But he was doing more than that."

"He felt terrible about Sinan, Melik."

"I know that as well, Wen. I was in too much pain to share it with him at first. I wish . . ." He presses his lips shut.

"What are you doing with the machines?" I ask, needing to move away from talk of Bo. His loss is so heavy that it is hard to breathe.

"We have positioned five in the canyon, and they will hold the troops back. The others are leaving tonight for the northern front."

My unsteady hands push Melik's hair back from his face. "Are you going with them?"

His jade eyes bore into mine. "I must." He turns his head and kisses my palm. "Wen, I need to know . . ." His eyelashes flutter against my fingers. "Will you be here when I return? Your father is here now. He said he could take you back to the Ring. It might be safer there. We do not know what will happen. I could have someone guide you if you want to return." He mumbles all of this against my skin, and I feel every word.

It is shocking to me, after what we have shared, that he would say this. I can tell it hurts him to do it, and I am glad, because it certainly hurts me. But I understand it. This time, I understand it. I turn his face back to mine. "Melik, I am not letting go."

I kneel in front of the grave, the chill wind whipping my hair. My body aches from another long day by my father's side, tending to patients who come from every village on the Line. I am so tired that I could lie down right here and sleep, but I think that is normal, and being tired is not the worst thing. Besides, there is always something to do, and that is when I do best.

I brush a bit of dirt off the grave marker. The stones are carefully placed, the corners squared, the earth smooth. "I hope you can hear me," I say quietly. "I think you would be very happy today."

A gust of wind tugs and twists the strip of cloth tied to the grave-post. I smooth down the crimson fabric, the delicate green leaves and black diamonds, but it wants to fly. It is identical to the one next to it, the one that marks Sinan's grave. The two banners flutter, straining to take flight. They are so alike, and so like their owners. It is hard to hold them down, to suppress their boundless energy.

I hope they are together. It is a silly kind of wish, but I like to think of them that way.

Hands close over my shoulders, and I cover them with my own. "Thank you for claiming him," I say.

"Do you think that's what he would have wanted?"

I lean my head back and look up at my red Noor. "It is hard to know what he would have wanted. But I think he would have been glad to call Sinan his brother."

Melik's mouth curves into a half smile. "Then he is my brother too, whether he wants to be or not."

Melik's arms wind around my waist as we look down at the two graves. Bo did not want to be alone, and he isn't. He will never be. He might have been a ghost in the east, long dead and known to no one at all. But I will never forget him, and neither will the Noor—he is a hero to them. He is the reason there is a truce. He is the reason Melik's arms are around me. He is the reason we are safe.

He gave power to those who had none, just enough to make them hard to stomp on. It was such a startling and expensive loss that our government reconsidered the invasion. After weeks of stalemate the balance was struck. The negotiations began.

And the fighters came home. Yesterday Melik and several of the other men from Dagchocuk rode their horses along the Line and came running down the lanes, into the arms of their families. Tonight there will be a feast. Already there is singing in the square. One would think the drought had ended or that the government had granted Yilat autonomy, but neither has happened. We do not need the rains or a permanent peace to celebrate, though—we will not assume there is a better time than now to be happy.

I close my eyes and inhale the scent of sage, my heart picking up a heavy, fearful rhythm. But there is nothing wrong with being scared. It simply means that something important is at stake. My hands slide along Melik's arms. "Do you think we will meet either of them again?" I ask, my voice tentative, filled with the hugeness of this moment.

Melik kisses the side of my head. "I am choosing to believe souls that bright will find a way to return, though there is no way of knowing how or when."

Maybe he feels the tremble of my body against his, because he leans back and looks down at me, his brow furrowed. I bite my lip and guide his hand over my belly. He blinks, staring at his fingers spread over my middle, and then looks into my eyes. "Are you happy?" he whispers, his voice breaking over the words.

My eyes sting. "I am very happy, Melik."

He grins, and then our lips touch. I relish the reality of it, how warm, how perfect in its flaws. Our people have an uneasy peace at best. Our lives are so fragile. The world can break nearly any promise we make, but the risk is one I will accept.

I will live inside this hope until the very last grain of sand falls.

Acknowledgments

When I finished *Of Metal and Wishes*, I thought it would be a stand-alone. Not because the story was complete, though. And so the first thank you goes to Ruta Rimas and the team at McElderry for allowing me the opportunity to continue Wen's story. I want to thank Justin Chanda, Paul Crichton, and Siena Koncsol for helping my books get the visibility they needed. To Debra Sfetsios-Conover and Michael Frost: thank you for putting so much thought and effort into my covers. To Erica Stahler: thank you for your brilliant and meticulous copy editing. And to Ruta: thank you for pushing me to deepen this story in the way it deserved.

Kathleen Ortiz, my tireless agent, deserves a lot of credit for helping me manage my schedule and for cheering me on and holding me together when things felt too hectic to stay on the rails. I also want to thank the team at New Leaf Literary, specifically Joanna Volpe, Danielle Barthel, and Jaida Temperly, for their patience and constant support.

A massive thank you goes to my beta readers and writer friends, including Lydia Kang, Virginia Boecker, Brigid Kemmerer, and Jaime Lawrence. I am so fortunate to have cheerleaders like you. I'm also grateful to my colleagues, Paul, Catherine, Anne-Marie, Chris, Casey, Kristal, Bethany, and Erica especially, for understanding my strange double-life and making it possible for me to do both things I love.

As always, my family is my constant. Mom and Dad, thanks for long morning phone calls and abundant, unwavering sympathy. Joey, thanks for being patient. Asher and Alma, thank you for being fascinating and delightful.

And finally, to my readers: thank you for wanting to continue this journey with Wen, Melik, and Bo.